WAITING FOR GOD

WAITING FOR GOD

PAUL ABLEMAN

BBC BOOKS

Published by BBC Books,
a division of BBC Enterprises Limited
Woodlands, 80 Wood Lane, London W12 0TT

First published 1994

ISBN 0 563 37086 6

Set in Linotron Meridien by Phoenix Photosetting, Chatham
Printed and bound in Great Britain by Clays Ltd, St Ives PLC
Jacket printed by Lawrence Allen Ltd, Weston-Super-Mare

ONE

'Come on, Tom!' called Dicky urgently. 'No time to waste.'

Captain Ballard glanced up from the letter he was writing and saw the Chief of the Escape Committee beckoning eagerly from a big hole in the floor where the pot bellied stove usually stood.

'I'm not on digging detail tonight, Dicky,' Ballard explained. 'I did my bit yesterday, shifted seventy-eight cubic feet of heavy clay with my bare hands. In addition, I had to gnaw through the roots of an oak and three elms with my bare teeth. I fancy I've done my share of tunnelling for the time being.'

'Of course, you have, you old duffer,' exclaimed Dicky affectionately. 'And it's because of your sterling achievements that we're in a position to try and bust out tonight. Had you forgotten?'

'By George, Dicky,' exclaimed Ballard apologetically. 'I really believe I had. Well then, I'll just finish this letter to Ginger in Hollywood and —'

'Can't wait for you to complete a hot missive to one of your filmstar girlfriends, Tom. It's Blighty time. We're going home. Now heave your lithe, athletic form off that bunk and get into line. This time tomorrow we'll be crossing the Swiss border and then – what about a few flagons of ice-cold lager to celebrate in a wonderful little bar I happen to know in Alex?'

'Sounds good to me, Dicky, and I'll be with you in half a mo. But I really must finish this letter first. You see, Ginger's in a dreadful state. She's finally agreed to use another dancing partner until I can join her once more when the lights come on again all over the world, but she says he's no good. Legs all over the place, keeps trampling on her toes. Fellow called

1

Astaire – Bill, Jim – no, I have it, Fred Astaire. She'll be over-joyed to hear that I'm on my way back to join her on the old back lot at Paramount and —'

'Will you kindly answer my question, you exasperating old idiot?'

What? Now that hadn't sounded like Dicky at all. Dicky was normally the most courteous of chaps. He wouldn't insult a fellow in that way. True, he was under a lot of stress. As Chief of the Escape Committee it was up to him to ensure that the escape went off smoothly. No point in busting out if you didn't get back into action and ... Come to that, what was the point of escaping at all when it was really so pleasant here in Colditz? Tom raised his eyes and glanced all round the cosy turret where he had spent so many jolly hours with such fine chums as Dicky Butterbean and Bruce Bonker-Batman and Bill Bastable-Burgundy and Boris Banks-Beaglebuster and Benjamin Baxter-Bulstrode and —

'Oh, do wake up, you dolt!' snarled Dicky and prodded him in the stomach with a stick.

Tom Ballard frowned and looked up indignantly. Yes, the fellow really was standing over him with his stick raised to prod him again. This behaviour was completely unlike Dicky. And it was, moreover, conduct unbecoming – but hang on! Dicky was not only behaving unnaturally, he was looking rather odd too. For one thing, he was wearing a shapeless old dress, and his hair had become iron grey and his moustache had disappeared. It was an almost unbelievable transforma-tion! The Chief of the Escape Committee now looked exactly like a fierce old woman.

'What? Who are you?' asked Tom Ballard, blinking at the apparition.

'My name is Diana Trent and I've been asking you for the last five minutes if you play Scrabble? I'm sick and tired of playing on my own.'

'Scrabble? I don't believe it exists yet, does it? It's a post war invention, surely?'

'And just what war would you be referring to?' asked Diana shrewdly. Then her eyes narrowed as she contemplated the tall, large, broad-faced old chap who had been sitting almost immobile in his deck chair and staring straight ahead as if in a trance. 'Look here, what do you think the date is anyway?'

'It is 1942 and I and these other brave chaps are about to escape from Colditz. You could have put the whole operation into jeopardy prodding me like that. Suppose I'd squealed out loud and alerted the guards?'

'Oh, my God, another fruitcake,' exclaimed Diana, 'and I specifically instructed Bains that I wanted a neighbour who was totally *compos mentis* just for once.'

Shaking her head wearily, Diana turned and stumped off back to her own half of the conservatory, leaving Tom Ballard gazing after her reproachfully.

After a while, Tom rose and retreated into the interior of his new home. He was feeling very forlorn. He wanted to go back to Colditz, wanted it with a keen yearning that tore at him like a winter wind. There, in the familiar turret at Colditz, he would be young and eager again and of some use to the world again. He frowned slightly. Had he, in fact, ever been in Colditz? Well, what did it matter anyway? He had seen innumerable films about the place and the chaps in the turret there were more familiar to him than – than – well than Geoffrey and Marion for a start.

Geoffrey and Marion – his son and his daughter-in-law! He had lived with those two for the past five years, ever since he had retired. Geoffrey was his own flesh and blood – his and Maggie's – but nevertheless he often seemed to Tom like an utter stranger. How, for example, could any son of theirs have married someone like Marion? She was an alcoholic and a nymphomaniac and those were her good qualities. Otherwise, Marion was lazy, cold-hearted, selfish and ruthless. Compared to her a king cobra would seem a civilized and agreeable companion. Indeed, so ghastly was Marion that it had become clear to Tom after five years under her roof that nothing in the world would induce him to spend more time with her. He had therefore agreed to move to Bayview, a rather posh retirement home, at least for a trial period.

Geoffrey had none of Marion's really vile qualities but on the other hand he lacked her sole tolerable one: a kind of dotty energy she sometimes displayed when she surfaced from her private world of tranquilizers, sex and booze. Geoffrey was simply dull – numbingly, mind-blowingly, almost inconceivably dull. Geoffrey was even duller than pine shelving which was one of the few subjects of conversation on which he ever became animated.

That very morning Geoffrey and Marion had brought Tom to Bayview in their Volvo, and Geoffrey had assured him:

'You're going to love it here, Dad.'

Marion, who would, Tom knew, have given a year's supply of vodka to get him out of her house, added eagerly:

'Yes, it looks really super, Tom.'

Tom had smiled and put on a happy face as he enthused, 'Oh yes – it's lovely. Very well kept grounds. Yes, I'm sure it'll be a great new adventure.'

But Geoffrey, who was not an unkind person (although Tom sometimes wondered sadly if he could really be considered a person at all) had picked up the ironic note in his father's voice and urged him, 'Dad, if you don't like it here, we'll forget the whole thing and go home.'

But Tom shook his head.

'Thank you, Geoffrey, but I don't think so. If I stayed with you one more night, I think poor Marion here would probably strangle her psychiatrist.'

'No, no –' urged Geoffrey.

'Yes, yes,' insisted Marion. 'And I'd strangle you too, darling!'

Tom smiled faintly. One thing you had to admit about Marion. She was no hypocrite. If she hated you she made no attempt to hide the fact.

'Stop feeling guilty, Geoffrey,' Tom urged. 'We'll all be glad to see the back of each other.'

'That's not true, Dad.'

'It is as far as I'm concerned,' said Tom candidly.

'Really?' asked Geoffrey dubiously.

'Oh yes. I'll love it here,' insisted Tom. 'Have to have adventures in this life, Geoffrey, and this will be my next one. It will be the upper reaches of the Nile, the trek to Lhasa, the Brazilian jungle.'

There was silence for a while and then Geoffrey murmured reprovingly.

'This is Bournemouth, Dad.'

And so it was, thought Tom several hours later after

Geoffrey and Marion had departed. It was uncompromisingly, paralyzingly, irrevocably Bournemouth.

He gazed about at his new quarters. They were pleasant enough. Big living room, big bedroom, decent kitchen and bathroom. Even the little conservatory where he had just been assaulted by the old woman that Dicky had mysteriously turned into, was quite nice. But – oh, how he yearned to get back to Colditz.

He plonked himself down into one of the big armchairs in front of the television but he did not switch the set on. Instead, he leaned back and closed his eyes. Colditz! Colditz! Colditz, where are you? But he knew the answer. Colditz was in the country of the mind and only the imagination knew how to get there. Colditz couldn't be reached by sheer willpower.

Tom had found that out long ago. There were times when he could wander almost anywhere in time or space – but not whenever he wanted to. His imagination had to lead the way and it was capricious. Sometimes it would respond and some-times it wouldn't. And now – when he needed desperately to keep the bleak new reality at bay – his imagination simply could not be roused. Colditz remained as unattainable to him as happiness had been ever since his dear Maggie had died. He sighed deeply. He was too old to cry and that, he felt strongly, was most unfair.

While Tom was trying to acclimatize himself to his new life, Harvey Bains, the young manager of Bayview, was sitting at his desk in the administrative office of the retirement home saying to Jane, his assistant, 'Oh, dear, I do hope that new chap's not going to prove a troublemaker. What's his name? Tim Bollard?'

'I think it's Tom Ballard, Harvey,' Jane suggested deferen-tially. She continued to gaze at Harvey adoringly and went on, 'And I'm sure he won't be any trouble.'

Harvey was quite a good-looking young man, but he was deficient in qualities such as decency and consideration which are such ornaments to a human being. He was not actually bru-tal but he regarded Bayview much as a grasping dairy farmer might regard his herd. It required a good deal of monotonous attention but, managed skilfully, could be turned into a nice source of profit. Of course, you had to feed and house the live-stock but if you were prudent about these inescapable outlays you could end up agreeably in the black at the end of the year. This was important to Harvey because although he received a salary his contract also entitled him to a share of the profits.

Unhappily, however, Harvey's unceasing efforts to maxi-mize profits sometimes encountered opposition from the old folk he theoretically looked after. This was chiefly because of his endless attempts to minimize expenditure. For this pur-pose he used techniques such as serving cheaper cuts of meat in the dining room and employing illegal immigrants who spoke little English at starvation wages to do the dirty jobs. But, and tediously from his point of view, whenever he thought up some new and ingenious way of turning the economy screw a little tighter one or the other of the more bolshie wrinklies was liable to complain. At present, Diana Trent was the chief critic of Harvey's prudent fiscal policies, but something about the cut of Tom Ballard's gib suggested to the young manager that the new arrival might also prove an agitator.

'You're not really worried about Mr Ballard, are you, Harvey?' asked Jane.

'No, of course not, Jane. But I happen to know that during the war he worked for MI3 or some such organization.'

'I think you must mean MI5, Harvey.'

'Possibly, Jane. The point is that he was a kind of James Bond figure, always parachuting into unlikely places and assassinating people.'

'Goodness, Harvey, how exciting.'

'Yes, but is it what we want at Bayview, Jane? I mean, those fellows were taught to kill. What if this old thug, Bollard, still has some deadly device for doing so in his possession? I mean, just suppose I found it indispensable to add a small charge for table service to the residents' bill, I wouldn't want to find myself threatened with a cigarette case that fires pellets of nerve gas or some such thing, would I?'

'Oh, he seemed quite a decent sort to me, Harvey. But how do you know so much about him?'

'He told me all about his exploits when his son and daugh-ter-in-law had gone for a walk in the grounds. Apparently his great achievement was catching a whole panzer division in a gigantic net suspended from a hundred helicopters.'

'Still, he is old now, Harvey.'

'True, Jane, but he looks a big, powerful chap for all that. I think he'll bear watching.'

'Would you like me to watch him for you, Harvey?'

Jane's idea of bliss was to do something – anything – for Harvey. If he had asked her to hang by her hands and feet over a deep ravine so that he could stride across her suspended body she would have regarded it as an almost celestial privilege. Jane loved Harvey deeply but alas he failed to reciprocate her feelings. One of the reasons for his coldness was undoubtedly the fact that Jane was no beauty. She looked in fact rather like a lovesick hen.

'That might be a good idea, Jane,' agreed Harvey thoughtfully. 'You see, if this place fails financially, people won't put their money into other Bayviews. So I would be depriving thousands of senior citizens of a place in the sun. Troublemakers spoil things for everyone, Jane.'

'I do understand, Harvey.'

'So I really would be grateful if you could keep an eye on Mr Ballard and warn me if he starts getting bolshie.'

'I will, Harvey.'

'All right, you can go, Jane.'

But Jane showed a tendency to linger.

'Erm, I just wondered, Harvey, did you know that there's a very good film on in town? It's called *The Master of Manor Lodge*?'

Harvey nodded with interest and said, 'Oh yes, I've heard interesting reports about that one. It's supposed to be excellent.'

'As it happens I've got two tickets.'

'Have you really, Jane?' asked Harvey, sounding intrigued.

'Yes, and I wondered if you'd like to go?'

'Yes, I would, Jane. I'd love to.'

'Really, Harvey?'

'Absolutely, Jane. When are the tickets for?'

'Tonight, Harvey. I don't suppose you're free, are you?'

'Yes, as it happens, I am.'

'Oh,' exclaimed Jane, unable to imagine the fulfilment that

seemed to be beckoning. 'And does that mean that you'll come with me, Harvey?'

Harvey smiled and, with an incredulous sigh, shook his head.

'No, of course not, Jane,' he said, as ever astonished by the girl's inability to grasp that an upwardly-mobile executive such as himself could hardly consort socially with the likes of her. 'I can't be seen about with a plain little skivvy like you. It would destroy my image. I'll catch the film later in the week.'

Jane stared at him in dismay, her chin trembling.

'Now whatever is the matter, Jane?' asked Harvey, sighing with irritation.

But he received no answer. Choking back tears, as she had done so often before, Jane had rushed out of Harvey's office.

Having failed to get back to Colditz, Tom Ballard fell instead into a short but quite refreshing doze. Awakening and glancing at his watch he discovered that it was lunchtime. He was not especially hungry, but he was quite glad to have an excuse to leave his quarters and explore a bit.

A short walk brought him to the main building which, unlike the purpose-built structure which housed his flat, was a fairly old and quite stylish small manor house. This, as he recalled from his original tour of inspection, was where the dining room was located. He entered the building, along with the other residents, and made his way to the dining room. This was a fairly large, bright and comfortable room with separate tables, each of them seating four people.

He was peering about uncertainly when a hand smote him heartily on the back and the voice of Harvey Bains sounded in his ear.

'Hello, Tom. Looking for some new chums, eh?'

Tom turned with a smile and explained, 'Looking for some food actually.'

'Follow me,' urged Harvey, a faint, but crafty, smile on his face. He led the other across the room towards the table where Diana Trent sat in solitary splendour. Harvey knew that when the police wanted to keep the lid on a criminal gang they did not disperse them, and thus make them harder to spy on, but concentrated them. The police, for example, never closed down clubs and pubs and other places where criminals were known to congregate. No, they used them for their own purposes by infiltrating their agents into the clientele. Harvey followed the same policy at Bayview. Jane was his chief infiltrator.

When they reached Diana's table, Harvey said ingratiatingly, 'Miss Trent, I've got someone to meet you. Tom Ballard this is Diana Trent. Now I know that you two are going to get on marvellously together, so I'll leave you to do just that. Enjoy your lunch.'

And smiling in a smug and self-congratulatory way he departed. Tom hovered awkwardly for a moment.

'Do you mind if I sit down?' he asked finally.

'Suit yourself,' said Diana indifferently. 'But I'm afraid you won't get any iron rations. Just ordinary disgusting Bayview fare.'

'Oh, that's all right,' agreed Tom. 'I'm not very hungry in any case.'

'Glad you made it,' said Diana.

'What?' asked Tom, puzzled.

'Back here to Blighty,' elaborated Diana. 'You were just busting out of Colditz the last time we met.'

'Oh that,' said Tom, completely without embarrassment. 'Yes, I usually tunnel on Wednesdays. I find by mid-week I'm ready for some excitement.'

Diana eyed him shrewdly. Perhaps this chap wasn't quite such a fruitcake as she had initially thought. She was about to probe further when Jenny, the cheerful and very pretty black waitress, arrived with their lunches.

'Hello, Tom,' she said with a smile as she put the plate in front of him. 'Settling in all right?'

'Oh yes, Jenny. I'm having the time of my life. Wonderful place.'

'That's the spirit,' Jenny complimented him. 'Pity everybody doesn't have such a positive approach.'

As she said this she glanced meaningfully towards Diana who responded with a baleful glare.

'Each to his own, Jenny,' said Tom sunnily. 'Some people like being cheerful and others enjoy being miserable. The main thing is for people to enjoy themselves in the way they like best.'

'Bully for you, Tom,' said Jenny with a laugh and departed to serve more food.

There was silence at Tom's and Diana's table for a little. Then Diana said bitterly, 'It's cloying old fuddies like you who give the elderly a bad name. Trotting out your trite little homilies like some refugee from the *Reader's Digest*. Now *you* might enjoy being a quaint old parody of a human being but I've still got my balls, thank you very much.'

'Is that so?' queried Tom with interest. 'I suppose you wouldn't consider serving on the escape committee back at Colditz, would you? I think you're the type we need.'

The flicker of a smile crossed Diana's face. Then she returned grimly to sawing away at the cutlet on her plate.

'This meat's not very good,' remarked Tom, doing the same.

'It never is.'

'What is it?'

'Squirrel.'

'Indeed? These carrots seem to be from a tin if I'm not mistaken.'

'Yes, well, the grub gets a little better at weekends. That's because relatives are here to observe the wretched fodder they chuck at us.'

'Doesn't anyone complain?' asked Tom.

'Not often. We're British. Bad food is in our genes. If the kitchen served dead dog the residents would complain to the RSPCA rather than the chef.'

Tom smiled, but then asserted firmly, 'Well, I'm going to have a word with Mr Bains.'

Diana shrugged and said cynically, 'Won't do a bit of good. He merely runs the place.'

However, later that day Tom did have a quiet word with Harvey Bains and when the two parted Tom was distinctly hopeful that his arguments had impressed the young manager.

Tom then spent the afternoon arranging his new living quarters to his liking and putting his personal effects, such as the picture of him and Maggie taken on their honeymoon, into appropriate places. He made no further attempt to return to Colditz and contented himself with a sandwich and a bottle of lager in his room for dinner. He spent the evening watching an old film on television.

The film was a special favourite of his. It starred one of his most happily remembered ex-girlfriends, Dorothy Lamour. He and Dorothy had spent several years exploring fascinating parts of the world together. The only drawback to their voyaging had been the incessant company of two hangers-on of hers called Bob and Bing, one of whom told jokes while the other crooned.

At about noon the following day Tom was taking a brisk walk in the grounds when he passed a bench on which Diana Trent was sitting and moodily firing stones from a catapult at some squirrels. He paused and remarked:

'Why are you persecuting those small animals?'

'If I get them then Harvey won't be able to serve them up for dinner.'

'Oh rubbish,' said Tom positively. 'That wasn't squirrel being served yesterday.'

'Then it must have been rat. It was quite definitely some kind of small rodent. Incidentally, did you have a word with Bains about the food?'

'Yes, I did,' said Tom firmly.

'And?'

'And I am hopeful that there will be a noticeable improvement at lunch today.'

Diana chuckled and said positively, 'I'll bet you a pound to a pinch of three-day-old beefburger that there won't.'

'No, I only gamble for high stakes,' affirmed Tom. 'Now when I broke the bank in Monte Carlo —'

'Oh, for God's sake put a sock in it!' ordered Diana sharply. 'It's far too early in the day for your lunatic babbling. And why on earth are you marching about our boring grounds like a demented colonel?'

'I'm taking a constitutional.'

'What for?' asked Diana sourly.

'Because it promotes a healthy mind and body.'

'And what good are those?'

'They help you to live a long and vigorous life,' offered Tom reasonably.

But his argument fell flat.

'And what is the point of living a long and vigorous life,' inquired Diana bitterly, 'if you spend half of it stuck in this place waiting for it to end?'

Tom shook his head sadly. It had seemed to him, when he set out on his walk, to be a fine and sparkling morning. But now he perceived that above the area occupied by Diana a small but very dark cloud was hovering.

'Dear, oh dear,' he murmured. 'Tell me, Miss Trent, what did you do when you were still alive?'

'I was a spinster.'

'Is that a profession?'

'It's an attitude. I was a self-contained unit. I did exactly as I pleased until the dismal iniquities of age turned the tables on me and made me into the sick joke you see before you. What's your excuse for continuing to clutter up the planet?'

'Well, I used to enjoy life. No, damn it, I still do.'

Diana shook her head in a wondering sort of way and exclaimed: 'It must be wonderful to be a simpleton.'

'Oh it is. And it's quite an easy thing to achieve really. I could give you lessons, if you wanted —'

'I might,' said Diana, quite meekly to Tom's surprise. 'I'm famous for trying anything once. But tell me – before you became a simpleton, did you have an occupation?'

'Oh yes,' said Tom, seating himself beside her. 'For many years I was a bull fighter. I fought under the name of El Cordobes. Maybe you've heard of me?'

'I've not only heard of you,' said Diana glumly. 'I saw you fight in Malaga twenty years ago. You were badly gored.'

Tom nodded agreement.

'Indeed I was.' Turning towards Diana he pulled the tail of his shirt out of his trousers and lifted it up to reveal a scar on the right side of his abdomen. 'As you see, I still bear the mark.'

Diana eyed it moodily.

'The bull seems to have had surgical training. That looks just like an appendix scar.'

'Bulls are very smart animals,' agreed Tom, tucking in his shirt again.

'When you'd despatched all the bulls in Spain, what did you

do then?' asked Diana, without, apparently, feeling any burning interest in the matter.

'I became an astronaut.'

'Ask a silly question. And when you'd explored the whole of space, what then?'

'A financier.'

'Ah,' said Diana, catching on. 'Now I get the picture. You were really an accountant, weren't you?'

Tom smiled at her perceptiveness.

'Yes,' he admitted.

'A humble accountant,' said Diana, unable to keep all trace of scorn from her voice.

'That's right,' agreed Tom. 'One of very many humble accountants in a very big firm. I sat at the same desk every day for forty years.'

'And that gave you absolute laboratory conditions for your endless neurotic fantasizing.'

'True,' agreed Tom with a wry smile. 'But you should know that we all received a three-week holiday every year and that gave me the chance to put at least some of my fantasies into practice.'

'I see,' said Diana adding cruelly, 'You're really just a boring man who's led a boring life, aren't you?'

Tom chuckled.

'I suppose so. And that's doubtless why I'm such a determined poseur. I'm afraid that if I don't make myself noticed I might find it hard to go on believing that I really exist.'

'But you don't,' said Diana firmly. 'I am simply having a conversation with a figment of my own diseased imagination.'

'But surely,' protested Tom, beginning to realize the steel of his opponent, 'you wouldn't even bother to imagine someone as negligible as me?'

'Reasonable point,' admitted Diana.

'And besides,' continued Tom, 'I had a look in the mirror before I came out and I really was there – in the mirror. So I have to infer that I must really exist. Assuming, of course, that the mirror really exists.'

'Assume nothing!' urged Diana fiercely. 'The only thing you can ever be sure of is an absence – and that's essentially all that you consist of.'

Tom shook his head with a wondering smile at her effortless malice.

'You really are a sweet person,' he said softly.

Diana shrugged fiercely.

'Just because we're old doesn't mean we have to be polite to each other.'

'I suppose not,' admitted Tom.

Diana suddenly stood up and glared fiercely down at Tom. When she spoke next there was real bitterness and hostility in her voice.

'Listen Ballard – you're not the philosopher you pretend to be. You can't fool me into accepting your gibberish as original thinking. You're just like the rest of us. Living out a long, boring, pointless life. We're born. We consume. We die. You and I have done the first two and we're simply waiting around for the third. We've come here to die.'

'But not just yet,' exclaimed Tom and he stood up again. 'Come along. You're going to take a little walk with me and, who knows, perhaps you may even enjoy it.'

And with that he took Diana by the arm and led her off down the walk. To his surprise she did not either resist or, apart from a few muffled murmurs, protest very much. And quite soon they were strolling together in silence but nevertheless, Tom felt, with a certain amount of enjoyment in each other's company. It was at about this point that they both saw the youthful director of the retirement home approaching them.

'Oh my God,' exclaimed Diana. 'That's all we need, the idiot Bains.'

'Good,' said Tom. 'Now tell me what you would like for lunch?'

Diana smiled a wolfish smile.

'Why? Are you going to instruct him to have it prepared for me?'

'Precisely,' said Tom.

'Very well,' said Diana, going along with the joke. 'In that case, I think I'll have poached salmon.'

'Mr Bains?' said Tom with a warm smile, stopping in the path of the director.

Harvey looked distinctly unnerved when he saw the pair confronting him but he paused and asked, 'Yes, Tom?'

'Miss Trent would like some poached salmon for lunch.'

'Poached salmon?' repeated Harvey incredulously. 'I mean, not caviar or plovers' eggs or —'

'No, just a nice cut of poached salmon, new potatoes and a fresh lettuce and tomato salad. You'll organize that, won't you?'

Harvey swallowed and glanced about desperately. Then he nodded meekly.

'Of course, Tom.'

Then, to her complete bewilderment, Harvey smiled at Diana and asked, 'And to follow? Would you care for the home-made chocolate pudding with fresh cream? That's our featured desert. But you might prefer fresh, home-made ice cream? Or a cheese board? Or a slice of home-made pear tart or —'

'No, no,' said Diana faintly. 'The chocolate pudding will be quite acceptable.'

'Good,' said Bains with a weakly affable smile. 'Well, I'm sure you'll enjoy it. And now I'd better hurry along to the kitchen and arrange for the salmon.'

And with another feeble smile Harvey Bains trotted away in the appropriate direction.

'What,' said Diana weakly, 'is going on? Was that real or did I imagine it?'

'Oh, it was real all right,' said Tom lightly, 'just as real as I am. 'You see, there's been a revolution in the catering around here. I brought it about yesterday after that revolting lunch.'

'You?' asked Diana helplessly. 'But you're just an ineffectual ex-accountant? You're about as forceful as a stuffed squirrel. How could someone like you get the better of Harvey Bains in a matter where money is involved?'

'Oh, it wasn't really all that difficult,' Tom assured her modestly. 'I first went back to my flat and drafted a letter. Then I took the draft to the office and asked Harvey if I could have a few sheets of Bayview headed notepaper in order to send the letter to *The Times*, the *Telegraph* and several of the tabloids. He was quite enthusiastic. He seemed to assume that I'd written a letter commending the facilities at Bayview. He asked politely if he might read the letter and I said "certainly" and handed it to him. He read the letter and then immediately promised that the catering would be completely transformed and that, in future, I could supervise the kitchens if I wanted to. He also requested me not to post the letter.'

'I see. And what exactly had you said in this miraculous missive?' asked Diana sceptically.

'Well, the letter contained an invitation to various newspapers to send a reporter to the town hall tomorrow – which is now today of course – to witness an event that would take place on the steps there precisely at noon.'

'What event?'

'Hara-kiri – Japanese ritual suicide, an art which, I informed the editors, I had mastered during my seven years apprenticeship in a Zen monastery on the island of Hokkaido. I explained in the letter that the food served at Bayview was an insult to the honour of a Zen master such as myself and I felt I had no option but to purge the dishonour in the traditional manner.'

'Wonderful!' exclaimed Diana. 'But were you really an apprentice in a Zen monastery? Oh my God, you've got me doing it now. Yes, but wait a minute – there's a logical contradiction in what you wrote. You couldn't have practised the art of hara-kiri for seven years and still be in one piece?'

'My impression,' said Tom gravely, 'is that our young leader, Harvey Bains, is not blessed with anything very substantial in the way of brains.' He glanced at his watch. 'I say, it's lunchtime. I do hope the salmon will be poached properly. Shall we go and see?'

And this time he extended his arm for Diana to take. She did so without demur and then the two wrinklies, arms linked, walked with great dignity towards the main building. Their dignity was, however, compromised now and then when they both, almost in unison, doubled up in laughter.

TWO

Jane was tidying up Diana's conservatory which, as always, was very much in need of this attention. Diana herself was attempting, despite Jane's unsought and undesired activities, to read. It was a lovely early spring day and the daffodils in Bayview's grounds, planted and tended by Antonio, the Portuguese illegal immigrant whom Bains employed as gardener, were in heavy bud. Indeed, one or two of the bolder plants had already put their heads out to sniff the air.

'What do you want doing with this envelope, Diana?' asked Jane, picking up a buff, stamped and addressed envelope from the floor.

'Mmm?' asked Diana glancing up from her book. 'Oh, could you pop it in the post for me when you leave, Jane? It's for my solicitor. I want him to get it as soon as possible. It's important.'

'I'll see to it, Diana,' said Jane obligingly, putting the envelope safely into the capacious pocket of her smock. 'Did you enjoy having your niece here yesterday?' she then asked in the emollient voice, half-motherly and half-matronly, she often used when talking to the residents. This tone, based on the assumption that the paying inmates were all either senile or half-witted or both, worked well in general but often came unstuck with Diana who regularly shocked Jane with the bluntness of her replies.

'Would you,' retorted Diana, 'enjoy having Jack the Ripper come to visit? My niece wants to see me dead.'

'That's nice,' cooed Jane who had stopped listening because she had resumed wondering, as she spent much of her time doing, how she could win the heart of Harvey Bains. 'She's such a nice woman.'

Diana eyed Jane narrowly for a moment. 'Yes, delightful.' She then said sardonically, 'And guess what? She tried to throttle me with her rosary beads.'

'That was thoughtful,' murmured Jane, who was now glancing about to see if she could spot anything significant to report back to Harvey.

'No, it wasn't, you simpering imbecile!' exclaimed Diana fiercely. 'It was homicidal. Don't you understand? My niece is after my money. It's not as if I have any objection to shuffling off this Bayview coil but I'm blowed if she's going to benefit by it. Anyway that letter you're going to post for me should regulate my financial affairs. You won't forget about it, will you, Jane? It might be needed quite soon.'

'No, of course I won't forget, Diana. But honestly I'm sure you're wrong about your niece. Do try to remember that, as Mr Bains puts it, persecution mania is very common amongst senior citizens.'

Diana gave a cry of anguish.

'I will not be called a senior citizen.'

'Really? Well what do you want to be called then?'

'I want to be called Diana. What do I look like to you, Jane?'

'Well,' said Jane, with a faint sniff of reproach, 'in my opinion you look like a senior citizen.'

'Don't push your luck, Jane!' warned Diana grimly. 'Now in your further opinion – and I am well aware that someone as vacuous as you can hardly be said to have opinions at all – just when did I become a senior citizen?'

'Well – after you turned sixty, Diana.'

But, surprisingly, Diana failed to erupt at this assertion. Instead, she blinked, opened her mouth to speak and then closed it again. And then, to Jane's gratified surprise, she simply leaned back in her chair with a fond, reminiscent smile on her face.

'What would you say, Jane, if I told you that on my sixtieth birthday I spent much of the day hanging out of a helicopter on the Cambodian border while various warlords tried to shoot my arse off?'

Jane gave a little shiver of distress at the language. 'So tasteless,' she shuddered. But she rallied and went on, 'I would have to say, Diana, that you were probably playing one of those dreadful video games. Surely it would be more becoming to leave those things to adolescent boys, wouldn't it?'

'But it's true, you ninny!' bawled Diana. 'I was a freelance photographer – just about at the top of my profession and – oh, what's the use?'

Shaking her head morosely she buried herself once more in her book. Jane went on needlessly tidying up behind Diana's back. But before long, discouraged by the other's silence and also by the lack of anything interesting to report back to Harvey, she prepared to depart. But when she had reached the conservatory door she beheld something which made her change her mind. She turned back.

'Oh, Diana?'

Diana glanced to left and then to right as if puzzled.

'That's funny,' she murmured, clearly intending her words to carry. 'I could have sworn I heard Jane's voice. But Jane has long since departed.'

'No, she hasn't,' Jane corrected her. 'I'm still here, Diana – just behind you.'

'Well, lucky old me,' said Diana grimly, although she was secretly rather pleased by Jane's continued presence. She found it exhilarating to let off steam by bawling at the placid and lovelorn wench. 'Found another lurking scrap of fluff to persecute, have we?'

'No, we've found a car, a "porch" if I'm not mistaken.'

Diana smiled ironically at Jane's attempt to cope with the pronunciation.

'Would that be a front porch or a back porch, Jane?' she asked interestedly.

'What?' asked Jane, puzzled.

'It's Porsche, you ninny.'

'All right then, Porsh,' said Jane, still not getting it quite right. 'As it happens, I don't speak Italian. Anyway, would I be correct in thinking that this – this very posh Porsh,' and Jane giggled at her own little joke, 'belongs to your niece?'

'Perfectly right, Jane,' Diana confirmed. 'My homicidal niece is going on holiday and since it seems that most of her neighbours are car thieves she has asked me to look after that valuable automobile.'

'But is it safe outside your flat, Diana? Cars have been stolen from the grounds of Bayview before, you know.'

'Ah, but I have the ignition key here in my handbag, Jane. So the machine is perfectly safe. And if you're thinking that a thief might try to break into the car by force, let me assure you that if anyone so much as brushed its wing with a silken kerchief that machine would emit screams like Lucifer descending into hell.'

'But that's just my point, Diana.'

'What is your point?'

'Well, my point is —' floundered Jane, unsure quite how to advance the momentous project she had conceived the moment she had set eyes on the car. 'Oh, yes I know. The thief would realize that an expensive car like that would have an alarm. So he would almost certainly come into your flat to try and find the key. And in that case he might assault you, Diana. So I think it would be best if you gave me the key so that I can lock it in the safe in Harvey's office. So could I have it, please, Diana?'

And Jane held out her hand tremulously.

Would her little ruse work? Goodness, how marvellous it would be if she could return to Harvey's office with the key to the Porsche in her possession. She was well aware that Bains – like most aspirant yuppies, and especially those like Harvey who could only afford to drive two-year-old Ford Escorts – had an all but uncontrollable desire to get behind the wheel of fast, expensive motorcars. Harvey would give his ears for the chance to drive the red Porsche. Even better, he might be prepared to give Jane – well, a kiss was probably more than could reasonably be expected but a kind word at the least, and quite possibly even permission for her to walk beside him when he next went down to the bakery to order bread.

'Don't be silly, Jane,' said Diana impatiently. 'I may want to go for a spin in it.'

'A spin? What do you mean, Diana?'

'It is a vernacular expression, Jane, meaning a brisk pleasure run in a motorcar.'

'But you couldn't drive a powerful car like that, Diana.'

Diana shook her head sadly.

'Jane, Jane – in my time I have driven vehicles ranging from

Land-Rovers to Sherman tanks. I have even landed a plane when the pilot was shot dead beside me. I could quite easily handle that Porsche with one hand while shaking a flawless dry Martini with the other.'

'Well, perhaps you could have done when you were younger, Diana. But now you'd probably kill yourself.'

'Could you guarantee it? I'd be off like a shot if you could. But whether to hell or Brighton, I still may want to go somewhere in that car and so I intend to hang on to the keys.'

'But – but –' sputtered Jane, grievously disappointed at the failure of her scheme. 'I simply don't know what Harvey will say about it.'

'Quite honestly, Jane, I don't give a whiff of burnt rubber what Harvey says about it. And now could you please transfer your attentions to some other region of this geriatric inferno? I have nearly reached the end of my whodunit and I am all agog to discover who, in fact, dunit. Incidentally, the plot of the book concerns a particularly nasty confidence trick perpetrated on decent, honest folk by an unscrupulous swindler. Someone rather like Harvey Bains, wouldn't you say, Jane?'

'Oh,' exclaimed Jane reproachfully, but knowing that basically Diana was just trying to upset her. 'That's a terrible thing to say, Diana.'

And then, sighing deeply at the loss of the opportunity for ingratiating herself with Harvey which had beckoned so brightly, Jane left the conservatory.

Diana gazed after her with a sly and gratified smile. She knew exactly what Jane had been after. And while she pitied the poor creature for her disastrous passion she had no doubt that Jane was better off being denied any hope of achieving the object of her desires. Diana's only regret was that she could not think of some way of letting Harvey know that he had missed a wonderful opportunity to get behind the wheel of a Porsche.

Meanwhile, Tom Ballard, in the adjoining flat, was addressing the Congress of the United States of America.

'Senators and representatives,' he thundered, 'and Italian ice-cream salesmen —'

From the rear of the great domed chamber the voice of

Congressman Grimes, a notorious critic of government policies, cried out:

'Out of order. No Italian ice-cream salesmen are allowed in during joint sessions of the American Congress.'

'I stand corrected,' called Governor Ballard. 'Strike the ice-cream salesmen from the record.'

'Will the Governor yield?' called an exasperated senator from one of the Eastern seaboard states. 'We came here to listen to Jimmy Stewart playing the role of Mr Smith coming to Washington. You're not in the script, Ballard.'

'I most certainly am in the script,' insisted Governor Ballard. 'And I am here to tell you that the great script of life proves that it is not much fun getting old. Look at you chaps. Most of you are pretty old. Well, I ask you, do you find it much fun?'

A strange seething roar, sounding rather like a whole zooful of animals at feeding time, rose from the ranked politicians. Ballard knew that it signified agreement with his views.

'Exactly,' he insisted. 'You're discontented. You're old fogies playing at being powerful leaders, although every day you find that a few more bits and pieces have fallen off you. You're stuck in here making laws when you'd rather be out playing truant and swinging round lampposts. That is my point. Society is topsy-turvy. Old people should skip and gambol through the streets as a reward for having survived while the young should be cooped up in offices and congress halls as a punishment for – well, just for being young. Now who would like a scoop of this excellent Italian ice cream?'

'Order, order!' called the Vice President.

'The order is for a double scoop of Italian ice cream all round,' called Ballard generously. 'There will be one scoop of strawberry and one of vanilla for every single congressman. And it doesn't matter a bit if you slurp some of it down the front of your suits. My friend, Jimmy Stewart, the film star, will pick up the bill for the ice cream and settle the national debt as well. It's his way of saying "sorry" because he wasn't able to come to Washington today, as he'd promised he would.'

'Stop this filibustering,' called Senator Grimes angrily. 'And remember, Dad, you can always come home with me and Marion if you want to.'

'What was that, Grimes?' asked Tom, puzzled by the change of both tone and subject.

'I said you can always – ouch, stop that, Marion. Dad can certainly come home if he's not happy at Bayview.'

'Of course, he's happy,' insisted Marion. 'But why is he just sitting there, gazing into space?'

'He's meditating.'

'Well he looks ghastly,' shuddered Marion. 'As if he'd died in the lotus position.'

'He's probably mentally in some foreign place and time,' said Geoffrey thoughtfully.

'You tell her, Geoffrey,' called Tom. 'Actually I'm in Washington, standing in for my friend James Stewart who developed laryngitis this morning and couldn't make his celebrated speech to Congress.'

'He's here in Bournemouth,' said Marion.

'Yes, in one sense,' agreed Geoffrey, who was surprisingly sympathetic to his father's spiritual adventures. 'But he's also travelling on an astral plane.'

'Well, let's hope the bloody thing crashes,' said Marion vindictively.

'I think he may be up Everest,' said Geoffrey thoughtfully.

'No, I'm not up Everest, Geoffrey,' bellowed Tom. 'I'm in Washington with Mr Smith. And we're all about to have two scoops of Italian ice cream. Would you care for a scoop or two?'

'He's not only out of his body,' said Marion sourly. 'He's out of his mind as well. And I think all this astral stuff is very creepy. I'm going home.'

'But we can't just leave him —' muttered Geoffrey weakly.

At that moment, Diana entered Tom's living room and took in the situation at a glance.

'Don't worry,' she said. 'I'll stay with him. I'm his neighbour, Diana Trent.'

'God, how I hate wrinklies,' said Marion under her breath but not so far under her breath that Diana did not catch the words. 'Come on, Geoffrey.'

And she tugged her hapless husband hard by the hand. He looked apologetically at Diana.

'If you really don't mind?'

'No, of course not. I'm getting used to Tom's out-of-body voyaging.'

'Then perhaps we really should be going,' admitted Geoffrey. 'I have to inspect some new pine shelving at the DIY shop. Nice meeting you.'

'And you,' said Diana with an acid smile.

Geoffrey and Marion made their way out through the front door of the flat.

When the door had closed behind them Diana touched Tom lightly on the shoulder and said, 'It's all right. You can come out now. They've gone.'

Tom opened his eyes and murmured, 'Was there someone here? I have been away in another world.'

Diana put her hands on her hips and pursed her lips.

'Now look here, Ballard,' she said sourly, 'you may fool your cretinous relatives with your dithery doodahs, but don't try it on me.'

Tom shook his head as if to clear it, smiled sweetly at Diana and then rose to his feet.

'You know your trouble, Miss Trent?'

'Oh, for God's sake, this isn't a royal garden party. We're neighbours. Diana and Tom from now on.'

Tom smiled broadly.

'Very well. But as I was saying, your trouble, Diana, is that you're earthbound. You have no wings.'

'While you're Doctor Who, I suppose?' urged Diana, seating herself in an armchair.

'Precisely. And my imagination is my tardis.'

'Well, which quarter of the galaxy have you been infesting this morning?'

'Washington, actually. I went with my friend Jimmy Stewart and we addressed Congress on a matter of grave injustice.'

'There are so many to choose from,' pointed out Diana ironically.

'I spoke on the grave injustice of growing old. Look at us. We have worked hard all our lives and what is our reward?'

'I give up – what is our reward?'

'Two scoops of ice cream.'

Diana stared at him.

'I beg your pardon?'

'No, sorry, that came later. Our reward is quite simply death. You see it's all the wrong way round.'

'What is?'

Tom shook his head unhappily.

'I'm not quite sure any longer. It all seemed so straightforward when I was addressing Congress, but now – the point is, I want to do something really youthful.'

Diana squinted at him thoughtfully.

'Do you indeed?' she said finally. 'Well, as it happens, Ballard, I may just be able to help you there.'

About quarter of an hour later, Jane burst into Harvey Bains' office. Inside she found Geoffrey and Marion with Bains. The pair had called in without an appointment to ask Harvey if he thought Tom was settling into Bayview happily or not.

'They've gone! They've gone,' cried Jane, breathless from her dash through the grounds.

'Jane, would you please knock before entering, especially when I'm in a meeting?' asked Harvey with a sigh of displeasure.

'But I tell you they've gone, Harvey. In the "porch".'

Harvey smiled wearily at Geoffrey and Marion and apologized.

'I must ask you to forgive this unseemly intrusion. My assistant, Jane, gets a little incoherent when she's feeling emotional. Jane, who has gone where and in what porch?'

'Tom and Diana. The red porch that goes at two hundred miles an hour.'

'We haven't got a red porch, Jane,' said Harvey patiently. 'And anyway porches don't go at two hundred miles an hour. They don't actually move at all. So would you please begin again, take it very slowly and tell us all just what the hell you are talking about?'

Jane swallowed and tried to pull herself together.

'Diana's niece left her the keys to her car. It's a big red – you know—'

'Oh, a Porsche?' exclaimed Harvey reverently. 'Yes, I've seen it. Glorious car. '

'Well, I told Diana she should give me the keys to keep safe for her but she refused,' gabbled Jane. 'I said she was too old to drive a car like that and might kill herself in it and she said "good". And now they've both gone —'

'Both?' asked Geoffrey.

'Yes, she and Mr Ballard, your father. They got in the porch – the porsh – and shot away like a guided missile just missing the big oak and making Antonio dive for cover and – well – taking into account what Diana said, I can't help fearing the worst.'

'What worst, Jane?' asked Harvey curiously.

'I think they're intending to have a crash, Harvey. I think they've driven off on a suicide pact.'

Marion pricked up her ears at this. Not only was Geoffrey Tom's sole heir, but Tom's residence in Bayview was rapidly reducing the value of the estate.

'I say, wouldn't that be wonderful?' she exclaimed.

'No, it wouldn't Marion,' Geoffrey reproved her. 'I'm quite fond of Dad.' He addressed Jane. 'Surely the fact that they've gone off for a drive together doesn't mean they want to die together, does it?'

'Yes, but there's something else,' said Jane. 'This envelope.' And she took from her pocket the envelope she had picked up from Diana's floor earlier in the morning.

'And what is that, Jane?' asked Harvey sceptically.

'I think it's Diana's will,' said Jane. 'See, it's addressed to her solicitor and she told me she wanted it posted immediately because there was no time to lose.'

After this announcement there was silence except for the faint gurgles of pleasure that periodically issued from Marion. Finally Harvey, shaking his head solemnly, asked Geoffrey: 'Could there be anything in Jane's theory?'

'Yes,' said Geoffrey, 'there could. Dad's quite unpredictable. The truth is I've been a bit worried about him ever since we installed him here. I think perhaps we'd better call the police.'

But at this suggestion Harvey blanched perceptibly.

'No, no, no, no, no – not the police!' he pleaded. 'We certainly don't want the police in on this. Think of the possible headlines: "Bayview Runaways in Motorized Suicide Pact". What would that do for the annual profit statement?'

Geoffrey, who was in fact a small shareholder in the retirement home – one of the reasons why he had encouraged his father to choose it – nodded thoughtfully.

'Still we must do something,' he pointed out.

'Of course we must,' agreed Marion. 'So I suggest that we order a crate of champagne and book dinner at The Vineyard which is probably the best restaurant around here so that when we get the good news we can cel —'

'Shut up, Marion,' suggested Geoffrey mildly and, apart from continuing to chuckle with glee from time to time, Marion did.

'Jane,' said Harvey, turning to his love-slave and second in command, 'have you any idea where they might have been heading?'

'No, Harvey —' began Jane, but then a keen light appeared in her eyes and she amended this. 'Oh, I've just remembered. Diana did mention Brighton when she and I were talking earlier. That's right, she said she might decide to go to hell by way of Brighton or something like that.'

Harvey turned to Geoffrey.

'We'd better use your Volvo. We wouldn't all fit in my Escort.'

Tom and Diana, each holding an immense cocoon of pink candy floss, strolled out to sea along the pier. It was too early in the year, and the breeze was too sharp, for the pier to be crowded but nonetheless a few other citizens, well wrapped up, were also making the promenade above the waves. And over the wooden planking seagulls wheeled and mewed. Diana took a huge bite of candy floss and it promptly shrank to a wisp of sweetness in her mouth.

'Revolting stuff,' she declared.

'Oh, I don't know,' said Tom. 'It's nice to still have taste buds.'

'What's that supposed to mean?' asked Diana suspiciously.

'Well, there was a spell back there – when you were doing ninety down the wrong side of the road – when I really thought that my taste buds, along with the rest of my poor carcass, were destined for the chop.'

'Are you implying that I'm a poor driver?'

'No, you may be as rich as Croesus but you did have a spot of bother driving that big car, wouldn't you say?'

'Only for the first ten or fifteen miles. After that I was completely at home in it.'

'In that case why did we do the whole trip in second gear?'

'Because that's where the acceleration is,' insisted Diana, not very convincingly. 'A Porsche will do ninety in second. Didn't you know that?'

'I do now. My eyes were glued to the speedometer the whole time. And I can confirm that we did hit ninety once or twice albeit with a roar like a jumbo jet taking off. I actually saw a flock of Sussex sheep, which are pretty much innured to traffic noise, stampeding across the downs as we approached.'

'We got here, didn't we?' asked Diana grimly.

'Yes, I think so. There is a pier beneath us, isn't there? I mean we're not just walking on water, are we? That might have rather sinister implications.'

'Oh —' said Diana peevishly and she reached out and pushed Tom's cloud of candy floss into his face. 'If you're going to go on carping like this you can walk back to Bayview.'

'No thanks. But perhaps we could keep to first gear for the return journey?'

They reached the end of the pier where the wind was too fierce for all but a few fishermen and small boys. But the day was a dappled wonder of racing clouds and stilts of sunlight above a restless, foamy sea. They stood in silence for some time, gazing across the Channel towards France, and then Diana said, 'I used to come here during the war. I was a WAAF then. We used to watch the air battles – the dogfights – over the sea. There was something mysterious and touching, as well as deadly, about the silver planes – our boys and theirs – weaving patterns in the sky on a lovely summer day. If one of theirs went down then everyone would cheer but if one of ours was hit it seemed that even the wind would stop blowing. Time froze until you either saw the pilot parachute to safety, or his plane plunge into the sea with him still inside it. If he didn't get out it was as if you died with him. I would think: for nineteen or twenty years he has been his mother's love and light and now he's just been – switched off – and she's been left in a dark universe.' Diana was silent for a moment or two.

Then she went on quietly, 'You see, that's why I never had any children. I simply could not bear the thought of losing them. But I know now that my cowardice meant that I would never really have much that mattered at all.'

For once Tom could think of nothing very useful to say. He reached out and briefly patted Diana's hand which was resting on the guard-rail. Then, after a little pause and in a brisk voice, he asked, 'Which shall it be? High gastronomy in one of the best chow houses or fish and chips?'

'For goodness' sake, Tom,' urged Diana in her usual brusque tones, 'do you take me for a snob? High gastronomy of course.'

So they went and had a lobster in Wheelers. And very good it was too. They washed it down with a full bottle of Pouilly Fumé and Tom repeatedly, thinking of the red missile in which they had come and which had somehow also to be got back to Bayview, urged Diana against over-indulgence. But she put away her fair share of the wine and then, to Tom's dismay, drank no fewer than three armagnacs to finish off the feast.

'Perhaps,' suggested Tom hopefully, when they were once more out in the street, 'it might be sensible to leave the car here and go home by train and bus. We could then pop back tomorrow for the Porsche.'

'Nonsense,' insisted Diana. 'It is my intention to achieve at least third gear and possibly top on the homewards journey. I think I can promise you a most exhilarating run.'

'Very kind of you, Diana,' said Tom humbly. 'But I'd be just as happy to drum along in first.'

'It's no good, is it?' asked Diana wonderingly. 'You simply haven't got any balls, have you?'

'It doesn't really matter,' said Tom, 'because I'm quite sure you've got enough for both of us.'

Nevertheless, in spite of Diana's brave promises, it took her a good deal of dithering to get the car started at all this time. She was clearly a little tight and had forgotten the settings for some of the controls. But in the end the big engine gave a throaty roar and immediately afterwards a hideous grinding noise as Diana, treating the gear lever as if it were some kind of muscle-building device, shoved the car into first without bothering about trifles like depressing the clutch first. The Porsche thereupon leaped forwards like a released greyhound and Diana just managed to swing the heavy machine round the corner from the side street where it had been parked onto the promenade. There, rattled by the turn of events, she pulled up sharply.

'Don't you think,' suggested Tom mildly, 'it might be an idea to park at the curb rather than here in the middle of the street?'

'No, I do not,' said Diana testily. 'I like it here. Besides I don't intend to remain here for very long. I just want to – well to *reculer pour mieux sauter.'*

'Ah yes,' said Tom. 'Draw back in order to leap further. But that's just my point, Diana, should we go leaping along in this powerful machine? A car is much better used if it simply floats above the road. I have read somewhere that the really expert driver is the one whose passengers cannot tell, if they shut their eyes, whether the car is actually moving or still stationary.'

'Pah, lily-livered lounge lizards!'

'Well done,' said Tom heartily. 'I would have thought you were past the stage of being able to cope with tongue twisters. But don't you think we ought to get cracking?'

'Why? It's quite pleasant here.'

'True. But we are blocking about two-thirds of the road. And I think people are beginning to notice. Take that Volvo behind us – good heavens.'

'What is it?'

'It looks very much like Harvey Bains. Yes, and that's Geoffrey at the wheel. Of course, it's his car. And there's Jane and Marion in the back. I say this just could prove to be a very happy coincidence.'

'What do you mean? Are you tired of my company?'

'No, of course not. I can never get enough of it. That's why I suggest we get one of those in the Volvo to drive the Porsche home to Bayview while you and I commune rapturously in a bus or a train. What do you say?'

'I say "never!"' roared Diana and once more shoved the gear lever forwards, this time prudently depressing the clutch as she did so. She rather spoiled the effect, however, by failing to release the clutch gently but simply taking her foot off it. As a consequence the Porsche once more took off in a manner more reminiscent of a ballistic missile than a motorcar.

'And now,' proclaimed Diana, 'for second.'

But she didn't make second gear. She seemed to have lost the trick of changing up and no matter how much she jerked the lever and stamped on the clutch the only result was to send the Porsche bounding down the promenade like a motorized kangaroo.

'That was an admirable meal, Diana,' groaned Tom. 'But I have no particular desire to see it again.'

'Damn!' exclaimed Diana fiercely and she stepped hard on the brake and brought the Porsche to an abrupt halt. She then switched off the engine and began practising the use of the gears and the clutch.

'Ah,' said Tom, looking backwards through the rear window. 'They've caught up with us, I'm pleased to say. And – yes – Geoffrey and Bains are getting out. I think they're coming to have a friendly word.'

'Are they indeed?' asked Diana with an evil chuckle.

And as Geoffrey tapped on the window on Tom's side and Harvey did the same on Diana's side, Diana turned the ignition key and the Porsche once more exploded into life. But this time it seemed Diana had mastered its controls. With barely a click she slipped smoothly into first and a moment later the car shot out of the grasp of Geoffrey and Harvey, causing them both to jump back in alarm and almost topple over.

'That wasn't very polite, Diana,' urged Tom.

'It wasn't meant to be polite. It was intended to teach the idiot, Bains, a lesson. Never try to put one over on Diana Trent.'

'What's he been trying to put over on you?'

'Well, you know why he's here, don't you?'

'As a matter of fact, I don't,' admitted Tom. 'My telepathic powers are at a low ebb today.'

'He wants to get his clammy little hands on the Porsche. The essence of Bains is that he's a yuppy without any capacity for upwards mobility. So he drives a Ford Escort and yearns for a Porsche. He's followed us in the hope of getting to drive this one. So we're going to have some fun with him. Are they still following?'

Tom turned with difficulty in the passenger's cockpit and gazed back.

'Yes. But they're a long way behind.'

'They'll be a lot further before I've finished with them,' promised Diana.

Diana's evil designs involved first slowing down to about forty so that the Volvo could again catch up with them. As it began to draw alongside, Tom was able to observe that three of its passengers were making urgent signals at him and Diana to stop. The fourth passenger, Marion, was drinking vodka from a quarter bottle in her hand and grinning inanely.

'They want us to stop,' said Tom.

'Really?' asked Diana. 'Well in that case, we'd better, hadn't we?'

She slowed down a little more and the Volvo actually began to pull ahead of them. This was precisely what Diana had intended. With a titanic roar and a burst of well-nigh incredible acceleration, she once more sent the Porsche rocketing away from the other car.

'If the objective is self-destruction,' urged Tom mildly, 'wouldn't it be simpler, and less of a risk to innocent bystanders, if we were simply to abandon the car and just leap off the cliff?'

'You're perfectly safe,' Diana assured him. 'I've got the knack now.'

And for the next twenty miles or so, she demonstrated just how thoroughly she really had got the knack. Time and again the Volvo caught up with them and whenever it did so its passengers, except for Marion, tried to wave them to a halt. And each time, at the very last moment and by means of some ingenious manoeuvre, Diana tugged the great machine from their grasp and sent it rocketing up the road again.

The last time she did this was on the motorway. She had slowed down to about a hundred miles an hour and it took the Volvo five minutes or so to come labouring up beside them. Then Diana glanced out of her side window and saw Harvey beckoning wildly and Geoffrey grimly intent on keeping the wheel steady and Jane making agitated faces and Marion draining the last of her vodka. With a triumphant smile, Diana thereupon put her foot down almost to the floor and shifted down into second. The Porsche sprang away and Tom watched in awe as its speedometer swung round the dial showing: 120, 130, 140, 150, 160. And at about the highest speed, which felt more like flying than motoring, they reached a point where they had to brake hard in order to turn off the motorway for the run into Bournemouth. It was then that Tom noted with reluctant admiration that Diana was laughing with sheer delight.

But an hour later, she was no longer laughing. She and Tom were waiting grimly in Harvey Bains' office. Tom was seated on the visitor's chair and Diana was stomping up and down tensely.

'I did suggest you slow down,' Tom pointed out.

'Don't worry,' said Diana sombrely. 'I accept full responsibility. You need feel no qualms of conscience. And just as soon as we get confirmation from the police, I shall know what to do.'

'What will you do?'

'Well, join them, of course.'

'There's no need for that. And besides we can't be sure that they crashed.'

'Of course we can. They'd have been here long ago if they hadn't. After all we were only about ten miles from Bayview when I took off on that last – glorious – run.'

'Yes, but they might have stopped or broken down.'

'Oh nonsense. Basil said they'd gone out looking for us in the belief that we were on a suicide pact. Absurd notion, of course. As if I'd have taken a wonderful machine like that to the grave. No, it's perfectly clear. They've had a crash trying desperately to catch up with us and now they're all dead.'

'Well, I think —'

And at that moment the 'phone rang. Diana went to it and put out her hand. But then she paused. She said, 'No, it seems I haven't quite the balls I thought I did. Could you answer it, Tom?'

Tom nodded, rose and went to the 'phone. He picked it up. He said, 'Yes? What? My God, all of them? I see. Oh yes, I'll take the necessary steps. Thank you for notifying me. Goodbye.'

Diana gazed at him and Tom noticed that her cheeks were sunken and her eyes seemed to burn in their sockets.

'Well?' she asked.

Tom nodded.

'Yes, it was the police,' he said quietly.

'Oh God!' exclaimed Diana. 'What have I done?'

She covered her face with her hands and stood for a moment like a statue. But then she heard something which puzzled her. It was a kind of gulping, snorting sound. Of course, that must be Tom sobbing for his poor, dead son. But, hang on, it didn't actually sound quite like sobbing. No, it sounded more like – like – yes, like laughing. Diana uncovered her eyes. And found she had been right. Tom was, in fact, standing before her rocking with merriment and with tears of delight streaming down his cheeks.

'All right!' she said grimly. 'What exactly did the police say?'

'They said that they couldn't catch the Porsche although they tried like Billy-o. So they settled for Geoffrey instead. He and Harvey and the two girls have all been done for speeding. They are being held in custody in the local nick. Marion, apparently, is waving her vodka bottle around and singing rude songs. The police say Geoffrey wants us to go down to the police station and bail them all out.'

Tom and Diana gazed at each other for a moment. Then Diana, gently at first, also began to laugh. And after that it wasn't long before they were both staggering about Harvey's office practically convulsed with merriment.

THREE

Tom was crouching in the snow on the top of Mount Everest peering up at the sky. He had reached the summit in record time and, having a couple of hours to spare before supper with good old Sherpa Tensing back at base camp, he had decided to see if he could make contact with God. Tom told himself that he was, after all, stationed at the top of the world and God should be visible from there if anywhere. Of course, he knew very well that people could get a lot higher than he was if they really tried. They could use aeroplanes, helicopters and even spaceships to do so. But he was convinced that no one would ever find God by using a flying machine because God would hear you coming and hide. But up here, hunkered down amongst the eternal snows, there was just a chance that God might fail to notice your presence and inadvertently reveal himself.

Tom had, however, been scanning the heavens for quite a long time now without result. True, he had at one point observed a few tendrils of cloud which just might have been flowing silvery hair on the head of a gigantic benign old gentleman. Tom had therefore strained his eyes to see if he could also perceive a pair of vast, but shrewd and benevolent, eyes peering down at him from beneath the hair. But no luck. He had also tried to discern the outline of an immense chin or a strong aristocratic nose the size of the Empire State Building but – nothing doing. And before long, the strands of what might have been silvery hair had begun to disperse and Tom had felt virtually certain that it had just been wispy cloud.

So, what conclusions could he draw from the failure of his search? That God didn't exist? Certainly not. It might only indicate that God was simply not visible from the top of Mount

Everest on this particular day. The Almighty could still be on, or near, the summit of some other mountain. Then again he might be on the moon or on Mars or Venus or on a planet in some other solar system revolving around some other star. God could, at this very moment, be in another galaxy a million million million million light years away. It was not inconceivable that God was simply taking a short holiday from his arduous labours. He might possibly —

'Psst!' said a voice.

'Hello? Who's that?' asked Tom, feeling a sharp pang of excitement.

'It's me,' said the voice clearly.

'Good Lord – and I mean that most sincerely. So you are here after all? And you've decided to reveal yourself to me? I must say I am both thrilled and flattered.'

'Tom?'

'That's right. And I appreciate your using my first name. The informality means that I don't need to stand in quite as much awe of you as I would have done if you'd addressed me as Mr Ballard. I fear that I am unable to reciprocate, however, since I have no idea of your first name.'

'It's Jane.'

'Jane? Really? Now that is astonishing. And yet, looked at rationally, why shouldn't you be called Jane? Names are merely conventions after all. Jane God undoubtedly has a simple strength and dignity. What surprises me, however, is that you're a woman. I'd always assumed you would prove to be a bloke. And don't think I'm knocking your sex. I can see that it has certain important advantages. For one thing it will, once I have proclaimed the fact of your gender to an astounded world, take the wind out of the feminists' sails. They won't be able to grumble that your Creation is just a stomping ground for macho chaps any more. And I doubt if they'll pursue the argument that we males have been making a mess of running this corner of the universe when they learn that the boss has really been one of them all along.'

'Tom, can you hear me?'

'Yes, I can hear you, God. Just about. But why are you whispering?'

'I don't want Diana to hear.'

'Good gracious, are you scared of her too? I would have thought you could have humbled her with a bolt of lightning or something. Anyway she's not with me up here on Everest.'

'I'm behind you, Tom.'

'Really? I'd assumed you were above me, sitting on a cloud or something.'

'I'm in your conservatory.'

'That is quite astonishing. I would have thought it was far too small for the creator of the universe. But I suppose you have the power to change your size at will. Is that it? I must say I'm eager to see what you look like, God, and very sensible of the tremendous honour of being the first human being in history, with the possible exception of Michelangelo, to actually look his Deity full in the face and —'

Frowning, Tom came to an abrupt halt. A face had just swum into his field of vision and it was one he knew well.

'Jane?' he asked doubtfully. 'Is that you?'

'Yes,' Jane confirmed, 'that's what I said. But what have you been muttering about?'

'Hm? Ah, well, nothing very important really. It's just that I've been, as it were, up a mountain – Everest actually and – I say, Jane, did you know that you and God have the same name?'

'Oh Tom, I can't play games with you now. I've come about Diana.'

'Really? Well then, join me here in the living room, Jane, and tell me what it is that you want to discuss.'

Gazing around stealthily as if she feared that Diana might suddenly pop up from behind a pot plant, Jane crept out of the conservatory into Tom's living room. Although a little disappointed that she hadn't proved to be God after all, Tom rallied and smiled warmly at his visitor.

'Sit down, God – er Jane,' said Tom hospitably. 'Can I get you a cup of Nescafé or something?'

'No, I haven't time, Tom. But it's nice of you to ask. It's a pity everyone around here isn't as courteous and thoughtful as you are.'

And she glanced demonstratively in the direction of Diana's quarters.

'Ah,' said Tom understandingly. 'Well then, what can I do to help?'

Jane glanced about cautiously once more and then said: 'I have to ask you something, Tom – has Diana been behaving normally lately?'

Tom frowned slightly and asked, 'By whose standards, Jane?'

'By your standards, Tom.'

'Oh yes,' said Tom positively. 'By my standards she's been behaving perfectly normally.'

'And by other people's standards?' pursued Jane.

'Utterly bonkers.'

Jane swallowed and her eyes took on a disquieting gleam.

'Really?' she asked thoughtfully. 'Well now, could you describe to me exactly how she's been behaving – well, in a disturbed way, Tom?'

'I could indeed. Only last week, for example, she proclaimed that God was a squirrel. God is, in fact, a woman called Jane. But that is perhaps a somewhat scholarly issue. Diana also keeps hitting people with her stick.'

'But she's always done that,' protested Jane.

'Of course she has. And it's always been a crazy thing to do.'

'I suppose that's true,' agreed Jane. 'Well now, taking these – these peculiarities of behaviour into account, Tom, would you agree that Diana is incapable of handling her own affairs?'

'I wasn't actually aware that she'd been having any affairs. She certainly hasn't with me. Mind you I have observed Antonio, the gardener, looking a bit cocky once or twice recently. Maybe he and Diana have been having bouts of wild Latin passion in the potting shed or conceivably bouts of wild Latin potting in the passion shed. Does that answer your question, Jane?'

Jane nodded with a slightly puzzled expression. But a moment later, Tom was astonished to see tears running down her cheeks.

'Yes, it certainly does answer my question, Tom,' Jane gulped. 'And – and – I'm sorry. I'm really so very, very sorry!'

With that Jane turned and rushed out of the flat. Tom gazed after her in surprise. But a possible clue to the mysterious conversation and to Jane's baffling distress emerged later that morning when Tom and Diana took a little stroll together.

'Hang on,' said Diana.

She was carrying her impressive looking photo-journalist's camera, with its great telescopic lens protruding from the front. The camera was slung round Diana's neck and every once in a while she unslung it in order to take a snap of Tom. Most of these attempts required placing Tom in a special pose or place and he was getting a little bored with the process.

'Just there,' said Diana. 'In front of the bench with the budding rhododendron behind you.'

'All right, but get on with it,' urged Tom.

'No, no, not a still shot. Action – how many times do I have to tell you? I only take action shots. I'm famous for it. Diana Trent, the action girl, I was known as, and not for the reason that may occur to you. Now back up a little and when I give the signal just stroll forwards casually past the bench.'

Diana hurried to what she considered the best position from which to take the shot only to find it already occupied by Antonio who was rooting up daffodil bulbs from the lawn. He was under the impression that they were a peculiarly noisome variety of weed.

'Out of my way!' cried Diana and slashed at him with her stick. The unfortunate gardener fell backwards with a strangled cry. 'And stop attacking those daffodils, you halfwit from the Algarve. Don't you even know a daffodil bulb when you see one?'

Antonio hurriedly picked himself up and retreated beyond range of Diana's stick. Diana then pointed her camera towards the bench and called out to Tom: 'Action!'

Tom obligingly strolled past the bench and Diana pressed the shutter release. Then Diana returned to Tom's side.

'It's very interesting,' she acknowledged.

'What is?'

'What you've been telling me about Jane. It ties in with certain experiences that I've had myself.'

'What kind of experiences?'

'Ominous ones. I have received the impression that our beloved leader, Harvey "pea-brain" Bains, is up to something.'

'Oh? What makes you think that?'

'Well, just for example, he came into the dining room this morning and kept smiling at me.'

'Perhaps,' suggested Tom, 'he's on one of those mind-altering drugs.'

Diana shook her head.

'No, that would be impossible. There'd be nothing for the drug to alter. I am convinced that a smiling Bains can only mean that he's dreaming up a new way to save money. And one such method would be to get rid of you and me, Tom. Now that we're running the residents' committee Harvey's having to shell out for long overdue improvements. To him that must be like sharing a bed with Dracula night after night. So we must guard our flanks, comrade.'

Tom nodded thoughtfully. Diana slashed at a passing squirrel with her stick but it was far too agile for her.

'So in your opinion, Diana,' said Tom soberly, 'Bains' new found affability ties in with Jane's questioning me as to your state of mind?'

'It seems a possible hypothesis. Oh, hang on – I must get one of you and the birdbath.'

Tom recoiled in alarm.

'I am not going to strip off and flap about amongst the bluetits.'

'No, what I had in mind was you standing on the bath on one leg looking like a geriatric Eros.'

'Diana —'

'Just stroll past it when I give the word.'

'You seem to be using up rather a lot of film. Could it be that you have developed an erotic fixation on me?'

'Fat chance,' jeered Diana. 'Right, start walking. Gotcha.'

Once Diana had clicked the shutter, Tom paused until she caught up with him again.

'Admit it,' he urged. 'You're going to use these shots for a pin-up calendar, aren't you? For raunchy grannies? Tom Ballard, the pensioner's Chippendale.'

'The wrinklies' ruin would be more like it.'

'Then why are you taking photos of me?'

Diana shrugged.

'Just to keep my hand in,' she averred. 'After all, I used to be a world-class photo-journalist. I might still take to the field again some day. There's plenty going on in the world, you know.'

'I do know. But I am not, in case you have failed to notice the fact, a small war or even a coup d'état.'

'You might qualify as a natural disaster. Anyway, there's no film in the camera.'

Tom stopped walking and said incredulously, 'You're not serious?'

'Well, of course I am. I wouldn't really waste a lot of expensive film on you, would I? I just need to practise the moves in order to maintain my mastery of the art.'

'Diana, I think I will spank you. You are a ruthlessly selfish superannuated brat and if only your parents had applied the rod as I am about to —'

Tom bent down and picked up a fallen willow wand. Then he made a bound forwards and seized Diana by the back of the neck. But as he tried to manoeuvre her into a position for administering the threatened corporal punishment, she suddenly shook him off with a cry:

'I was right! Look! Look!' she exclaimed urgently.

'It's no good. You can't get out of it by —'

'No, you great oaf. What we were talking about! I was right. There *is* treachery afoot!'

And she pointed dramatically. Tom followed the line of her pointing finger but saw nothing very interesting.

'Well?' he asked sceptically, his hand tightening on the willow wand again.

'My niece. The Clapham strangler herself. She's just gone into the house. I saw her.'

Tom let his hand holding the rod fall to his side. He frowned.

'Yes, and that's her car, isn't it? The Porsche which you nearly put into orbit the other day with me inside it. So what does this mean?'

'Skullduggery of some sort. She's here to confer with the bandit Bains and it can only mean trouble for me. And you too, I'll be bound.'

'Come on,' said Tom, chucking away his willow wand. 'Let's go to the office and find out.'

'Oh splendid scheme,' said Diana ironically. 'We'll knock on the door and say: "Harvey, we get the impression that you're trying to harm our interests in some way. Could you explain exactly what you intend?"'

'Well then, what do you suggest?' asked Tom a little helplessly.

'Jane knows something,' said Diana darkly. 'That's what all that spooky questioning was about, I'll be bound. So I suggest you go in search of her and when you find her wring the truth out of her.'

'Using force?'

'Definitely. But don't wring her too hard or you'll get covered in that ghastly perfume she uses to try and snare Bains with.'

'Oh is that what it is?' asked Tom with interest. 'I assumed it was an aroma she acquired from helping Antonio to manure the roses.'

'While you're interrogating Jane, I'll go back to the flat and load some film into my camera.'

'What for?'

'Well, if there is really a conspiracy against our physical or financial wellbeing it might be a good idea if we armed ourselves with photographic evidence of it. From the flat roof, using one of my superb telephoto lenses, I can get a picture of the interior of Harvey's office which will show not only the assembled conspirators, but even the gleam of greed in their eyes.'

'Righto, Colonel,' said Tom, saluting. 'Shall we set our watches?'

Diana automatically put her hand to her wrist but then irritably shook her head and abandoned the gesture.

'Oh, this isn't a game,' she snapped. 'It's for real. So get after Jane.'

Tom saluted smartly once more and trotted away. Diana, less active, nevertheless stumped off energetically with her stick beating a tattoo on the path. But when she reached her flat she had a surprise. Jane was waiting for her there.

'Hello, Diana,' Jane said with one of her faintly martyred smiles. 'Could I have a word with you?'

'Why certainly, Jane,' purred Diana but with somewhat narrowed eyes. 'How can I help you?'

'It's just that I'm a bit worried about Tom.'

'Really, Jane? Well, I admit he is rather a bizarre result of five billion years of evolution but I imagine that's not what you mean.'

'I'm worried about his mind, Diana.'

'Why, what's it been up to?'

'I just feel that Tom's been behaving a bit oddly. Not very responsibly, if you see what I mean?'

'No, I don't. I would say that Tom's mind is a magnificent instrument. It strikes me as combining all the best qualities of a supercomputer with those of an especially responsible and compassionate doctor.'

'Then why does he pretend that he's having a – a relationship with a Californian teenager called Peggy Sue?'

'Does he? I've never heard him mention it. Are you sure you're not imagining it, Jane? Remember that you do have a slight tendency to hallucinate.'

'Ooh, Diana, you fibber,' Jane said reprovingly. 'I have a very firm grasp of reality.'

'Don't be absurd, Jane. Anyone who can believe that the barracuda Bains is a wonderful human being has about as much grasp of reality as King George the Third. He, you will recall, believed himself to be an elm.'

At this point, there was a bellow from the conservatory area.

'Diana? I can't find her anywhere. But I do have news for you —'

And Tom came bustling into the room.

'Hello,' he exclaimed, stopping dead when he saw Jane. 'So she's in here? Have you been applying the thumb screws?'

'She's worried about your mind, Tom,' said Diana grimly. 'Seems to think you're going round the twist.'

'That's not true, Diana!' cried Jane shrilly. 'You mustn't say wicked things like that. Just because I – I worry about you – both of you – and so does Harvey – and we both are very concerned for your wellbeing and that's why Harvey has decided that it might be in your own best interests if – well if – well, anyway, I'm sure Harvey's right because he always is.'

And bursting into tears, Jane turned and rushed out of the flat.

'Very sinister,' said Diana gazing after her with pursed lips.

'That girl,' said Tom soberly, 'is clearly suffering from a very guilty conscience about something. But what?'

'You said you have news for me?'

'Oh yes – whatever's going on – Geoffrey and Marion are in on it. As I was scouring the grounds, I saw them roll up in the Volvo and go into Harvey's office.'

'So —,' said Diana, concentrating hard. 'The mafia top brass are in evil conference. And Bains, the *capo di tutti capi*, is probably appointing a hit man to finish us off at this very moment. But how? That's the question. All right, Tom, I'm afraid it's Everest time.'

'How do you mean?'

'A climbing job. You and I. Roped together. Although I fear that you're probably going to have to haul me up the North Face.'

'What are you talking about?'

'I must get onto the flat roof overlooking Harvey's office. So I can take some pictures. With my gammy leg I won't be able to do much serious climbing, so I'm afraid it's your powerful biceps which will have to get me up there.'

'Diana, I have some sobering news for you. It's only my astral body and not my physical one that goes up Everest. I doubt if I could get my physical body up Primrose Hill without a chair lift.'

Diana shook her head in disgust.

'No balls!' she exclaimed. 'I've said it before and I'll doubt-less say it again. No balls.'

A gloomy silence fell on the pair and persisted for some time. Finally Diana said, 'Well I suppose a chair is better than nothing.'

'For bringing down hard on Bains' head?'

'Afterwards perhaps. But first for me to stand on so that I can take pictures through his office window. I'll doubtless be spotted before long but at least I may have acquired some hard evidence of wrong doing by then. You get the chair and I'll get my camera and film.'

But at this point there was a knock at Diana's front door. Tom and Diana looked at each other.

'Possibly it's Jane come back to confess all?' suggested Tom.

Diana approached the door and called, 'Hello? Who's there?'

'It's Sarah,' came the answering call.

'Good God, she's got a cheek,' whispered Diana to Tom. 'No,

44

more likely she's the chosen hit man and she's here to polish me off.'

'Aunty?' came the voice through the door. 'Are you in there?'

'Just a minute,' called Diana. 'I'm just finishing dressing.'

'Anyway,' Tom pointed out. 'It seems that their meeting's over.'

'I'll have to let her in or she'll get suspicious,' said Diana. 'You go back to your flat and I'll come over when she's left.'

'Will you be all right?'

'Oh, I can look after myself. After all, I once walked unscathed out of the jungle in Nam after spending a month taking pictures of Johnny Cong. So I should be able to handle my niece all right.'

'Well, if you do want any help, just whistle a bar or two of "Men of Harlech" loudly and I'll come charging in with my samurai sword drawn.'

'Aunty?' came the plaintive cry once more.

'Coming,' called Diana and, as she went to open the door, she shooed Tom out through the conservatory. Diana then pulled open her front door to reveal a pretty young woman standing there smiling.

'Hello, Aunty,' said Sarah hopefully. 'May I come in?'

'Why?' asked Diana coldly.

'Well – just for a friendly visit. I won't stay long if you're busy. Here, I've brought you some chocolates.'

And Sarah handed Diana a sumptuous looking box of obviously very expensive chocolates.

'What are these for?' asked Diana suspiciously.

'Well, perhaps to thank you for looking after the Porsche for me when I was away.'

'Are the chocolates spiked with cyanide?' asked Diana ungraciously.

'No, of course not. And I do think you ought to get over this absurd notion that I'm trying to poison you.'

'Not so absurd. You tried to strangle me with your rosary.'

Sarah sighed in frustration.

'It was not a rosary. It was a present for you – a necklace that mother used to own and I thought you'd like to have.'

'But you didn't need to pull it tight around my neck.'

'It slipped as I was putting it on you. Now are you going to invite me in or not?'

'Oh all right,' agreed Diana sullenly. 'But don't expect me to make a fuss over you. I'm not going through any tedious ritual of providing tea or coffee.'

'You don't have to. I just want to be with you a little.'

Diana stood back to allow Sarah in, closed the door after her and then led her through into the sitting room. They sat down opposite each other.

'Would you mind explaining,' Diana resumed on the same morbid note as before, 'why you've come if it's not to try and kill me?'

Sarah shook her head in dismay.

'For heaven's sake, Aunty —'

'And don't call me "aunty"!' Diana flared. 'It's sickly and twee. If you want to have any kind of serious discourse with me, you can call me Diana.'

'All right then, Diana, I am not trying to kill you. As you may have noticed I visit you every month. You swear at me, accuse me of having homicidal intentions, try to wreck my car, but still I come.'

'And what I want to know is – why?'

'To see how you are.'

'Just as I thought,' said Diana grimly. 'Well you needn't bother any more. You're not mentioned in my will.'

'Your will?' echoed Sarah in exasperation. 'You haven't got anything to leave.'

'Oh yes, I have,' proclaimed Diana.

'Not by my standards. Good heavens, Aunt – Diana, how do you think I dress so well? How do you think I drive a Porsche and live in a huge apartment on the river?'

Diana frowned thoughtfully for a moment and then suggested, 'Because you're a high-class tart?'

'Because I started – and now own – one of the best model agencies in Europe. I make a great deal of money. I have no need of the few bob you have tucked away in your piggy bank.'

'Don't be a rude little girl,' snapped Diana, forgetting all the years that had passed since Sarah's childhood.

'I'm sorry. But I do sometimes get a little fed up with trailing all the way down here and getting nothing but a slagging off for my trouble.'

Diana was silent for a moment or two. She fiddled with her stick. Then she said, 'You still haven't explained it. Why do you come?'

'Because you're my family – practically all I've got left.'

'So what?'

'Well families do keep in touch with each other.'

'I never did.'

'That's just not true. When I was little you were all over me. Presents whenever you got back from one of your wonderful trips. Lots of hugs – and you never forgot my birthday. You were just lovely to me.'

Diana blinked in astonishment.

'I was?'

'Absolutely. So now I come here because I like you. No I love you. I'm sorry if that makes you squirm with embarrassment but it's true. You're my only close relative and I do love you. So there.'

Diana shook her head as if to clear it of unwanted emotion and asked gruffly, 'What have you been doing closeted with Harvey Bains and the others?'

'Well,' said Sarah.'Mr Bains is very concerned about your health. Yours and Mr Ballard's.'

'That's what he tells you.'

'Yes, it is, and I believe him. He's afraid that you and Mr Ballard are not really capable of managing your own affairs. So he has thought up a plan to help you with that task. Do you want to know what it is?'

'You bet your sweet Nellie I do,' said Diana.

And so Sarah told her.

Four days later, a short but distinguished-looking man was shown by the faithful Jane into Harvey Bains' office. The man was a reasonably eminent clinical psychologist called Dr Darrow. Harvey greeted him warmly and then, as a supreme mark of respect, seated him at his own desk.

'Tea or coffee? Or perhaps a drink?' he asked hospitably.

'No, nothing, thanks. I find these occasions rather painful.'

'But it's in their own best interests, isn't it?' asked Bains hopefully.

'Possibly. We'll see.'

'Have you read the notes? The ones taken by my young assistant, Jane, here? She obtained them by closely questioning the two luna – residents we're concerned with.'

'Oh yes, I've studied them. Most interesting.'

'I thought that's what you'd think. The point is these two trouble – er guests of ours suffer from practically every kind of delusion going. Ballard keeps taking off on these potty astral travels and Trent believes her niece is trying to kill her and it's pretty clear they've both gone so far round the bend they're practically out of sight.'

'Perhaps it would be best if we left the diagnoses to me, Mr Bains? Naturally, if I find that these people are not of sound mind I will of course sign the papers giving you power of attorney.'

Harvey smiled and accompanied the cordial expression with just the hint of a wink.

'And it goes without saying that if you do sign those papers, I will be very grateful. Yes, very grateful indeed.'

'I'm not sure I follow you, Mr Bains?'

'Oh nothing. Nothing at all. I wouldn't dream of trying to br – er, put pressure on a reputable practitioner such as yourself. So now I think we'd better have them in so that you can feel their fetlocks or whatever is necessary. Jane, could you get Tom and Diana in here, please?'

'Of course, Harvey – er – Mr Bains,' said Jane obediently.

She left the office and returned in a moment or two escorting Tom and Diana, Harvey hurried towards them, beaming.

'So good of you two to come,' he purred. 'This is Dr Darrow, the clinical psychologist that I told you about. He's conducting a survey of the elderly care establishments in this area and I thought that you two, as our most prominent residents, should be the ones to answer his little questions.'

Diana smiled sweetly – perhaps a little too sweetly – and greeted the doctor with, 'How do you do?'

'Pleased to meet you,' said Darrow, rising slightly from his chair.

Tom was more brusque. He contented himself with a nod and the words, 'What ho, quack.'

Dr Darrow frowned slightly. Tom went on, 'Dr Livingstone I presume? Or could it be the flying doctor in which case I should have said: "G'day, sport." Ho, ho, ho. Ha, ha, ha. He wants to cut my leg off – whip out my kidney – stuff me full of bicycle parts? Be my guest, quack. Think of my body as your body.'

Diana shook her head and looked deeply distressed as Tom gibbered on in this way. But he seemed quite unconcerned by her manifest anxiety.

Darrow cleared his throat and suggested: 'Would you two care to sit down?'

Diana seated herself demurely but Tom promptly turned his chair round and sat with his back to the group. Jane was watching the proceedings with a dismal expression. Indeed a close observer might have noticed that, from time to time, her chin trembled suspiciously.

'Now, Miss Trent,' said Darrow genially, 'perhaps I could first ask you a few questions. Are you happy here?'

Diana clasped her hands in front of her and, with a beatific smile, assured Darrow: 'Deliriously happy. This is the most wonderful place in the world – quite possibly in the entire universe.'

Tom, meanwhile, was snatching at invisible flies buzzing about his head and making growling sounds in his throat as if eager to devour them. He still had his back to the company.

'I see,' said Darrow, nodding thoughtfully. 'And now Mr Ballard – are you happy here?'

'Good Lord, yes,' Tom enthused, his back to the doctor. 'I particularly love the clear, fresh air at this altitude.'

'Altitude?' asked Darrow.

'Well Everest is the highest mountain in the world. Surely you knew that? Some people even get somewhat short of breath up here. Should you begin to suffer from that, Darrow, old shrink, I'll send Tensing back to base camp to get you a spot of oxygen. But, my God, just look at that view! You can practically see Tibet. On a really clear day you can even see the Bayview retirement home in Bournemouth. But that's a bit of an eyesore.'

'Very impressive,' said Darrow with a faint shrug at Bains who tried to smother a smile of delight.

'For goodness' sake, Tom,' said Diana angrily. 'Do pull yourself together. To begin with, turn round and face us.' Tom did as she ordered and then Diana urged Darrow, 'Don't think he's always quite as gaga as this. He can be quite rational – sometimes for as much as half an hour at a time.'

'I'm delighted to hear it,' said Darrow soothingly. 'Now, Miss Trent, you didn't tell me what it is that you find so pleasant here.'

'That's easy. There are very few assassins.'

'Assassins?'

'Exactly. Bains here is, of course, a killer. He has a vast armoury of weapons and practises grenade-throwing in the dining room. And the gardener runs amok with a hatchet occasionally. But the barbed wire, watch towers and dogs keep outside assassins at bay. And we have our body armour to protect us from Butcher Bains. Now, come on, Tom. It's time to treat the good doctor to a chorus of our special version of "Land of Hope and Glory".'

The two venerable patriots thereupon rose to their feet, stood side by side with their right hands raised in a military salute, and bawled a dissonant chorus of 'Land of Hope and Glory'. It was too much for Jane. The song was soon drowned out by her cry of anguish and subsequent loud sobs. Tom and Diana stopped singing and stared at her in astonishment.

'What's up with her?' asked Diana interestedly.

'Mad as a March buffalo,' suggested Tom.

'Oh,' sobbed Jane, 'I just can't bear it.' She turned to Bains. 'Oh, Harvey, I'm sorry. You know I'd do anything in my power to help your schemes but I simply can't be a Judas. I know I got the dirt on Tom and Diana for you but at the thought of what it might do to them I – I —' She then turned to the two in question and spluttered, 'Please, please, don't behave the way you are doing. You're in terrible danger. I know because I've helped to put you in it. If this mad doctor – I mean, if this doctor to mad people – decides that you're really loonies then you could lose everything. Harvey and your families will get power of attorney over your affairs and control all your money and so on. So please, please – I implore you both – pull yourselves together.'

'What's she talking about?' asked Diana curiously.

'Mad as a March sperm whale,' suggested Tom.

And Dr Darrow stood up and clapped vigorously.

'Bravo!' he cried. 'Excellent. Most entertaining.'

Harvey stared at him in dismay for a moment and then said urgently, 'But you see what they're like, don't you? I was right, wasn't I? They're both barking mad, aren't they? They have no idea what they're doing.'

'In fact,' said Darrow, a trifle ponderously. 'They both know exactly what they are doing.'

'How can you say that?' screeched Harvey.

'Come, come, Bains. People who can put on such closely observed and brilliantly acted displays of lunacy have total control over all their faculties. These two are perfectly capable of handling their own affairs. Thank you so much, Diana. And you too, Tom. Wonderful show. I particularly enjoyed the Everest bit.'

'I'm so glad,' said Tom, with a warm smile, extending his hand to take Darrow's proferred one. 'Now, you're quite sure you wouldn't like a whiff of oxygen before you go?'

'Tom!' exclaimed Diana, and this time there was a hint of real warning in her tone.

But Darrow had apparently not noticed anything untoward. He shook hands with Diana, saying, 'And now good bye to you, Diana. Oh, and please don't forget to give my regards to your charming niece.'

'What?' exclaimed Harvey, comprehension and rage fighting for supremacy on his twisted features. 'Are you saying that you know Sarah – Diana's niece?'

'Oh indeed, yes,' Darrow assured him. 'We're very old friends.'

And Darrow walked out of the office.

Harvey nodded with a pathetic attempt at a smile.

'Well,' he said, and it was clearly a tremendous effort. 'I'm glad we've got that sorted out. Naturally, I knew all along that you two were both perfectly sane and just putting on an amusing act. So, what is there left to say but, see you about, Tom and Diana?'

'Oh you will, Harvey,' said Diana warmly. 'You certainly will. And Judas – er, Jane – perhaps this will teach you to be a little more careful to whom you give your heart in future. Come along, Tom, we've got a date.'

'With Tensing? Up Everest,' asked Tom eagerly.

'No, Sir Edmund, with my niece, Sarah, for a celebration tea in my room. She'll be dying to know how we got on. It was her idea that we should put on the loony show. She said that Darrow really appreciates good theatre and she would warn him in advance so that he could put himself in the right frame of mind to appreciate it and —'

Prattling cheerfully together, the two old conspirators stomped out of Harvey Bains' office and off across the spacious grounds of Bayview. At one point Tom stopped, shielded his eyes and gazed up to catch the magnificent spectacle of the sun beginning to set behind Mount Everest.

FOUR

Tom was lying on his back in his bed staring at the ceiling. He looked rather like a dead fish. The two women gazing down at him were not, however, seriously worried. Tom's chest, under the covers, was clearly rising and falling and just occasionally his eyes, a bit like those of a lizard on a rock, blinked swiftly.

Jane said anxiously, 'See? He won't get out of bed.'

Diana, the other woman at the bedside, passed a hand in front of Tom's face as if testing for blindness. She shook her head knowingly at the lack of response.

'He's off on his travels,' she said with a sigh. 'He's working through his immense library of B-movies. For most of the past week he's been Scott of the Antarctic.' She leaned forwards and whispered in the supine man's ear, 'Tom, where are you?'

But there was still no response. She tried again, 'Tom, Jane Russell is outside. She's wearing hardly anything. And she hopes you'll give her a massage.'

'Diana!' exclaimed Jane, deeply shocked. 'That's a disgusting thing to say. It's sheer pornography.'

'Works wonders with chaps sometimes,' Diana maintained. 'But he's not responding, is he?'

'Well, Harvey's sent for Geoffrey,' Jane disclosed. 'Perhaps he'll be able to get him out of it. Otherwise we'll have to send for the doctor.'

'Oh, this isn't a medical matter,' said Diana irritably. 'He's just got the Bayview blues. You run along, Jane. I'll stay with him.'

'Are you sure?'

'Yes.'

'Well then, I'll report back to Harvey. You know how upset he gets if any of his dear residents aren't well.'

53

'Oh I do. The thought that they might snuff it and stop paying good money for their hovel and swill causes him terrible anguish. Well, you can reassure him that his investment is safe, Jane. Tom will be with us – insofar as he can ever really be said to be with us – for a long time to come.'

'I think you're very cynical, Diana,' said Jane more in sorrow than in anger. She turned to flounce out but then recalled something important and turned back, 'Oh, you won't forget, will you? About the new arrival?'

'No, never fear, Jane. Give me a buzz when she arrives and I'll take her on a guided tour of the compound, pointing out all its pitfalls and horrors.'

'Now, Diana —'

'Buzz off, Jane.'

With a doubtful final glance, Jane slipped away through the conservatory.

Diana gazed down at the motionless man, nodding sympathetically.

'I don't blame you for getting out of Bayview any way you can, old chum. But did you hear what she said? If you don't show some life they'll bring your idiot son and his revolting wife round to terrify you into responding. Marion's idea of an effective resuscitation technique will probably be something like sticking pins into your eyeballs.'

There was still no response. Diana leaned over him and said firmly but not too loudly, 'Ground Control calling Captain Tom. Come in, Captain Tom. Time to tell Aunty Diana all your woes.'

And at last Tom's eyeballs moved and he looked up at his neighbour.

'Oh, Diana —' he said with a huge, heartbreaking sigh.

'Yes?'

'Oh, Diana —'

'Well, do get on with it, you lame fish.'

'Diana —' Tom shook his head pathetically. 'How can a fish be lame? It has no legs.'

'Which is why you're so remarkable. You can actually manage it. But what's wrong? Why are you skulking in your bed? Why don't you get up?'

'There doesn't seem much point.'

'Of course there isn't much point. And that, of course, is the whole point about everything. If you were a little better acquainted with modern cosmology, and especially with chaos theory, you would realize that the real point, and by that I mean the metaphysical point —'

'Diana,' interrupted Tom with a little sigh. 'I only said I didn't want to get out of bed.'

Diana was silent for a moment. Then she nodded.

'Want to tell me why not?'

Tom heaved another heart-rending sigh, and explained, 'I'm lonely.'

'Oh rubbish,' said Diana, but not too fiercely. 'You've got friends all around you. I'm just next door. You're just suffering from a fit of the blues as we all do sometimes. Now what I do when I'm feeling really low is to go out and do something really horrible to some innocent person. Listen, the mobile library will be here soon. Why don't we both hobble down there and make the librarian's life a hell on earth by refusing to pay our fines and demanding books she hasn't got? How about it?'

Diana smiled enthusiastically, but the proposed therapy failed to commend itself to Tom. Ignoring Diana's words, he said simply, 'I miss my wife.'

Diana frowned uncertainly for a moment and asked, 'Are we talking about Mae West, Betty Grable or your real wife?'

'I'm talking about Maggie, Diana,' said Tom pathetically. 'My beloved Maggie who slipped away ahead of me fifteen years ago yesterday. And I wish I'd gone with her.'

Diana sighed and looked uneasy. Tom was getting beyond her emotional grasp. Tom went on, 'It's not too bad during the day. You're doing things, chatting away, but at night you climb into bed and switch out the light and then you're on your own. There's no one to share a thought with. No one to share a hope with. No one to light the darkness just a little.'

'Yes, well —' murmured Diana helplessly.

'So what I don't see,' went on Tom, 'is the point of getting out of bed at all. All that happens is that you dodder about all day knowing that when the night comes you'll get back into bed and be lonely again. Might as well stay there in the first place. Just stay in bed until – well – until —'

There was quite a long silence in the spruce, cheerful room that harboured not one but two lonely old people. Then Diana sighed even more deeply than Tom had been doing and murmured, 'I can see that today is going to be one long fun trip.'

After a short pause she went on, 'Now look, old chum, if you want to go back to the Antarctic or wherever you feel most cosy, I'm not the one to impede you. But just remember, if you decide you'd like to have a game of, say, explorers and ice maidens or if you just feel that you could do with a spot of company, you have only to tap on the wall and I'll come running. OK?'

But Tom had once more sunk back into his pillow and was doing his cod-on-a-slab imitation. Diana stole quietly away to her flat.

She had, however, hardly reached her living room and set up the chessboard in order to embark on the seventh game of her Bayview Championship Match against herself (in which she was at that point leading six nil) when Jane arrived once more. The matron and factotum of Bayview informed Diana that Geoffrey and Marion were in Harvey's office and that Harvey would deeply appreciate it if Diana would consent to make her way there and give the interested parties a brief account of Tom's condition. Naturally, Diana, although far from an enthusiast for the company of any of those named, agreed.

'So what you think,' said Geoffrey ponderously after Diana had, a little while later, made her report, 'is that Dad's behaving this way because he misses Mum?'

'No,' exclaimed Diana in exasperation. 'He misses Maggie, his wife.'

'Exactly,' said Geoffrey, who resembled a respectable but not very athletic pigeon. 'He misses his wife, Maggie – who was, in fact, my Mum.'

'Good God,' exclaimed Diana, appalled by the implications of what Geoffrey had said. 'Are you seriously suggesting that some unfortunate woman actually had to give birth to you, Geoffrey? I've always assumed that you were plucked by mistake from the shelf of a DIY shop just before your sell-by date. No offence intended.'

Geoffrey bore this assault stolidly, but Marion said tartly,

'And what about you, Diana? I've always assumed that you were slung out with the rubbish just after birth and then suckled by a misguided werewolf.'

'Ladies, ladies,' said Harvey diplomatically. 'There'll be time for socializing later. I think now we should concentrate on Tom.'

'What a ghastly notion,' said Marion, shuddering. 'No, I didn't really mean that. What I was trying to say was that Tom is basically an old – well, an old – just an old sort of person, isn't he? I mean he's erratic and unpredictable in his moods, wouldn't you all agree? After all, his wife has been dead and buried – cremated actually – these fifteen years.'

'Did either of you happen to know that it was, in fact, exactly fifteen years ago yesterday?' asked Diana pointedly.

'No, we didn't and what does it matter, anyway?' asked Marion brusquely. 'Is there any hope of getting this boring matter settled? I have a migraine coming on.'

'There's an infallible cure for that,' suggested Diana sympathetically. 'Cut your head off. Or get someone to do it for you.'

Marion smiled tightly. 'What a wit you have, Diana,' she applauded. 'Considering all your talents, isn't it strange you should have ended up just an embittered old spinster?'

Seeing that hostilities threatened once more, Geoffrey quickly asked Bains, 'So what do you feel we should do, Harvey?'

Bains, who was not all bad – perhaps not much more than fifty per cent on a really good day – suggested solicitously, 'I was wondering if a short break might not cheer him up.'

'Well, I hope you're not thinking of anything expensive like a cruise?' said Marion decidedly. 'He can't possibly afford it and we haven't got any spare money. I need every penny in our bank account for my spring wardrobe.'

But Bains gently persisted. 'I was actually thinking that perhaps Tom might benefit from spending a little time with you two.'

'You're not serious!' Marion exclaimed. 'You can't mean with Geoffrey and me? Not actually in our house?'

'Yes, that is what I was suggesting,' said Harvey, with a gentle smile.

'Well —' began Geoffrey.

'You're right, darling,' said Marion firmly. 'It's out of the question.' And then to Bains, 'Tom smells. It's not his fault of course but it upsets the children. And we just don't have staff, as you do here, qualified to deal with – well, with all the valves and things that old people have such trouble with. I love Tom dearly, of course, and would adore having him with us for as long as he wanted to stay if only he weren't incontinent.'

'You heartless, lying witch!' exclaimed Diana fiercely. 'Tom is not incontinent and compared to you he's as fresh as a daisy.'

'Perhaps he is,' said Marion pertly. 'But surely we are all foregathered here in this dreary little office because the saint would seem to have gone off his holy chump?'

'Dad has always been a little eccentric,' pointed out Geoffrey mildly. 'I think we'd better go and see for ourselves how he is.'

And Geoffrey got to his feet.

'All right,' agreed Marion. 'And while you're doing that I'll just take the car and pop down to the White Bear for a quick —'

'Marion,' said Geoffrey with faint reproof.

'Oh God!' exclaimed Marion desperately. 'There's no point in my coming. Tom and I hate each other.'

'Dad doesn't hate you,' said Geoffrey, patiently. 'He just feels that you're a terrible wife and mother.'

'And a ghastly human being,' added Diana. 'Otherwise he holds you in the highest regard.'

'I warn you, Diana —,' began Marion.

But Geoffrey, having started towards the door, gave her arm an unexpected tug and she stumbled after him out of the office.

Diana looked after them both anxiously.

'I think I should go too,' she said. 'I wouldn't put it past that woman to have a syringe full of cyanide stashed in her knickers and when Geoffrey's back is turned —'

'Oh, Diana, really,' remonstrated Bains with a pained smile. 'Marion is not a monster.'

'Well, she may not have been admitted to the union yet,' said Diana positively, 'but she's considered an exceptionally promising candidate.'

58

At this point, Jane bustled excitedly into the office.

'Diana, Diana,' she exclaimed, 'I've just shown Daisy Williams to her flat.'

'Well, what do you want, an MBE?' asked Diana irritably. 'You must learn to perform these little duties, Jane, without getting quite so self-important about it.'

'Oh, Diana!' chided Jane. 'You've forgotten, haven't you? Daisy Williams is the new arrival. You're going to show her round Bayview.'

'Oh my God, so I am!' groaned Diana. 'That's all I need on this abysmal day. All right, let's have it straight – what's she like?'

'Ever so nice. Ever so ladylike. Ever so —'

'I get the picture,' said Diana despondently. 'A complete nonentity. Well, you'd better lead me to her, Jane. No Trent ever shirked an assignment, no matter how challenging or disagreeable.'

But in fact, when they met a few minutes later, Diana was favourably impressed by Daisy who seemed to her a vital and intelligent person. Physically Daisy was small with an almost doll-like perfection of countenance. Indeed, so smooth and yet animated were her features and so vigorous her movements that Diana felt initially that she was too young for Bayview. She didn't seem much over fifty. Then Diana recalled what Jane had told her about the new arrival. Daisy was, in fact, almost Diana's age. At this recollection, Diana could not suppress a slight feeling of envy at the other woman's apparent gift of eternal youth.

As part of the introductions, Daisy told Diana that she was the widow of a Guards lieutenant colonel and she certainly displayed all the qualities of intelligence and breeding that such a background implied. 'My God,' thought Diana. 'If there were only five or six more like her amongst the zombies who infest this place, a life sentence to Bayview might be almost bearable.'

'Well,' said Diana with something quite like a friendly smile after introductions had been completed, 'I've been detailed to take you on the grand tour of Bayview. Don't be deceived by the lawns and the general air of genteel opulence. This place is actually a cultural and spiritual desert.'

'Really?' said Daisy, surprised. 'I've been thinking how pleasant it seemed.'

'Well it can be tolerable – when the sun is shining – and in the brief intervals when there are no brain-dead inmates shuffling past. I must say you seem in pretty good physical shape.'

Daisy smiled in acknowledgement of the compliment.

'I go in for riding, swimming, sailing —' she explained, 'but also reading, playing the piccolo, directing plays in remote garrisons – *mens sana in corpore sano* – a healthy mind in a healthy body. I've been very lucky. I've had a rich and rewarding life. And I've loved every moment of it. Especially making a team with my husband. Do you know he often got me to drill the subalterns. He said I was a better PT and drill instructor than the sergeant major. The Lady Colonel – that's what I was known as in the regiment. The Lady Colonel.'

This boast struck Diana as just a tiny bit complacent as well as slightly twee, but she found Daisy's vitality so attractive that she was prepared to overlook it. Their tour had by this time taken them close to the main building and Diana explained:

'This place has been at different times a monastery and a lunatic asylum. Nowadays, of course, it combines both those functions in the ghastly aberration we know, but fail to love, as the Bayview Retirement Village for the Almost Dead. As you can see, it was designed by an architect who was probably under sedation at the time. Either that or he had even less natural intelligence than the cloth-headed shyster who at present runs the place.'

'Oh?' asked Daisy, surprised by the ferocity of her language. 'Do you mean Mr Bains?'

'That's the one,' confirmed Diana. 'Harvey Bains. Some people maintain that, contrary to appearances, he really is a member of the human race but this remains a minority view challenged by all the best authorities. The same applies to his sidekick, the barely sentient, if harmless, animated flannel called Jane Edwards. But Jane does at least provide us all with a steady source of entertainment. Everyone has great fun making her life a misery.'

'Oh dear – is that true?'

'Absolutely. Of course, she's so sluggish she usually fails to notice. But then again, Jane is a fountain of energy compared to the average inmate. In fact, a convention of Bayview residents would make a gathering of three-toed sloths seem lively.'

'I say, you are nasty, aren't you?' said Daisy, unexpectedly.

'Oh, thank you,' said Diana genially, assuming that Daisy intended a compliment. 'Now, let's take a look at the inside of the stalag, shall we?'

They entered the main building and made their way to the dining room where lunch was being served.

'This is the slops trough,' said Diana cheerfully. 'Oh, and there's our leader.' She thereupon called across several tables. 'I say, Harvey?'

Whereupon Harvey Bains, who had been doing his rounds, looked in their direction and, seeing who it was, approached the two women, smiling his hopelessly insincere smile.

'Hello, Diana and – Rose, isn't it?'

'Daisy, actually,' Diana corrected him.

'Of course, flower-like name – flower-like face,' and Harvey purred with bogus gallantry. 'Settling in, Rose? Er, Tulip?'

Daisy smiled tightly.

'Yes, thank you.'

'Excellent,' said Harvey warmly. 'You'll forgive me if I leave you so that I can continue my lonely search for perfection? Indeed the quest for ever-improved conditions here at Bayview leaves me hardly any time for socializing with my dear residents. Enjoy your lunch.'

'It's hedgehog today, isn't it?' asked Diana quickly as Bains began to depart.

'That's right,' said Harvey, half-turning back. 'Delicious, stewed he —' Then he realized what she'd said and shook his head with mock severity. 'Ah, Diana, you are a merry prankster.' And, waving a reproving finger at her, he moved on across the room.

'Search for perfection!' exclaimed Diana. 'Where's the sick bucket? Oh, but Daisy, now here's one of the few thoroughly certificated, one hundred per cent human beings in the establishment – our Jenny.'

Jenny smiled warmly at the new arrival and cautioned, 'Don't pay any attention to Diana, Mrs Williams. She's a professional gloom merchant.'

'Oh, it's all right,' said Daisy brightly. 'I understand her perfectly. She thinks it's awfully clever to shock people. It's a common trait amongst people who are ill-mannered and ill-bred.'

Diana gaped at her.

'Hang on,' she said. 'Did you actually mean all that?'

'Decidedly,' Daisy assured her.

'Yes, but – let me get this straight. Are you really saying that we're not just having an amusing girly chat as I'd supposed? You genuinely do think that I'm ill-bred?'

'I should say that you were one of the most ill-bred people I've ever met. And now —' she turned to Jenny, 'I wonder if you could find me a table somewhere well away from this frightful woman?'

Jenny looked embarrassed but said, 'Well, I suppose – over by the window perhaps —'

Daisy turned to Diana once more with a frosty smile.

'Good day to you, Miss Trent. Thank you for the tour which you failed to spoil for me because I am capable of judging things for myself. Incidentally, I assume that it is "Miss" rather than "Mrs" Trent? It seems almost inconceivable that anyone with such a sour disposition as yours could ever have been married.'

And then Daisy turned sharply away from Diana and followed Jenny to a table over by the window. Diana gazed after her in astonishment and also, she was distressed to discover, dismay. Finding that her appetite had abruptly left her, and not primarily because of the quality of the food, Diana then made her way to the door of the dining room and continued on out of the building. She told herself that she was leaving because she wanted to check up on Tom. But if she had been completely honest with herself she would have admitted that she felt publicly humiliated and quite severely hurt by Daisy's sudden attack.

For the first time in her life, as far as she could remember, Diana felt compelled to ask herself if she might really be an unpleasant human being. Could Daisy's notion of her be the way others normally saw her? Diana's customary relationship with herself was, while not uncritical, still a reasonably comfortable one. She credited herself with being, whatever else, an independent thinker, someone who had the guts to say what she meant. But was it true? Was she a genuinely strong and outspoken person or just a selfish old biddy who sneered at those weaker than herself? What was it that Daisy had called her? Oh yes, ill-bred. So in the final analysis was Diana Trent merely an ill-bred bully?

She paused in the doorway to the main building. Across the path, Antonio was hoeing one of the flower beds. Seeing Diana emerge, he quickly moved to another bed further away. Observing this caused a new wave of self-criticism to assail Diana. Why was she always making, or trying to make, this man's life a misery? True, he was little better than a clown as a gardener and his English was so sketchy as to be nonexistent, but did that give her the right to persecute him? He was, after all, as human as she was. Had she ever tried to get to know him? To find out the circumstances that had compelled him to leave his native Portugal? Did she know anything about his mind and spirit? No, she did not. Then what, except for accidents of money and social position, gave Diana Trent the right to torment Antonio, the gardener?

'My God,' she thought, 'that woman's castrated me. If I don't get my balls back soon I'll start feeling sorry for Harvey Bains.'

She set off down the path towards her flat and was soon greeted by a cheerful voice.

'What ho, Diana?'

She looked up to see Tom beaming at her. She said, with a faint smile, 'You got up then?'

'Yes. And I think I've found the solution to my problem. I'd like to talk to you about it.'

'Really? Now?'

'How about over lunch? Or have you lunched already?'

'I'm not – hungry today.'

'Of course, it's reconstituted hedgehog on Thursdays, isn't it? I must have another go at the committee. The catering has slumped again since my kitchen revolution of a month ago.'

'Anyway,' said Diana with slight impatience, 'what's this solution?'

'Hm?'

'Oh, Tom, you said you've thought of a solution to your loneliness. What is it?'

'Ah yes. It's simplicity itself. I'm lonely. You're lonely. So why don't we shack up together?'

'Do what?' asked Diana, gazing at him in astonishment.

'Not talking of searing passion – not necessarily anyway. We could have separate bedrooms. Anyway, look, I'm starving. So I'll pop in and have a quick lunch and when I get back, you can tell me how you feel about it. How's that?'

'Well —'

'Good,' said Tom ebulliently. 'See you soon.'

And he hurried away towards the main building.

Diana gazed after him with, she was dismayed to find, her thoughts once more in a whirl. My God, she thought, what a day. First I get savaged by a colonel's lady and now I've had an offer of illicit cohabitation that has made me come over all giddy and breathless like a schoolgirl. Will life at Bayview ever be the same again?

Back at the flat, Diana found herself pacing up and down her living room trying to order her thoughts. Naturally, she had rejected Tom's offer in her mind the moment he had made it. After all, who the hell did Tom Ballard think he was? In his fantasies, she knew, he often figured as the consort to dishy film stars. But in reality he was just a portly, staring, half-crazy pensioner.

Did he imagine that all he had to do was snap his fingers and women would flop into his bed? And even if Diana did have a soft spot for him, it was only as a neighbour. Good heavens, they had only known each other for – what? Three or four weeks? And they had spent a good deal of that period having rows.

True, they had also shared a few amusing adventures, especially the Porsche trip to Brighton with that wonderful swoop at a hundred and sixty down the motorway on the way home. But that was hardly the basis for an enduring relationship.

All right, she was prepared to concede that old Tom Ballard was quite a decent bloke in a barmy sort of way. But, if she went along with his suggestion what exactly would she be letting herself in for? Would she have to act as his bearer up Everest? Help him to tunnel out of Colditz? And in the real world? Cook him meals? Nurse him when he was sick? Fat chance. Diana was a loner who had never – no, who had only once – found living with a man a tolerable experience. Of course it was true that on that one occasion she had found it not only tolerable but such a miracle of joy that it had almost provided enough happiness for a lifetime.

It had happened during the war when she had been just twenty. The living together had only lasted three weeks and had occurred in a borrowed flat in London during the Blitz. Diana had purely by chance found herself sharing the place (which belonged to a mutual friend) with a Spitfire pilot called Buck. Buck had, before two days and nights had passed, seemed to her to be the companion and lover of her dreams made flesh. And they had laughed and loved for the whole three weeks even when cowering under the dining-room table as sticks of bombs raced towards them like giant exploding footsteps.

But within a week of his having returned to his squadron Buck had been shot down over Kent and had burned to death in the air hanging from his parachute. When the rescue people had found him on the ground Buck had, from the ferocious flames that had engulfed his plane, seemed more like a charred log than a human being. So terrible were his burns that his brother pilots had been unable to figure out how he had even managed to get out of his cockpit in those days before ejector seats. Anyway, since those unforgettable three weeks with Buck in wartime London, Diana had hardly ever spent more than a night with a man. Oh yes, Ballard really had an infernal cheek. And she could hardly wait for him to get back so that she could snub him.

But Tom was a long time over lunch. Diana looked at her watch quite often and began to feel rather cross about his failure to return. He was not, after all, feasting in the Savoy Grill but spooning up stewed hedgehog, or whatever it was, at Bayview. How could that take – what? Yes, he'd been gone an hour and a half. Damn it, the man had asked her to live with him. Surely elementary courtesy should have brought him hotfooting back to her flat for her response?

So she paced and consulted her watch and felt indignation grow and paced some more until she found that over two hours had passed since she had bumped into Tom outside the main building. Well, enough was enough. She was going to bed. She usually had a nap at this time. If this was a foretaste of the shared life he had imagined for them then he could jolly well – and then she heard something. What? It seemed to be a strange kind of noise, a bit like a fire crackling. Where was it coming from? She listened intently. Yes, it was coming from Tom's flat. But what could be causing it? Thieves? She might be cross with Tom but she couldn't just let him be burgled.

Very cautiously Diana edged out into her conservatory and there, with the sound just that little bit louder and clearer, she realized what it was. It was not being caused by a thief at all. It was, in fact, laughter, female laughter. And it was now followed by speech. And with a stab of such intense anger and disappointment as she had not felt for decades, Diana realized that Tom was entertaining Daisy Williams in his quarters.

Diana knew what she should have done. She should have turned haughtily and strode back into her flat, firmly closing the door behind her. What she actually did, after a moment's anguished pause, was to steal quietly through her own conservatory until she reached Tom's adjoining one. And then, loathing herself as she did so, she eavesdropped.

And she heard Tom and Daisy chatting about their marriages. And as each unfolded the story of a happy and loving relationship, the other listened sympathetically. It was clear that they were united in instinctive understanding and each was able to supplement the other's memories. And strangely, to Diana's way of thinking, Daisy and Tom were not sad or elegiac but laughed quite a lot about the past.

As she listened guiltily, Diana realized that the jokes they were telling about married life were not like her own bitter and mocking witticisms. Daisy and Tom, it seemed, had often found married life to be something of a farce. But they had also known it as a joy and a blessing.

Diana shook her head crossly. Well, so what? Daisy had loved her colonel and Tom had loved his Maggie and where were the loved ones now? They were dust, weren't they? And Tom and Daisy were now just as alone as Diana. The only difference was, Diana congratulated herself, that she could get by without such treacly orgies of nostalgia.

And yet, sickening though she was finding the scene going on next door, Diana was astonished to experience moments when her heart seemed to pause in her breast. These moments occurred when, perhaps following a joke, there was a long, inexplicable silence from within Tom's living room. But why, Diana wondered, did these silences trouble her so? Surely it couldn't be because she saw on a mental screen two old but vital people inside looking at each other as they laughed and then, falling silent, continuing to look at each other as their heads moved imperceptibly closer together until, reaching out, Tom pulled Daisy gently into his arms and their lips —

'Oh, rot and rat droppings!' growled Diana to herself.

What the hell did she care if they were kissing and cuddling or not? What the hell did it matter to her if they were rolling naked on the hearth rug? And yet, once, when the silence was especially protracted, Diana imprudently leaned further and further over until she suddenly found she could see the two culprits. And what she actually beheld was them sitting side by side on Tom's big sofa, gazing ahead with faint reminiscent smiles. But why, she wondered, having seen this and thus established that their conduct was still well within the bounds of the strictest propriety, did Diana feel such an extraordinary sense of relief? Furious with herself, she abandoned her shameful station, stepped back very slowly and cautiously and then returned through her own conservatory to her living room once more.

Then she went into her hall, put on her coat, took her stick and stumped off out of the flat, through the grounds and along the road to the bus stop. She took the bus into Bournemouth and spent the afternoon window shopping and having tea in a chilly café on the seafront. And when she got back to Bayview late in the afternoon she tried to read the copy of *Vogue* that she had bought in town. But she tended to sit with it on her lap, staring into space, rather than reading much.

At about six, she heard, with a sudden and almost alarming thump of her heart, Tom calling to her from his conservatory.

'I say are you there?'

'Where?' Diana called back, trying to sound perfectly normal.

'There in your place?'

'No, I'm not. Try somewhere else.'

'I have done. And I couldn't locate you. I say, Diana, can I come over?'

'I don't know. Can you?'

'Ah, here you are,' said Tom, grinning broadly as he appeared from her conservatory. 'I looked in earlier. You were out.'

'Yes, I buzzed into Bournemouth for a breath of sea air and to drown myself. But the water was too cold.'

'Now tell me – what do you think of Daisy Williams?' asked Tom eagerly. 'I mean, wouldn't you say that she was wonderful?'

'Absolutely,' affirmed Diana, dismayed by a feeling that her leaden heart had torn loose and was sinking rapidly towards her shoes.

'Of course,' said Tom cheerfully, 'I know you two had a little bust-up earlier. Daisy told me about it. We sat at the same table over lunch.'

'Oh, it was nothing that major surgery won't fix,' said Diana, attempting her standard breezy manner. 'So you think Daisy is wonderful, do you?'

'Yes, she's so full of life. And what an interesting one she's had. We talked for hours – all through lunch and then after it at my place.'

'Which must account for that high pitched buzz I heard. I went out to escape it.'

Tom laughed merrily at what he took to be a jest and then said, 'Listen, there's something I want to ask you?'

'Really?' asked Diana, her heart suddenly, and very disconcertingly, giving a thump. 'I wondered when you'd mention it.'

'Mention what?'

'Well – I mean – whatever it is that you want to ask me.'

'Right. I just thought it might be a splendid idea if we all three had a drink together?'

'Oh that is indeed a wonderful idea,' enthused Diana. 'You mean you, me and Cary Grant?'

'Or even better,' said Tom, ignoring her facetious remark, 'why don't we have dinner together? There's a new Thai restaurant out on Elm Avenue? Daisy and I have both heard good reports of it.'

'Yes, I believe their fricasseed dog is superb.'

'Give it some thought – and let me know if you'd like to join us. Now I must go and write to the Prime Minister about my pension. He promised he'd jack it up a bit and he hasn't done so. I shall remind him in no uncertain terms.'

Tom turned and began to move towards the conservatory. Diana suddenly called:

'Tom?'

He turned back.

'Yes?' he asked, with a smile on his broad face.

'Erm, you remember you wanted to ask me something?'

Tom frowned.

'Really? When was this?'

'Well, it was – it was —' Diana licked her lips slightly. 'It was when you first arrived at Bayview. You wanted to know if – if it was possible to have an allotment in the grounds.'

'Me?' exclaimed Tom incredulously. 'I find it hard enough to grow hair never mind cabbages.'

'No, how silly of me,' exclaimed Diana. 'It wasn't you at all. It was Harry Walton, and he died last week, didn't he? I don't know what made me recall it just then. All right, I'll think about the dog supper. Is there anything else you want?'

'Not that I can think of,' said Tom. And this time he departed.

After he had gone, Diana sat for a long time just staring straight in front of her. But then she shook her head, picked up *Vogue* again and began to turn the pages. A close observer, however, would have discerned that she still wasn't actually reading the magazine. She was merely gazing past it into space.

FIVE

'What is it?' asked Tom, frowning suspiciously at the concoction.

'Raw eggs, sherry, cream and a dash of tabasco sauce,' explained Basil, holding the glass up to the light.

'Sounds ghastly,' exclaimed Tom.

'No, it's marvellous,' Basil assured him. 'Mind you, it tastes ghastly.'

'Then in what way is it marvellous?'

'For virility. The "stud's stand-by" is what we used to call it when I was a young officer. We always made sure we drank one before going on a date and it never let us down.'

'In what way?'

'In every way. And especially —'

'Yes, all right,' said Tom. 'Have you been drinking a lot of this stuff lately, Basil?'

'No, just morning and evening as usual. Why do you ask?'

'Because your virility seems to be getting a little rampant. As a matter of fact, that's why I'm here.'

'Really?' asked Basil, intrigued. 'Come for a few tips, have you?'

'No, I haven't,' said Tom irritably.

At this point, Basil took a deep breath, raised the glass to his lips and, closing his eyes, gulped down its unpleasant looking contents.

'Ugh – yugh – oof!' he exclaimed, wiping his lips. Then, with his silk dressing gown flapping about him, he rose from his chair and trotted three times round his living-room table. Tom watched this performance and marvelled that an old man who was as seemingly frail as Basil had become known in the retirement home as the Bayview Stallion.

'What was that for?' asked Tom curiously.

'What was what for?' asked Basil, reseating himself.

'That canter round the table?'

'Oh, that's the effect it has on me. Provides instant energy. After consuming it I need either a quick sprint or a woman. And, as you may have noticed, there doesn't happen to be a woman present.'

'Have you always been like this?' asked Tom curiously.

'Like what?'

'Well – as sexually active as you are now?'

'Oh, good heavens, no,' the little chap assured him. 'I realize I'm not much any more but when I was young I was a real goer.'

'Well, all I can say,' said Tom, shaking his head wonderingly, 'is that you've become a living legend around here.'

'Really?' asked Basil, smiling with pleasure. 'Well, I like to be of service.' Basil glanced about as if wary of eavesdroppers and then leaned towards Tom and confided, 'You know there are a lot of hot chicks in this place once you get to know them. You quite often find that behind the Zimmer frame lurks a real nympho.'

'Yes, well I'm here to tell you that Daisy Williams is not one of them.'

'Oh? And which one is Daisy Williams? Remind me.'

'The new resident. She arrived two days ago.'

'Ah yes,' said Basil, actually rubbing his hands together with enthusiasm. 'No nympho I grant you, but still a kind of geriatric sex kitten. I expect that Daisy and I will spend many a long winter afternoon together in the sack.'

'Well, I think you'd better abandon any such ambitions,' said Tom firmly. 'If you don't, you may find yourself up before the local magistrates on a charge of sexual harassment.'

'What?' asked Basil, his jaw dropping and his eyes widening. 'My dear fellow, I don't understand —'

'Well, it's really quite simple, Basil, old goat. Daisy has given me instructions to inform you that if you make any more unwelcome advances to her she will complain to the police. I think she also rather expects me to give you a good horse-whipping, but I seem to have misplaced my only good horse-whip.'

Basil stared at Tom in blank astonishment for a moment

before protesting, 'But this is extraordinary. I outlined my advanced sexual ecstasy course for her only yesterday and she was rapturous.'

'How do you know?'

'Well – she looked rapturous. They usually do you know. I have built into my course a number of highly effective Indian and Chinese techniques for maximizing physical delight and these usually arouse a girl's interest. Another way I can tell that the little darlings are responding is from certain physical signs such as the heaving bosom, the —'

'Yes, yes,' agreed Tom quickly. 'But can you be quite certain that Daisy was putting out the right signals?'

'Well, I think so. And I'm very experienced. She's a damned attractive gel. So much so that I went over my plans for her in far greater detail than I normally do. We were seated on the bench down by the greenhouse and I particularly noticed how pretty she looked with the daffodils on the lawn behind her. Now if she was upset by anything I was saying, well – why didn't she just tell me?'

'The answer to that question is quite simple, Basil. She was literally speechless with indignation. She told me that nobody, not even the neighbourhood louts when she was a girl, had spoken to her as you did.'

'I daresay that's true,' said Basil thoughtfully. 'As far as I am aware my sexual ecstasy programme is unique. I've had many offers of publication, of course, but I could never permit that. Some things must remain sacred.'

'Well, sacred or profane, I think you'd better lay off Daisy Williams.'

There was a moment or two of silence and then Basil said disconsolately, 'You know what I think?'

'What?' asked Tom in return.

'I think you're just being dog-in-the-manger about this. You want to keep her for yourself. I've seen you giving her the rush – a stroll by the lake one minute and a wild conversation over breakfast the next. But there's no need for all that, you know. I don't want to take her away from you but just to get my fair share. We might even consider embarking on an amusing little threesome or perhaps I could bring another chick along and —'

'That's quite enough,' said Tom forcibly. 'Mrs Williams and I are just good friends —'

'A likely tale,' grumbled Basil.

'Whatever you may think,' asserted Tom loftily, 'not every man is a rampant Casanova. Anyway I have delivered my message and I will now leave you to consider it. But for your own good, Basil, I would advise against any further approaches to Daisy Williams.'

'Horse feathers!' Basil retorted in the slang of an earlier era, as Tom stalked out of his flat.

At about this time, the lady in question was strolling in the grounds of Bayview in the company of Jane.

'I'm so glad you liked the flowers,' Jane was saying. 'It's so nice to get a little appreciation for one's efforts. Normally —'

Jane broke off, staring. Daisy glanced around, saw her eyes popping and followed their line of sight. When she saw what had silenced Jane, she too gaped at the strange procession approaching them. It consisted of Antonio, the Bayview gardener, wheeling his largest wheelbarrow piled high with all manner of miscellaneous bits of timber and planking. Behind Antonio marched Diana who was flicking the gardener from time to time with her stick as if he were a pack mule and shouting: '*Vite, vite,* you Latin moron. *Plus vite encore,* or I'll flay you alive.'

Jane swallowed and, as these two drew abreast, said politely, 'Hello, Diana. Whatever are you and Antonio doing?'

'Mind your own business,' snarled Diana. Her vile temper, it seemed, was fully restored.

'I think,' said Daisy, in icy tones, 'a civil question deserves a civil answer.'

'Do you indeed, Little Miss Muffet?' said Diana, pausing. 'Then think of a civil answer to this one: how would you like me to pull out all your hair and use it for stuffing my new scatter cushions?'

Daisy clicked in disapproval as the strange caravan passed on.

'I don't know what's wrong with Diana,' said Jane unhappily. 'She's never been a bundle of fun, but for the last day or two she's been pure poison.'

'It's frustration,' said Daisy positively.

'Do you think so?' asked Jane. 'What kind of frustration exactly?'

'Oh, I think it's obvious. She's frustrated because – not surprisingly with her vile temperament – she's never succeeded in attracting a husband. Women like that get increasingly bitter and twisted. The next stage is that they turn on all those about them and finally they go raving mad.'

'Oh dear,' said Jane. 'Does that always happen?'

'Well, perhaps not always but very commonly. I say, what's the matter?'

Daisy had noticed a trembling of the chin and a suspicious moisture in the eye of the other.

'I don't want to go mad,' gulped Jane.

'Well, why should you? You're married to Mr Bains, aren't you?'

Jane gulped again and said wretchedly, 'I don't think you quite understood what I was saying earlier, Mrs Williams. It's not that I'm actually married to Harvey —' and Jane could not refrain from moaning slightly at the intoxicating thought. 'No, it's just that I really want to be.'

'Oh dear,' said Daisy. 'Well, never mind. If you feel madness coming on I'm sure you'll be able to find someone to marry you. Oh, look, here comes Mr Ballard.'

'Hello, Daisy,' said Tom with a big smile.

'Hello, Tom,' said Daisy, smiling back.

'Hello, Jane,' said Tom with another big smile.

'Boo hoo!' said Jane, covering her face with her hands and rushing away.

'Extraordinary girl,' exclaimed Tom watching her flight. 'Whatever can be ailing her?'

'I think I know,' said Daisy. 'It was something I misguidedly said. But don't worry I'll cheer her up later. Now, did you have a word with that horrid little man?'

'Steady on,' said Tom. 'Basil is very popular around here and, perhaps surprisingly, even more with the ladies than the chaps. But the answer to your question is: yes. I made it clear to him that his attentions were unwelcome to you. I don't think you'll have any further trouble from that quarter.'

'Splendid,' said Daisy.

'I say,' said Tom, glancing up at the blue sky approvingly. 'It's a wonderful day and I've finished my tunnelling duties early. Why don't you and I take a bus ride into Bournemouth and then a stroll along the front?'

'Sounds good to me,' said Daisy, and she took Tom's arm and off they marched together.

A few hours later Tom returned on his own. This was not because discord had arisen between him and Daisy but only because the latter had decided to stay on and buy some clothes at a sale. Tom had to return to Bayview to play a previously agreed game of croquet and so he and Daisy agreed to part and then meet again for dinner either at Bayview or at one of the local restaurants. Tom had promised to call for Daisy.

Once back in his flat, Tom changed into suitable clothes for croquet in his bedroom and then, still tying his cravat, walked into his living room, calling out:

'I say, Diana —'

He knew that Diana was often to be found in her conservatory at this time of day, taking tea, or, occasionally, gin.

There was no reply and Tom, late for his game of croquet, hurried through into his own conservatory which was really the other half of Diana's.

'Diana,' he called more loudly as he went. 'Daisy and I have just come back from Bournemouth and you'll never guess —'

He then fell silent, staring. And the sight that had claimed his wondering attention was not Diana but – yes, well what, in fact, was it? It was odd. It was surreal. It was not something that had been present in his conservatory, or, come to that, in Diana's, a few hours before, and it raised a number of uncomfortable questions. How had it got there? Why had it got there? Would it ever go away again – to name but a few.

Tom approached it uncertainly and then raised his hands and pressed them against it. Yes, it really was what it had seemed to be – a wall. The wall was crudely fashioned from odds and ends of timber but for all that it was a solid and impenetrable structure which completely separated the two conservatories and thus, effectively, the two flats.

A sudden doubt assailed Tom. Was he actually in his own flat? There were, in the grounds of Bayview, several other units with shared conservatories of the kind he and Diana occupied and it was not totally unknown for Tom to mistake one of the others for his own. Yes, but that had only happened at night, in the dark, after a party. He glanced down at the cravat he had put on. Yes, it was his all right. He went back into the living room and glanced about. No, there could be no doubt: this room, which contained many of his most prized personal possessions, was quite certainly his very own living room.

So what on earth was that wall doing in the conservatory?

Tom went back out to where the wall now bisected the conservatory and addressed the structure diffidently. 'Excuse me, wall,' he said, 'my name is Scott – no hang on, it's Tom and – I was just wondering – I do hope you won't take this as a mark of unfriendliness, wall – but could you possibly be at the wrong address?'

Tom thereupon pressed his right ear to the wall as if listening.

'I see,' he went on. 'So you're saying that Diana put you there? Yes, well, I thought she might have done. The question is – why? Have you any idea? No? None at all? Then I suppose I shall just have to ask her.'

At this Tom knocked quite loudly on the wall. He had barely concluded his knock when – giving him quite a shock – a panel set into the wall at head height, and which he had not previously noticed, flew open and part of Diana's face became visible.

'Oh – er – hello, wall,' Tom stammered. 'You know you look remarkably like Diana Trent and it very definitely suits you. Has anyone mentioned that before, wall?'

'What do you want?' asked the wall angrily.

'Erm, you haven't seen Diana about, I suppose?' asked Tom diffidently.

'Stop playing the village idiot,' snapped the wall.

'Ah yes, of course,' agreed Tom humbly. 'I'll just slip off my smock and brush the hay out of my hair. There, that's better. But the truth is, Diana, I'm still a bit puzzled by this wall.'

'Really?' asked Diana, sarcastically. 'You mean, you have never seen one before?'

'I have never seen one in my conservatory before. And, candidly, I don't think it constitutes a significant improvement.'

'Oh yes, it does. It performs the function that all good walls do.'

'And what would that be?'

'It keeps the barbarians at bay.'

'Ah, I see. You're thinking of barriers like Hadrian's Wall and the Great Wall of China? Do you know, I thought I was the only one around here that had problems with reality? Well, would it increase your peace of mind, Diana, if I told you that there are neither Mongols nor wild Celts on this side of your wall?'

'Not in the slightest. There is you.'

'True, but I gave up raping and pillaging years ago. I'm now a model citizen and a good neighbour.'

'Rubbish!' snapped the wall and with a little bang its panel slid shut again and Diana's face was blotted out.

'Hey, come back,' called Tom. 'That's not fair. Even the most rabid barbarian can't be expected to reform unless he knows what his crimes are? Diana? How have I upset you? I say? Diana?'

But answer came there none.

Tom sighed and returned into his flat to get his bomber jacket and scarf. He then went to the croquet lawn, which was in the grounds of Bayview, played, won (which was not too difficult since his opponent was ninety-two and had only one good eye) and returned once more to his flat. When he got there he found, with small delight, that both Harvey Bains and Jane were lurking in his conservatory.

'Hoy,' he said. 'It's not really done to just walk into a chap's home while he's out.'

'Oh, Tom,' said Jane apologetically, 'you left the conservatory door open.'

'And you took that for an invitation to trespass, did you?' asked Tom sternly.

'Well, not exactly but —'

'The point is,' said Bains peremptorily, 'it was clearly my duty to inspect this outrage.'

'That is no way to refer to my home,' said Tom mildly.

Harvey pointed to the wall.

'I mean this – this wooden partition. What's it doing here?'

'Oh, nothing very much,' said Tom. 'Possibly a little fishing and tennis, but basically it's just come for a good long rest.'

'Did you put it up?' asked Harvey, ignoring Tom's somewhat ponderous humour.

'As a matter of fact, I did not. That barrier is Diana's brain-child.'

'Oh!' exclaimed Jane, 'I've just remembered.'

'Remembered what?' asked Harvey.'

'When I was walking in the grounds with Mrs Williams we saw Diana and Antonio with a wheelbarrow full of wood. He must have used it to build the wall for her.'

'Well, if that's true,' said Bains grimly, 'I shall have to consider terminating Antonio's contract.'

'Oh, he's got a contract, has he?' asked Tom. 'I always thought you just gave him a bowl of gruel three times a day and warned him that if he complained the authorities would have him broken on the wheel.'

Harvey shook his head wearily.

'Tom, this is quite a serious matter. Your humour is ill-conceived.'

'Yes, it's not really up to my usual standard, is it? But aren't you making rather heavy weather of this wall, Harvey? I mean it's not an actual threat to life and limb, is it?'

'You know nothing about estate management, Tom. That wall is a fire hazard and if the insurance people ever heard about it they could invalidate my cover.'

'Well, I agree we must avoid that at all costs,' affirmed Tom. 'You'd frighten some of the spinsters if you ran around Bayview with invalidated cover.'

'Tom —'

'Sorry. But it seems to me that the question is: why has Diana put it up – or had it put up?'

'To upset me of course,' maintained Harvey. 'Everything that woman does is designed to upset me.'

'But she told me only last week she was bored with that lark, Harvey,' Tom assured the distraught manager. 'She considers it too easy. No, the truth is I think this wall is here because of me.'

'Well then, surely it's up to you to ask her,' snapped Harvey.

'I have done. She refuses to discuss the matter.'

'Does she indeed? Well, my job is to run Bayview efficiently and economically and without illegal partitions popping up all over the place.' He turned to his secretary and aspirant spouse and said, 'Jane, I'm afraid you'll have to sort this out. Diana's gone too far this time. Tell her I want the wall removed and, if it has not been removed by the end of next week, then I shall have to recommend to the committee that her residency agreement be terminated. Is that clear?'

'Tell him to get stuffed, Jane,' said an acid voice nearby. 'And preferably with high-level radioactive waste.'

They all turned and – just before the sliding panel closed again – caught a glimpse of Diana's face, wearing a bitter smile.

For the next few days, Tom applied repeatedly to Diana for an explanation as to why she had put up the wall. But she gave him either no answers at all or such complicated ones that he could make small sense of them. Actually, he did not see a great deal of Diana during this period. He had taken to eating at Daisy's table rather than at Diana's in the dining room, partly as a protest against the wall and partly because he and Daisy were getting on rather better than he and Diana were.

No one else joined Diana at her table and Tom sometimes felt a pang of guilt when he saw her, grim and alone, spooning up her fare and occasionally snarling fiercely at Harvey, who might be doing his rounds, or perhaps at Jane. He also noted with surprise that she was once quite rude to Jenny who had always been the one person to whom Diana was relatively civil.

A few days later, in her chintzy and charming flat, Tom sat opposite Daisy, who had a steaming silver teapot poised above two dainty cups placed on a silver tray. There was also on the tray a cake stand with simple but clearly home-made and delicious looking cakes on it.

'Tea?' asked Daisy.

'Please,' Tom said.

'What's the matter?' Daisy asked.

'Oh nothing —'

'Yes, there is. Tell me.'

'It's just that I'm a little worried about Diana —'

Daisy stiffened slightly.

'I would have thought it was her victims that deserved your sympathy,' she said coldly.

Tom smiled wryly and said, 'True. But Diana's going to get chucked out of Bayview. And I don't think she's got anywhere else to go. I've just come from Bains' office. And he was adamant.'

'Adamant about what?'

'Well, I went there to ask him to give her a little more time, but he refused. He said that if she hasn't pulled down her silly wall by Saturday she'll be out on her ear.'

'Would you miss her?' asked Daisy, with a faint smile.

'Yes, I think I would,' said Tom with a sigh. 'Before you came, she was about the only person around here I could talk to.'

'By that I assume you mean trade insults with?'

'Oh, Diana's not always a vicious harpy. Come to think of it that's not true. She is always a vicious harpy. But then even vicious harpies have the right to life, liberty and the pursuit of happiness. Who said that? Abraham Lincoln? Or did I just make it up?'

'It was Thomas Jefferson in the preamble to the American Declaration of Independence,' said Daisy.

'Yes, not really up to my standard,' said Tom. He heaved a sigh and changed the subject. 'Anyway, what are you and I going to do this evening?'

'Who said we were going to do anything this evening? At least together?'

Tom smiled ruefully.

'No one, I suppose. But since the subject has now cropped up —'

'I ought to write some letters,' said Daisy.

'Letters?' repeated Tom with a frown. 'That reminds me —'

He reached into his breast pocket and withdrew a plain white envelope. 'Yes, Jane gave me this for you when I was in the office. She said it came by the second post.'

Tom handed the envelope to Daisy, who looked at it curiously. It bore the printed address of a firm of solicitors.

'Oh dear,' said Daisy.

'What is it?' asked Tom.

'From my solicitor. Almost always bad news. Oh well, no point in just waiting and wondering.'

She tore open the envelope quickly, withdrew a typed letter and scanned it. Her expression did not change.

'Bad news?' asked Tom.

Daisy shook her head slowly but she also sighed quite deeply.

'No,' she said. 'Quite the reverse really. And yet —'

She smiled a wistful little smile.

'What does it say?' asked Tom. 'If you don't mind my asking.'

In reply, Daisy simply handed him the letter and he read it slowly and carefully. Then he nodded and said sadly, 'I see. I didn't even know this was on the cards.'

He handed the letter back to her.

'No – well,' said Daisy, looking at Tom uncertainly, 'there didn't seem much point in telling you because I didn't think it would happen for months or even years.'

'And it's what you want, is it?' asked Tom, a trifle wistfully.

'Well, yes it is, rather. You see, it will be like – oh, like a wanderer returning to his native land.'

'I shall miss you,' said Tom.

'I hope so. But don't look so glum. We'll stay friends. And I've got seven whole days still. And in answer to your earlier question about what to do this evening. Well, I suggest that we really live it up. And not just for this evening but for the whole week.'

Tom brightened perceptibly.

'You mean wild parties? Night clubs? Drinking and carousing until the small hours?'

'Exactly. Or failing those we might settle for a tea dance, a few decent meals in tolerable restaurants and perhaps a good film or two.'

'You're on,' said Tom. 'But look here, is it still possible to find a tea dance? Even here in Bournemouth?'

It turned out that it was – in a small but picturesque hotel on the front and with a disco rather than a palm court orchestra. Tom and Daisy had a whale of a time there, drinking tea, eating butterfly cakes and waltzing gravely round the dance floor. They tried the foxtrot too but Tom had never learned it and his version was more like the bear shuffle.

And during the next few days they went on to do all the

other things that Daisy had suggested and they enjoyed them all enormously. On their last day together they made an addition to the programme. They hired a small car and drove along the coast, crisscrossing the downs, admiring the views and having a sumptuous picnic in a hollow of the hillside. Daisy had prepared the feast and it was based on cold pheasant, wine and apple tart but included an array of other goodies as well.

After consuming this alfresco banquet they lay side by side in the surprisingly warm spring sun and chatted until they both drifted off to sleep. An hour or so later they awoke feeling rather chilled and had to warm themselves up with the help of the car heater. Then they drove some more and that evening, having returned the car to the firm in Bournemouth from which they had hired it, they went for their last dinner together to a French bistro that they had found earlier in the week.

And in the bistro, when they were about half way through their second bottle of claret, Tom took Daisy's hand and said, 'I don't want you to go. In fact, I don't think I could bear it.'

'If that were really true,' said Daisy, smiling, 'why then I wouldn't go.'

'But it really is true,' said Tom.

'No, you only think it is, because you're lonely. I'm lonely too. But it's not the same as wanting to be together.'

'But I do want us to be together.'

'You wouldn't like it,' said Daisy. 'Not for long. You'd soon learn that I'm really rather a martinet. I wasn't called the Lady Colonel for nothing. I'd make you smarten up in all kinds of ways. And you'd begin to detest me. For my part, your fantasy life and general refusal to take things seriously would soon begin to drive me up the wall.'

'But we've had a wonderful week.'

'So we have,' agreed Daisy. 'But I suspect a week is about our limit. After much more than that the sparks would begin to fly. Anyway, there's nothing to prevent us having more marvellous weeks in the future. We'll be able to visit each other – if we want to.'

'But it's going to be absolutely dreadful,' said Tom, 'with both of you going.'

'How do you mean, both of us?'

'You and Diana.'

'Diana's not going.'

'Yes, she is. Harvey's having her thrown out. He's already arranged to get the fire department in to knock down her wall.'

'Tom, I think you should know that I was rude to Diana. I called her ill-bred. And it won't have helped that you and I have been seeing so much of each other. Your best plan is to talk to her.'

'But I keep trying. She won't listen.'

'Try once more. I think that when she learns I'm leaving it will make a big difference. But if that doesn't work – and only as a last resort – give her this.'

And Daisy produced from her handbag a small, neat, sealed envelope.

'What is it?' asked Tom .

'I'm not going to tell you. And now, it's our last evening, why don't we dance until dawn?'

'I didn't know one could in Bournemouth?'

'I don't suppose one can – in Bournemouth. But I've got a splendid selection of old foxtrot records in my flat and I left a bottle of champagne in the fridge. How about it?'

So they danced until dawn – well, damned nearly half past twelve anyway. At which point Tom found he could no longer hoist himself out of the chair upon which he was resting between records. Daisy thereupon kissed him gently on the brow, tugged him to his feet, led him to the door and aimed his lurching form in the direction of his own quarters. After that, it took him the best part of an hour of wandering aimlessly about the grounds of Bayview before he finally stumbled upon his flat, entered it and passed out fully dressed on the sofa.

When he awoke the sun was shining, the birds were singing and his head was aching. He rose unsteadily to his feet, tottered into his bathroom and surveyed himself in the mirror above his sink. On the surface he looked much the same as usual. There was no visible indication of the small factory for manufacturing car parts which someone had started up in the front part of his brain.

He filled the washbasin with water and plunged his head into it. He kept his head submerged until he was gasping for breath. Then he withdrew it, took a deep breath and plunged it in once more. And after that, he felt somewhat better. He turned and walked slowly and carefully into his kitchen where he put on a kettle in order to make himself some coffee.

But at this point he suddenly exclaimed, 'Oh God!' He looked at his watch, saw that it was half past ten and moved hurriedly to the telephone. He picked it up and dialled Daisy's number. But it turned out that it was too late for the farewell call that, before drunken sleep had claimed him the previous night, he had promised himself he would make. The 'phone just rang and rang. Daisy was on her way to Aldershot.

He sat down on his sofa and tried to ward off the huge sense of abandonment and loneliness which swept over him. It wouldn't have been so overwhelming if he and Daisy hadn't spent such a wonderful week together. True, they had never done anything more intimate than hold hands, except for once when Tom had leaned down and given her a quick peck on the lips when they were parting for the night. But Tom felt that he and Daisy had experienced a great romance.

'Play it again, Sam,' he murmured to himself in an atrocious Bogey accent.

And yet – he smiled ruefully. She had doubtless been right in what she had said. It had been an affair, if such a chaste relationship could be called that, that had taken place out of time. They had both been acting really; playing the parts of two aging people having a last carefree fling. Their real personalities had not been engaged. If they had been, the result would probably have been just as Daisy had warned: they would soon have begun to drive each other crazy.

So was Tom destined, he wondered, to spend his last years utterly alone? His beloved Maggie was long gone from the earth. True, if there really were a heaven then she might be waiting for him there. But, meanwhile, he could easily have many years still to spend in this strange world. And the only people that he could claim any kind of relationship with here were his son, Geoffrey, and Geoffrey's toxic wife, Marion. What a prospect.

Tom frowned and patted his inside jacket pocket. Yes, it was there still, the envelope that Daisy had given him for possible handing on to Diana. Talk to Diana, Daisy had urged. All very well but what if Diana wouldn't talk back?

Tom rose and went slowly into his conservatory. The wall, he noted at once, was still there. He paused and listened. He could hear no sound from the other side of the wooden structure. Diana would have been up and about for some time and might by now easily have left her flat. Still, Tom went up to the partition and knocked.

'Diana?' he called. 'Are you there?'

There was no answer. He knocked again.

'Diana? I have something important to tell you.'

There was still no answer. He tried once more.

'Daisy's gone, Diana. She's no longer at Bayview. I say? Diana? Did you hear what I said?'

There was a pause and then the slide in the wall opened and Diana's face, or part of it, became visible.

'Where's she gone?' asked Diana acidly. 'To have tea with the Queen?'

'Quite possibly,' said Tom smiling. 'Can I come in?'

'I don't see how,' returned Diana curtly. 'There's a wall here.'

'You do have a front door,' Tom pointed out.

'Oh, all right,' said Diana. 'But only to make your report. And the wall stays up.'

Diana pulled the slide shut and, shaking his head with a wry smile, Tom turned and made his way through his own flat and then to Diana's front door upon which he knocked. The door opened immediately and Diana said coldly, 'All right, come in.'

She led the way into her living room and then asked brusquely, 'Well? Make your report.'

'Erm, couldn't we sit down, Diana?' asked Tom, with an ingratiating smile.

'I'd prefer not to. It might give you the impression that you're a welcome guest.'

'No, I'll remember my place. But I've got a bit of a headache.'

'Hangover, is it? From carousing with Daisy?'

'Well – carousing is a bit strong. But we did have a few glasses of champagne last night. It was her last evening.'

'How touching,' said Diana sarcastically. 'Very well then, I suppose you'd better stop swaying on the spot and sit down.'

Tom did so gratefully and Diana sternly seated herself opposite him.

'You two have been having quite the springtime romance, haven't you?' she said disdainfully.

'Not exactly,' said Tom.

'Really? Anyway, where has she gone?'

'To the El Alamein Retirement Home in Aldershot. Apparently it's full of old officers and their widows. She'll be in her element there.'

'Why did she come here then?'

'There wasn't a place at the El Alamein. And she was warned there might not be one for months or even years. But it seems the grim reaper has been concentrating on old soldiers and their ladies recently and she had a letter from her solicitor about a week ago telling her that a place had become available.'

'I see. Well, their loss is our gain. You may go now.'

'Erm, Diana, Bains is serious, you know.'

'Nonsense, he's a complete idiot.'

'True, but he is nevertheless serious when it comes to wanting your wall down. And he has the power to get your tenancy agreement cancelled if you don't cooperate.'

'Well, this isn't the only retirement home in England. I held an honorary captain's rank when I was covering the Falklands War. So perhaps I could get a place at the El Alamein Home and make Daisy Williams' life a misery.'

'You seem to have been working overtime on making people's lives a misery recently.'

'Well, what would you expect? I'm so ill-bred. Or is it just a case of give a dog a bad name?'

'But you haven't got a bad name, Diana. You've helped a lot of people in Bayview. You saved Jenny's job when Harvey wanted to dump her. Jenny thinks you're the tops.'

'Oh, I only did that because it gave me a chance to clobber Bains. No, Daisy was right basically. The Wicked Witch of the West was Mother Teresa compared to me.'

'Diana —'

'Anyway, thanks to Daisy, I now know what people think about me. And I wouldn't be surprised if they weren't right.'

Tom reached carefully into his inside pocket and withdrew the small square envelope that Daisy had given him. He said:

'I promise you that I have no idea what is in this envelope. It's from Daisy.'

He handed the envelope to Diana who, frowning, contemplated it.

'Probably more character assassination,' she said grimly.

'Well, you could, of course, simply tear it up and throw it away unread,' said Tom. 'But the one thing no one has ever said about Diana Trent is that she lacks balls.'

Diana smiled faintly and opened the envelope. She pulled out a folded sheet of paper, closely handwritten. She read it carefully and slowly. Then she gave a faint and enigmatic snort and sat staring ahead of her.

Tom said: 'Well?'

Diana, with a shrug, handed the letter to Tom. He read:

Dear Miss Trent

During our first meeting I called you ill-bred and I have to say that in a narrow sense this still seems to me a fair assessment. However, I now know that there are other, and far more important, things to be said about Diana Trent.

Shortly after that meeting, I learned from Mr Ballard that you had once been a photo-journalist. I made it my business to look into this claim and I came across an account, in the newspaper files of the Bournemouth reference library, of how you were the first journalist to reach Goose Green during the Falklands War. During the journey, you took some superb photographs and you stopped to do what you could for several wounded men.

Amongst these was a major who had been shot through the upper leg and was in great pain. You stayed with him under fire until a helicopter could be brought in to evacuate him. I was intrigued to note that this particular officer was one Major Williams. That major, as he then was, happened to be my husband. I then remembered that he had often spoken to me of the courage and kindness of the woman photographer who quite possibly saved his life.

With your qualities, Miss Trent, breeding is something of an irrelevance. I, for one, am unrepayably in your debt.

Gratefully,
Daisy Williams

'Is this true?' asked Tom. 'Were you in the Falklands?'

'Yes, I seem to recall I dropped in there,' admitted Diana.

'And did you save Major Williams?'

'How should I know? I stumbled over some major or another who had been shot in the leg. We didn't talk much because he was out of his head with pain.'

'Well, I do think it's a bit thick!' exclaimed Tom.

'What is?' asked Diana, surprised.

'The fact that you've never saved me,' said Tom indignantly.

'You were never in the Falklands,' expostulated Diana.

'That's all you know,' replied Tom haughtily. 'In fact I spend at least one afternoon a month there.'

'Oh, get stuffed!' said Diana crossly. 'Tom, I'm bored with your childish fantasies. I wouldn't mind so much if you were prepared to trot out a bit of sanity when it's appropriate. You've forgotten, haven't you?'

'Forgotten what?'

'On the day you met Daisy in the bloody dining room, you asked me to shack up with you.'

Tom smote his forehead.

'By God, you're right. I had forgotten. Thanks for reminding me. Well, will you?'

'Damn you, Ballard!'

'Why?'

'You keep me waiting for weeks while you have a wild affair with Daisy Williams and then you treat your impertinent request as a joke. Would it surprise you to know that I would-n't mind a spot of romance myself?'

Tom smiled.

'There are better things than romance, Diana.'

'Really? What, for example?'

'Well, the things that make you such a magnificent person to begin with. Truth and courage. But, as regards any possible relationship between us, the most important quality you possess is a sense of humour. Daisy had none at all. Humour would see us through, Diana.'

Diana looked at him penetratingly for a moment. Then she shook her head and sighed but with a faint smile.

'That is your belief, is it, Captain Scott – or would it be General Custer today?' she asked.

'It's Tom Ballard. And it is my belief, Diana Trent.'

'Right then,' said Diana lightly, getting to her feet. 'Just wait here a moment.'

And she disappeared into her kitchen area. A moment later she returned holding a small domestic hammer. She handed it to Tom.

He considered it doubtfully.

'What's this for?' he asked.

'To knock the wall down with.'

'A little hammer like this? Impossible.'

'No, it's not. The wall is nothing like as solid as it looks. I knew Harvey might send for the bailiffs, so I had Antonio build it in such a way that it could be quickly dismantled in an emergency. The whole thing is held together by just a few pegs.'

'Really?' asked Tom, more enthusiastically. 'I'll have a go then. And once I've knocked it down, will you then shack up with me?'

'I shouldn't think so for a moment,' said Diana. 'But, you'll just have to wait and see. Still, I promise you one thing?'

'What?'

'I'll go on laughing at you.'

'Yes, but —'

'Take it or leave it,' said Diana.

Tom rose and, with Diana following, stumped out into the conservatory and up to the wall. Diana pointed out the fastening pegs. Tom raised the hammer and struck one of them a heavy blow. The peg remained unmoved but the head of the hammer flew off and fell on Tom's foot. He gave a cry of pain and went hopping frantically round the conservatory. As his pain abated he became aware of a curious sound in the vicinity. He looked up and saw that it was Diana laughing. For a moment he was angry but then he suddenly realized that he hadn't seen her look so happy for a long time.

With an effort, he smiled. And soon after that he sniggered with genuine amusement at his absurd mishap. And after that, of course, it wasn't very long before they were both staggering about, laughing their heads off.

SIX

Tom stood in the atrium of a great glass tower in the City of London and gazed up at the distant arching roof. After a while, he became aware that someone had approached him but he continued to look almost directly upwards. Then a voice asked softly:

'Is there anything I can do to help, sir?'

At this, Tom looked down with a cheery smile and saw a large uniformed man standing directly in front of him.

'No, I don't think so,' he said politely. 'I've just realized that in some ways this place is even better than Mount Everest.'

'I beg your pardon sir?' asked the security guard with a slightly weary note in his voice.

'Well, you see,' explained Tom, 'every second Tuesday I climb Everest. I enjoy it immensely but I do sometimes suffer rather badly from frostbite. Now if I climbed in here instead of in the Himalayas I would remain warm no matter how long the ascent took. I'm surprised that indoor climbing hasn't already become a craze. The only problems I can envisage would be transporting the Sherpas over from Nepal and finding some way to hammer in pitons. They don't work very well on glass or steel, you know.'

The security guard smiled in a resigned sort of way. 'You do realize where you are, don't you, sir?' he asked gently.

'Oh yes, perfectly.'

'It's just that you've been standing there gazing up without moving for nearly ten minutes.'

'I know. I'm planning the best route to the summit.'

'There isn't any summit, sir. This is the atrium of the United Investments Conglomerate building. You are not in Nepal, sir. You are in Bishopsgate in the City of London.'

'I am perfectly aware of that. And now that I've completed my preliminary survey of the ascent I would be grateful if you could direct me towards the firm of Sam Parry Promotions Limited.'

The security guard nodded.

'I'm delighted to do that, sir. It's on the first floor – in the foothills you might say – and you can reach it by taking that escalator over there.'

'Thank you,' said Tom. He turned to move in the direction indicated but then hesitated and turned back. 'Tell me, has anyone conquered this peak yet or is it still virgin?'

But then a hint, in the security guard's demeanour, of patience stretched to breaking point caused Tom to add hastily, 'Don't worry, I can look it up in the *Mountaineers' Gazette*. And thank you for your help.'

He turned once more and strode towards the escalator.

Some twenty minutes later, and after a very tedious wait in an outer office, Tom was ushered into the spacious and, in a glassy and glitzy sort of way, glamorous sanctum of Sam Parry himself.

'Tom,' exclaimed the tall and stylish, but a shade too slick-looking, man behind the desk who now rose and held out his hand. 'Sorry to have kept you waiting. It's always a madhouse here on Monday morning.'

'It's Tuesday,' said Tom, ignoring the outstretched hand.

'Exactly,' said Sam with seamless ease. 'The uproar often goes on for most of the week. Anyway, to what do I owe the honour?'

'Well,' said Tom, with an earnest smile on his large open face, 'I'm not sure you'll find it all that much of an honour. You see, I've come here to tell you exactly what I think of you.'

'I see,' said the other, sounding intrigued. He pointed to the comfortable chair facing his desk. 'In that case, why don't you sit down and fire away?'

'Right you are,' agreed Tom, seating himself. 'Well then, it is my judicious and considered opinion that you are a bent little weasel who could only play snooker with a spiral cue.'

The other looked thoughtful for a moment and then nodded.

'Yes, that sounds about right,' he agreed. 'Would you care for a cup of coffee? The spoons have been specially prepared by Uri Geller.'

'No, thank you,' said Tom. 'So my insult didn't worry you?'

The other shook his head.

'Oh no. I've been called far worse things than that. What you probably don't realize, Tom, is that I have absolutely no scruples. There are only two things in life that matter to me: making money and marrying Sarah.'

'That's extremely interesting,' said Tom. 'Because it seems to imply that if I threatened to tell Sarah the kind of cad that you really are then you would be genuinely upset. Is that the case?'

Sam nodded earnestly.

'It is indeed. And if you did that I would almost certainly feel compelled to make a counter-threat.'

'Would you care to tell me what the counter-threat would be exactly?'

'Premature. I'd have to give it a good deal of thought. But it would probably be something along the lines of saying that if you ever did blacken my character to Sarah then I would request a couple of odd-job men I happen to know to break both your legs.'

'Fascinating,' said Tom. 'I must say, I do admire your negotiating style. Crisp and to the point. No circling tediously round the nub of the matter. Yes, it's almost a pleasure doing business with you.'

'I feel rather the same, Tom. So why don't we dispense with further pleasantries and get down to some hard bargaining?'

'Why not indeed?' agreed Tom enthusiastically. 'But first – I wonder if you happen to know: has the atrium in this building ever been climbed?'

A few hours later, back at Bayview, Tom went in search of Diana. He found her seated on a bench in the grounds watching, through field glasses, three other lady residents having a race across the lawn. What made the spectacle a little bizarre was the fact that the three runners were all using Zimmer frames and the best speed of the leading contestant would hardly have equalled that of a not particularly fleet tortoise.

'Come on, Nellie!' Diana was urging loudly. 'Cut the other two off at the corner.'

'What on earth are they doing?' asked Tom who, lacking field glasses, could only just make out the scene in the distance.

'Trying to get to the bus first,' Diana explained, without taking her eyes from her glasses. 'It's an outing to Bournemouth organized by Geriatric Jollifications or some such ludicrous outfit. There's only one seat left on the bus and so those three are rushing to get it. However, if we're lucky the driver will get tired of waiting for them and drive off. Then we'll be able to enjoy the disappointment of all three as the bus roars past without them.'

'Diana, you are ghastly!' exclaimed Tom, genuinely shocked. 'Your glee is verging on the sadistic.'

'Well, I have to live up to my image, don't I?' asked Diana briskly, lowering her glasses. 'Diana Trent, the unspeakable swine of Bayview, as Daisy Williams christened me.'

'Oh, for heaven's sake, Diana. After that wonderful letter Daisy wrote you, I should have thought even your paranoia would have been assuaged.'

'Never. Giving your paranoia a good canter is one of the few pleasures left to us antiques.' She raised her glasses again and shouted, 'Keep it up, Lily, just a few more wobbles and you'll be on your way into town to meet the Queen.'

'Is that really where they're going?'

'Absolutely. They're going to a concert being given by Barry Wimpus, the soulful folk crooner, and after it they've been invited to take tea with him in his dressing room. Of course, Barry's practically a museum piece himself. I remember hearing his maudlin and mock-American voice over my first cat's whisker radio.'

'But you said they were going to meet the Queen?'

'Well the truth is, Tom, that Barry is not really as macho as some of the cowboy songs he specializes in tend to suggest – if you take my meaning. That's right, Charlotte, you're into the straight. Now a big final gallop and – oh dear, she's fallen at the last fence.'

Tom grabbed the field glasses and peered. One of the old ladies was indeed floundering on her back on the turf. As Tom watched, Jane hurried up and helped Charlotte to her feet and then all three venerable ladies, with Jane shepherding them, shuffled the last few feet to the waiting bus where they were helped on board.

'It wasn't a race at all,' said Tom. 'There's plenty of room on the bus for all three.'

'Well, it made it more exciting to think of it as the Disability Derby,' said Diana grumpily.

'You know, you'll regret your cynicism one day,' Tom warned. 'The Zimmer frame awaits us all in the end.'

'Not me,' said Diana firmly. 'The day I can no longer get about on my own pins is the day I pull the plug on my earthly existence. Anyway, how did you get on in the Great Wen?'

'You were absolutely right. Sarah's future husband, Sam, really is a gangster,' said Tom firmly.

'Yes, well I spotted that almost the first time I met him. I didn't succeed years ago in infiltrating the Krays' outfit and photographing some of their more disgusting practices without being able to recognize a gangster when I meet one. But how did you get on about the franchise?'

'After I'd put on the pressure and vowed that if he didn't play ball I would definitely tell Sarah how he'd tried to con you, he agreed to let you off the hook. He did this quite cheerfully I may say. And moreover, he gave me the franchise to do with as I will. But all on condition that I swore I wouldn't say a word to Sarah about his dishonest proclivities.'

Diana nodded and said, 'I see. What are you going to do with the franchise?'

'I thought of making a present of it to Marion. She's always saying that if she had a business to run she'd stop being a drunken slut and become a model wife. Well, running a beauty salon might be just the thing.'

'Rubbish. Marion couldn't run a birdbath. She'll end up drinking the face lotion. Still, you've done well to get me in the clear.'

Tom snapped to attention and saluted smartly.

'Thank you, sir. Does this mean I'll be mentioned in despatches?'

'Possibly. But that would still not put you into the same

category as Monty who was the last chap I commended for his resourcefulness.'

Tom smiled complacently and then asked, 'What are you going to do about Sarah?'

'How do you mean?' asked Diana.

'Well – her fiancé has proved to be a crook who tried to con her aunt into purchasing a franchise at a ludicrously inflated figure. How much was it? Twenty grand?'

'Thirty.'

'Good Lord! So – a manifest crook. I've had to give him my word I'll keep my mouth shut but surely you're going to warn Sarah?'

'No point. She'll find out soon enough.'

'Diana, for God's sake. They're going to be married soon.'

'Splendid. And once they've started sharing a roof, and especially a telephone, it won't take Sarah long to realize Sam's true nature.'

Tom shook his head in amazement and exclaimed, 'I think this is the most cynical and irresponsible behaviour that even you have ever displayed, Diana. Your own niece – whom you profess to love.'

'Oh, don't be such a naïve fool Tom,' snapped Diana. 'What do you think would happen if I told Sarah that her loved one was a crook? She'd simply stop seeing me and cling to him even more tightly. You don't know a thing about women, and particularly not about romantic women like my niece. But Sarah will be all right. She'll simply divorce Sam when she can no longer blind herself to the truth about him. And when she's divorced him she'll still be a millionaire in her own right.'

'Yes, but what if they have a baby?'

'In that case, it will be a smashing baby. With Sam's drive and initiative and Sarah's charm and scruples how could it help being a winner? And you and I will probably see him – or her – in Number 10. Then she paused and smiled ruefully, 'No, we're not likely to last that long, are we?'

Two weeks later, Tom was relaxing in an armchair in Diana's living room and sipping a cup of tea. Before long Diana emerged from her bedroom wearing something on her head that struck Tom as curious. He gazed at it, blinked, rubbed his eyes and gazed some more. Diana posed and smiled invitingly.

'Well?' she asked. 'What do you think of it?'

'I'm not sure,' said Tom. 'Perhaps a more important question is: what does it think of me? That thing looks as if it could turn very ugly if offended.'

'Oh, don't be absurd,' scolded Diana. 'You've seen hats before.'

'Of course,' exclaimed Tom. 'It's a hat! Yes, I knew I'd seen something similar riding on a female's head some time in the past. Of course, it actually looks rather like a giant bacillus.'

'How would you know? You're not a doctor,' said Diana, turning towards a mirror on the wall and primping.

'No, but in my early youth I owned a splendid children's encyclopedia and it contained fascinating and much-magnified pictures of the more common disease germs. I think your hat resembles the one that causes typhoid – or is it cholera?'

'It will be perfect for the wedding,' Diana affirmed. 'People wear hats like this at weddings.'

'Yes, but not in England, surely? Only in Brazil during the Carnival.'

'Now, just put a sock in it, Ballard,' ordered Diana firmly. 'My dear niece, Sarah, is the only family I have in this world and I intend to put on the dog a bit for her wedding.'

'I see,' nodded Tom. 'Are you planning to wear bells on your shoes?'

Diana removed from her head the elaborate creation and set off with it back into her bedroom. As she went, she said scathingly, 'Anyway, what do you know about fashion, you dull bumpkin?'

Diana was only gone for a moment and then she returned to the living room minus the hat. She thereupon sat down opposite Tom and poured herself a cup of tea.

'Another?' she asked Tom.

He glanced at his watch.

'Better not,' he said. 'I'm due for my facial.'

'Your what?' asked Diana incredulously.

Tom had the good grace to blush slightly.

'The thing is,' he explained a trifle sheepishly, 'Marion gives me a free facial every now and then – as a way of expressing her gratitude for the beauty parlour franchise.'

'Dear God!' exclaimed Diana. 'And he had the cheek to cavil at my chaste little hat. Have you considered having a spot of plastic surgery too? That second chin could profitably be subdued and you might give some thought to a bust job while you're at it. It's not considered seemly for a man to wear a bra.'

'I do not wear a —' began Tom angrily but then he pulled himself up and smiled to show that he could take a joke. 'Trying to provoke a chap, are we? But it's no use because I simply do not happen to be a transvestite, as you very well know, Diana. I do, however, believe that just because the clock's winding down it doesn't mean one shouldn't polish its case now and then. So —' he glanced at his watch again and then stood up. 'Yes, I must be off. I'm having the avocado face pack this week. See you in church.'

And singing: '"I feel pretty, oh so pretty – I feel pretty and witty and gay" – no, cancel that last item,' Tom danced out of the flat while Diana gazed after him, shaking her head in mock despair.

But when Tom reached the beauty parlour, which was quite a swish establishment in the posh Bournemouth suburb where Bayview was located, he found that all the chairs were occupied. To pass the time while waiting for a free one, he made his way to the office in order to ask Marion how things were going. She was not, as it happened, there but Tom's son, Geoffrey, was. Geoffrey appeared to be poring over the accounts on a computer screen.

'Hello, Dad,' he said, looking up with a sigh.

'Hello, Geoffrey,' said Tom cheerfully. 'How's it going? Making a mint?'

'Not exactly,' admitted the other, with one of his tight smiles.

'Really?' asked Tom, frowning. 'Why not? I mean I got you two the franchise for this place by cunningly outwitting Sarah's crooked fiancé. So surely Marion is not still just sitting around the house popping pills and slugging vodka, is she?'

'Oh, good heavens no, Dad,' said Geoffrey reassuringly. 'She's rushing about the beauty parlour here popping pills and slugging vodka.'

'But why?'

'Because she's utterly incompetent and she knows it. She

needs to drink and pop pills in order to have the courage to face herself. The truth is we're losing money hand over fist, Dad.'

'Losing money?' echoed Tom incredulously. 'I don't believe it.'

''Fraid so,' Geoffrey assured him. 'You might have got us the franchise, but the small print gives Sam a percentage of the gross. He slices it off the top before we've even deducted expenses. This might not matter if Marion didn't alienate the customers.'

'How does she manage to do that?'

'Oh, she has a variety of methods. One is cutting their hair while her hand is shaking from a hangover, which leaves them looking like mangy cats. Another very successful technique is confusing lavatory cleaner with face lotion, which produces widespread blistering.'

'But she can't do such appalling things to all the customers?'

'No, of course not. But word gets around. I reckon we'll be out of business within a month.'

'Geoffrey, is Marion totally beyond redemption?'

'Yes, of course, Dad, I thought you knew that,' exclaimed Geoffrey, clearly astonished at finding that his father still had even residual doubts about the matter.

'Well, I can't say it comes as a stunning surprise but surely —'

However, at this point the 'phone rang and Geoffrey answered it.

'Hello? I see. Oh, really? Yes, my father is here and I'll pass the message on. Is she all right? I see. Right you are then. Thank you for letting us know. Goodbye.'

He turned to his father.

'That was Jane. It seems that Diana has had quite a serious fall and she's been taken by ambulance to St Agatha's Hospital. Jane thinks you should hurry straight over there.'

Tom stared in dismay.

'But – but is she seriously hurt?' he asked anxiously.

'Jane wasn't very specific. She just said that Diana was being remarkably abusive and difficult.'

'Thank God,' exclaimed Tom. 'Clearly it can't be too serious.'

Then, not bothering about his facial, Tom hurriedly left the beauty parlour, succeeded – but only with a good deal of diffi-culty – in getting a taxi and so made his way to St Agatha's which was set in its own pleasant grounds on the other side of the dual carriageway.

Once inside the main building he inquired at the desk and, on receiving the appropriate information, hurried to the ward in which Diana – or so he had been told – had been installed. However, he failed to spot Diana and went in search of the staff nurse who, when he'd found her and stated his mission, told him that Diana had been given a single room off the corridor.

'Really?' asked Tom. 'Is she a private patient then?'

'Well, no not really,' confessed the nurse, 'but she was creating such an uproar that some of the other patients on the ward were getting a bit upset. So we put her in an individual room – at least for the time being.'

The nurse pointed out the way to the individual room and Tom made his way there and gently opened the door. Diana was not, at that moment, making an uproar but rather lying back with her eyes closed. Jane was seated at the bedside.

'What happened?' asked Tom.

'She slipped while throwing a brick at Antonio,' explained Jane lugubriously. 'She hit her head falling and knocked herself unconscious. She also hurt her hip.'

'But if she was unconscious,' asked Tom logically, 'how did you know what had happened?'

'Antonio was howling his head off. Diana had managed to hit him with the brick. Why can't Diana grasp that a quiet word of rebuke is often more effective than gratuitous violence?'

'It's a puzzle, isn't it?' asked Tom, shaking his head. 'So how badly damaged is she?'

'Well, she's got a severe fracture of the hip. They're going to operate on it almost immediately.'

'That's why she's so quiet is it? She's had a shot of sedative?'

'Oh no, she's just exhausted from swearing at the surgeon. She says he'll mess with her hip only over her dead body. I think she's probably a bit delirious. She seems to think the surgeon wants to imprison her in a Zimmer frame for some fiendish purpose.'

'Oh my God, I'd forgotten her Zimmerphobia!' exclaimed Tom. 'Yes, her attitude to Zimmer frames is somewhat similar to that of the Pope towards sin. She considers that they have no place in human society. Is she likely to need one?'

'Well, for some time after the operation I should think. I don't see how it can be avoided.' Jane looked at her watch and shook her head anxiously. 'Oh dear, I've got a million things to do at Bayview.'

'You run along, Jane,' Tom urged her. 'I'll stay with Diana.'

'Well —' said Jane doubtfully. 'If you really don't mind, Tom?'

'Of course, I don't. She'd do the same for me. Of course she'd accuse me of malingering and try to tip me out of bed but she'd stay with me.'

'I'll accept your kind offer then, Tom. Give me a ring if you need me.'

And Jane rose from the chair at Diana's bedside and left the ward.

Tom seated himself on the chair Jane had vacated and gazed down at Diana. She looked a bit pale and drawn and she was no longer young but he liked what he saw. Diana's face had strength, intelligence and attractive features. It was not a face that suggested Dresden-doll femininity but nor did it resemble the countenance of a fiend from hell, which was the kind of image Diana seemed to prefer. No, this was the face of a humane lady who had suffered a good deal, raged a good deal but had also done a lot of valuable work in the world. It was a face that a person could easily become attached to and —

'What are you staring at, you soppy old idiot?' asked Diana gruffly. Tom started and then noticed that Diana's eyes were not quite tightly shut. He realized that she must have been watching him all along.

'So you're awake, are you?' asked Tom, with a faintly embarrassed cough.

'Of course I'm awake. I just couldn't stand any more of Jane's sentimental prattling and so I pretended to have nodded off. Mind you, your mooning over me is not much better than her brand of loopiness. What's got into you?'

'Well, you've had quite a rough time, you know,' urged Tom. 'I mean, you're not a young person and the strain —'

'Oh, don't you start!' groaned Diana. 'I've had a little itsy bitsy fall. And if that imbecile of a gardener hadn't moved at the last moment I wouldn't have had to twist my body in order to hit him with the brick. It was that twist which made me lose my balance. But now all I need is a quiet hour or two in bed and then I'll be up and away.'

'Oh, don't be ridiculous, Diana. You're going to have an operation.'

'In a pig's ear. I'm not going to miss Sarah's wedding, Tom.'

'Oh well – perhaps some arrangement can be – hello.'

There had been a knock at the door and, almost immediately, a bespectacled, cheerful looking man in a chalk-striped suit entered. He was accompanied by a nurse with a tray of instruments that included, as both Tom and Diana noted, a hypodermic syringe.

'Hello, Diana, *fach*?' the man said with a broad Welsh accent. 'How are you doing?'

'Oh, my God!' exclaimed Diana. 'It's the surgeon – Taff the Knife.'

'And who is this?' asked the new arrival, offering Tom a quick smile.

'Tom Ballard,' replied Tom. 'A friend of Diana's.'

'Oh good,' said the surgeon enthusiastically. 'She's got one then?' He held out his hand. 'I'm David Davies. I do a lot of the carving around here.'

'Less of the chitchat!' urged Diana impatiently to Davies. 'And more of the diagnosis. What is your professional verdict?'

'Well, you've given yourself quite a hefty whack, my dear,' said Davies soberly. 'When I go in, the chances are that I'll have to give you a new hip – the old ball and socket job.'

'Don't be absurd!' exclaimed Diana loftily. 'It's just a bruise, that's all. My own hip is perfectly satisfactory.'

Davies shook his head positively.

'No, it's a bit brittle, you know – because of all the steroid treatments you've had. Best do the operation now. You'll almost certainly need one in a couple of years anyway.' He turned to the nurse. 'OK nurse – a bit of softening up, if you please.'

'No, hang on!' urged Diana. 'Tom, will you stop them? I

don't believe this is a hospital at all. I've fallen into the hands of bodysnatchers. Tom, knock him to the ground! Tom, do you – ow!'

The needle slid smoothly into Diana's arm. The nurse held Diana and lowered her gently back onto the pillow. It seemed no more than a few seconds before she was out.

Two days later, Tom was seated in a treatment chair in Marion's beauty parlour with his face covered in avocado paste. He had pads over his eyes to protect him from the messy stuff and so was unable to see. But he could hear and he was, in fact, listening with interest to a conversation that was taking place nearby. While the paste did its beautifying work, Marion and Geoffrey were having a chat with Sam, Sarah's fiancé, who had just called round to collect his cut of the gross. Tom could hear everything that was being said.

'I really am most awfully sorry,' said Sam unctuously.

'No, you're not,' said Marion positively. 'You're simply a liar and a hypocrite. Well, I hope your stars and planets get into horrible conjunctions and remain like that for the rest of your life. If I didn't have to manicure this stupid cow' – Tom heard a gasp of disbelief, presumably from the waiting customer – 'I'd stay and insult you properly. But as it is I'll have to hand over to Geoffrey who's not very good at it. Do try this time, Geoffrey. Give him a thorough roasting.'

'All right, dear,' said Geoffrey soothingly.

There was a pause, presumably while Marion moved some distance away to do her manicuring, and then Sam said earnestly, 'The truth is, Geoffrey, that I really am sorry about this. What with the wedding coming up I feel that you're almost family.'

'But,' pointed out Geoffrey quite mildly, 'that doesn't stop you from ripping us off, does it?'

'You mustn't think of it as ripping off,' urged Sam. 'It's simply a matter of fulfilling the franchise contract. You've read it. You know the deal: we get a piece of the turnover.'

'Still,' Geoffrey maintained, 'it means that we run at a loss.'

'That is very distressing, I admit,' said Sam. 'But I do feel it's fair to point out that none of the other salons run at a loss. And there are fourteen of them altogether.'

'The explanation,' said Geoffrey, 'is probably that none of the other salons is run by a total incompetent. What it all adds up to is that I am working simply to support my wife's losses.'

'Have you considered,' suggested Sam helpfully, 'changing your wife?'

'Yes, I have,' affirmed Geoffrey, 'but there are obstacles to that. We have an assortment of children to consider. I'd much rather change my wife's profession if you'd simply let us off the franchise agreement.'

'If only it were as simple as that,' purred Sam, 'but I too have responsibilities. There's my board of directors, the shareholders and – aah!'

His sudden, rather panicky, exclamation had been generated by the spectacle of a great green man, rather resembling the Incredible Hulk, rising up menacingly from a nearby treatment chair.

'Just one moment, please,' exclaimed this alarming monster, wiping avocado paste from its face and thus gradually disclosing that it was really Tom Ballard. 'Sam, what happens to those who default on their payments?'

'Oh, it's you, is it, Tom?' asked Sam with mild relief. 'You do have a way of popping up in the strangest places – and disguises. Well, in answer to your question, what happens is that the franchise reverts to me and the defaulters lose whatever they paid for the franchise.'

'Which, of course,' Tom pointed out gently, 'in the case of Geoffrey and Marion would be nothing at all since, at my urgent request, you granted them a free franchise.'

Sam looked none too pleased by this observation. He stammered, 'Yes, well – you may have a point there, Tom, but the fact of the matter is that although you could be technically correct —'

'Oh, dry up, Sam,' said Tom brusquely. He was almost totally clear by then of green gunge and he turned to Geoffrey and said boisterously, 'You're absolutely free, Geoffrey. There is nothing he can do to compel you to retain the franchise. So any time you want to, you can get back to your yoghurt and cheese slices. And Marion can resume what, for her, passes as a normal existence.'

'No, but hang on —' protested Sam.

'Be quiet, Sam,' ordered Tom. And then to Geoffrey, 'Still, I'd look nippy, if I were you, Geoffrey. Just grab Marion and run before Sam decides to 'phone for the heavies.'

'Well – well, if you think it will be all right, Dad?' stammered Geoffrey, a light of renewed hope dawning on his chubby face. 'I'm very grateful. Yes, you're certainly an ace, Dad, and —'

'Out,' said Tom. 'No time to lose.'

And at this, pausing only to tear Marion away from the customer whose hand she was savaging, Geoffrey, with Marion in tow, fled the sinking business.

With an effort, Sam smiled at Tom.

'You're a pretty smart mover, Tom,' he said. 'Mercedes standard – or possibly even Porsche. Ever considered trying your hand at business?'

'Frequently,' said Tom, 'but if you're offering the franchise to me now – no thank you. From this point on I'll pay for my own facials.'

Sam smiled appreciatively.

'Ah well, no hard feelings,' he proposed. 'And I trust that we'll see you on Monday?'

'Monday?' asked Tom, mystified. 'Oh yes, of course, the wedding. I suppose, Sam, that you and Sarah will pass out of the church under an arch made by two ranks of mafiosi holding up automatic pistols?'

'Oh, definitely,' said Sam. 'And then we'll drive off into the sunset in our bulletproof black saloon.'

'Wouldn't miss if for the world,' said Tom. 'And perhaps I'll get a mention in the report of it that will doubtless appear in the *Gangsters' Gazette*. I just hope Diana will be able to make it too.'

'Sarah and I are visiting poor old Diana this afternoon,' said Sam. 'So we'll find out how she's doing then.'

But what they found was not encouraging.

'No chance,' said Diana grimly when Sam and Sarah turned up at St Agatha's and after Sarah had inquired if Diana would be fit enough to come to the wedding. 'They say I'm making quite good progress, but I won't be up to things like weddings for some time yet.'

'Oh, you poor darling,' said Sarah, kissing her aunt sympathetically. 'But never mind, we'll keep you a slice of wedding cake. And anyway I don't suppose you're really interested in catching the bouquet, are you?'

'Oh, don't be silly,' said Diana petulantly. 'You can't possibly get hitched without me. You'll just have to postpone the ceremony for a week or two. By then I'll be leaping about with a pair of walking sticks.'

'Oh dear,' said Sam, shaking his head sadly. 'What a pity. The truth is that there is no way we can postpone the wedding, Diana.'

Diana glared at him.

'Why the hell not? It's your wedding, isn't it? So it follows that you can have it whenever you want to have it.'

'You're so naïve, Diana,' smiled Sam. 'The point is that the wedding has been timed to coincide with the end of my tax year. If we get married on Monday as arranged, we can get optimum income-splitting tax advantages for the next two years.'

'Well, it's plain to see that you're a dyed-in-the-wool old romantic, Sam,' said Diana bitterly.

'Oh Diana,' said Sarah sadly but firmly. 'Sam's right. It would cost us a fortune to delay the wedding.'

Diana looked from one to the other and then shrugged.

'All right then – no big deal. You don't need me there in any case. And don't tell Tom but I never really liked that hat.'

'Diana,' said Sam, with a pained smile. 'You could come if you really wanted to. Now I had a word with your surgeon and he said that there would be no difficulty about your being at the wedding if you used a suitable support.'

'I am astonished that you could make out a word old Taff the Knife was saying,' observed Diana sniffily. 'The only language he speaks fluently is old Welsh.'

Sam smiled but shook his head gently.

'Mr Davies is one of the most highly respected hip men in this part of the country,' he said accurately.

Diana shrugged and said breezily.

'Oh, I admit that it would be physically possible for me to grace your wedding in a wheelchair or even bring it grinding to a halt by processing down the aisle with a Zimmer frame. But neither of those alternatives would be the entrance that I had planned.'

'And what would that be?'

'I had intended to parachute into the church grounds from a low flying helicopter. No, the truth of the matter is, Sam, that we all have our little vanities and mine is that I would rather be dead in a ditch than seen in public in a wheelchair or using a Zimmer frame.'

Sam shook his head and lifted his hands in resignation.

He turned to Sarah.

'I'm afraid I must be off. Business,' he explained.

'Oh yes?' asked Diana scathingly. 'Which branch of it needs your attention today? Is it extorting protection money from small shopkeepers and restaurateurs?'

'No, no,' Sam reassured her. 'That was yesterday. Today is my day for grinding the faces of widows and orphans. It's absolutely amazing how much money they often have stashed away under mattresses and in piggy banks.'

And with a quick wink at Sarah, Sam strode from the room.

Aunt and niece contemplated each other with rueful smiles.

'Do you think he's ghastly?' asked Sarah finally.

'Is that a genuine query or are you merely seeking an aunt's blessing?' asked Diana roughly.

'I really do want an answer – what do you think of Sam?'

'Oh, he's clearly a saint amongst men. He's charming, witty, intelligent and quite exceptionally good-looking.'

Sarah sighed and shook her head.

'You're teasing. I know he's a dreadful conman but he would never harm anyone physically. Still, he has no scruples whatsoever about separating people from their cash.'

Diana nodded thoughtfully.

'Yes, I suppose there is a dubious side to him.'

'Then why,' asked Sarah desperately, 'do I love him so much?'

Diana shook her head firmly.

'God knows,' she exclaimed. 'And no one but God ever does understand what binds most couples together. Take your mother and father. She was a wet little mouse and he couldn't bear it if there was a virgin left on the planet. But what happened in the end? They got married. He stopped playing the field. She blossomed into a rare beauty with brains. And they had years and years of quite appalling happiness. There are simply no rules. If there were, we'd all play by them.'

Sarah laughed. Then, 'Why did *you* never marry?' she asked. Diana shook her head with a disgusted look.

'Oh Lord, why does everybody always ask that boring question? I never married because I was a photographer.'

Sarah frowned uncomprehendingly.

'What's that got to do with it?'

'A great deal. As a photographer I could see the whole picture. I could be objective. I knew exactly what qualities I wanted in a husband. And, of course, from time to time I would actually meet a chap who had those qualities. But somehow they never seemed quite so attractive on the hoof. No, the good guys, the responsible guys, the kind guys who conformed to my image of "husband" just never turned out to be the ones who could actually throw my magic switch. The ones who could were always the pirates, the swashbuckling no-good sods – quite often they were simply the rock-bottom bastards. And no girl in her right mind would have married one of those, would she?'

Sarah shook her head sadly.

'Except me. Sam's a no-good pirate. I have no illusions about him.'

'No illusions. I never had any either. But there is one big difference between you and me, Sarah. Here I am in my cosy little ward – all on my own.'

'Meaning?'

'That's how I've spent my life – all alone. So maybe I should have nailed my colours to one of those tall pirate masts. In other words, my advice to you is to marry your wicked gangster but the moment he steps out of line, string him up. If there's another woman involved drop a truck on her and if you're not gloriously happy forever and ever – well, in the last resort you won't feel too guilty if you have to strangle the sod.'

Diana laughed. Once again aunt and niece gazed long and fondly at each other.

Wedding Monday arrived and the scene just before noon in and around St Xavier's in Bournemouth was very lively. It was a day of intermittent showers and bright bursts of sunshine but the showers, with their attendant gusts of wind, were not protracted enough to discourage anyone. The exhilarating intervals of sun and scudding cloud, on the other hand, communicated a sense of joy and adventure to the well-dressed guests milling about in front of the church.

Big cars kept rolling up and discharging prosperous looking people, many of them business contacts of Sam's. Jane was there, ecstatic at being escorted by a morning-coated Harvey who, in honour of the occasion, was being quite pleasant to her. Gazing about, moist-eyed, on their arrival, Jane remarked:

'Oh, Harvey, aren't weddings wonderful?'

He replied, 'Yes they are, Jane.'

'Wouldn't you like to get married too, Harvey?' she continued.

Normally, of course, Harvey would then have destroyed Jane with some such follow-up as: 'Indeed I would, Jane. Not to you, of course, but if I could find a girl with both beauty and brains I would seriously consider the step.'

But on this occasion, he contented himself with the gentle rejoinder, 'No, not really, Jane. So it would be sensible if you abandoned any unrealistic ambitions you may be harbouring about marrying me and settled for a lesser man.'

With a sniff, Jane rejoined: 'Oh, no, Harvey, I'll wait for you forever.'

'As you choose, Jane. It means that you'll die a spinster, of course, but if that's what you want, go for it.'

Geoffrey was there with Marion who was wearing a gown she had been making for herself for the past fortnight and had only finished the night before. Unfortunately she had been popping pills as she applied the finishing touches and so the dress had a lot of strange tucks and pleats in it at inappropriate places. Nevertheless, as she reeled and lurched about the church forecourt Marion attracted many intrigued glances.

Finally, Tom arrived with Sarah, whom he was giving away, and with the bridesmaids who looked charming in their white gowns. Soon the whole company made its way into the church and the pews quickly filled up with guests. It took some time before everyone was seated. Then, at last, the organ boomed out and, with dignity and poise, Tom and Sarah processed down the central aisle and took their places before the officiating priest.

'Oh dear,' whispered Sarah to Tom from the corner of her mouth. 'I feel dreadful about Diana not being here. I almost feel as if I'm not really getting married at all.'

'Of course you are,' Tom hissed back. 'Only not to Diana – which is an excellent thing from every point of view.'

The organ music stopped. The priest stepped forward and opened his mouth to speak. But before he could utter a single word there was a loud grating sound from the rear of the church. Everyone, including Tom and Sarah, turned to see what had caused the noise and all observed that it had been produced by the massive rear door of the church being pushed open. For a moment, there was no explanation as to who had done the pushing but then, through the door, and moving strenuously at about one mile an hour with the help of a Zimmer frame, came Diana.

'Sorry for the interruption,' she called loudly, 'but the taxi was late. All right, look to the front all of you. Hasn't anyone ever seen a Zimmer frame before? This is the latest turbo-charged model with a one-speed gear.'

And then, in a long silence that was broken only by the shuffle and thump of the woman and her ungainly walking device, Diana's solitary figure moved gracelessly down the central aisle. On her head wobbled the big white hat which had so alarmed Tom at first sight. And when Diana finally – and amazingly without the hat falling off – reached the front row of pews, a place was, with some difficulty, found for her.

Then, having settled herself comfortably and while every-one was speculating in whispers on the meaning of the painful interruption, Diana called out, 'Sarah? You didn't really think I was going to let you get married without me, did you? All right, Reverend, you can unite them in holy wedlock now.'

SEVEN

Time passed at Bayview and some of the relationships changed. Amongst these was the marriage between Sarah, Diana's niece, and Sam, the suspected gangster, whose nuptials we described in the last chapter. The melancholy truth, however, is that by the time we reach the start of the present chapter, Sarah and Sam were no longer living together. Sam had provided Sarah not with, as Diana had hoped he would, a lifetime of happiness but with only a year and a half of it.

True it had been a pretty good year and a half. The honeymoon in the Pacific had been glorious. Sarah's pregnancy had been joyous and exciting and the birth of Diana the Second, as her girl baby had been christened in honour of her great-aunt, had been thrilling and deeply fulfilling. The baby herself had struck Sarah – and nothing but a cliché will do here – as being exactly like a bundle of sunshine. But then Sarah had discovered something about Sam which had induced her to break off relations with him.

No, it was not that Sam really was, as Tom and Diana believed, the Al Capone of South Kensington. In fact, by this stage of their shared life it had become clear to Sarah that her husband was not a gangster at all. He was actually a businessman, a very shrewd operator certainly, but one who never quite overstepped the narrow line that divides slightly dubious commercial activities from blatantly illegal ones – less Al Capone, one might say, than a kind of Arthur Daley who had made the big time. Sarah loved Sam so much that she might even have been able to cope with the discovery that he really was a crook – so long as he never physically harmed people – but what she could not tolerate was the discovery that he was a father.

No, not a father to Diana the Second. She knew about that, of course. But a little after the first anniversary of the wedding, anonymous letters from 'well-wishers' began to reach Sarah. Subsequent investigations, undertaken by a private detective that she hired, soon turned up proof that Sam had sired not only Diana the Second but no fewer than three other children by three different mothers. True, this procreative hyperactivity had all occurred before Sarah and Sam had even met. But the private eye also discovered that Sam still visited these mothers and their babies and was also seeing a number of other young women who were not, thus far anyway, pregnant.

In other words, Sam was unmasked not as a crook but as a womanizer of prodigious stature. To be fair, he also seemed to be a conscientious one who gave help and comfort to his far-flung network of families. But sharing a husband on this scale proved to be something that Sarah simply could not handle. So she sent Sam packing.

It hurt terribly at first. Sarah's lovely little mews house was profoundly lonely without Sam although even then little Diana proved a tremendous source of comfort. Diana the First's visits also helped Sarah through the darkest period. Then gradually Sarah began to emerge from despair and, by degrees, to redirect her energies into professional channels. Before very long she had re-established herself as a force to be reckoned with in the fashion and beauty worlds. She found a good woman to look after Diana the Second during working hours and spent her evenings and weekends either alone with the child or proudly taking her to visit friends.

Not all the relationships at Bayview had changed. That between Geoffrey and Marion, for example, had not changed very much. After the fiasco with the beauty parlour franchise Marion had resumed her normal lifestyle, which involved gulping vodka like a Russian general, popping pills like a film star and removing the trousers of any man, other than Geoffrey, incautious enough to get within grabbing range. The only man who fulfilled this condition with any regularity was the postman and he, after experiencing Marion's avid attentions several times, became very expert at sneaking up to the door and slipping letters through the slot swiftly and silently.

Jane and Harvey, too, were a couple who had remained much as they had always been. Jane continued to adore Harvey and Harvey continued to be appallingly rude and dismissive towards Jane. Their relationship, in other words, was proving to be a stable one.

And what of Tom and Diana? Did they belong amongst the couples that had changed or those that had remained the same? A bit of both actually. There had been no profound alteration in the nature of their relationship but there had been a steady deepening and broadening of it. A year and a half or so after the episode of the beauty parlour franchise, they had become accepted as Bayview's most enduring, if also most tempestuous, couple and, because they were also at the forefront of any movement or campaign to improve conditions there, they had been given the honorary rank of elder statesmen.

For all that, Tom remained to some extent dissatisfied. His innate loneliness persisted and he often renewed his appeal to Diana to share a home with him. But Diana continued, for complex reasons connected with her need to preserve freedom of both thought and action, to refuse any such arrangement. And so basically the relationship between these two continued pretty much unchanged. Until, that is, the night of Dave Cartwright's party.

At about half past six on the evening in question, Harvey Bains looked up from a list of potential wives ('lovely, lively and loaded', as the rather vulgar brochure he was using put it) that was on the desk in front of him. He had, for a hefty fee and much to Jane's dismay, obtained the brochure and list from a computer dating service and he was in the process of ticking off the names of what he considered to be promising candidates for marriage. Now he paused and exclaimed:

'What's that?'

'What's what, Harvey?' asked Jane, who was pretending to be making up menus for the dining room but was really casting furtive and miserable glances at what Harvey was doing.

'That din – music, happy voices, merriment – not what we want at Bayview at all. Where's it coming from?'

'The dining room, Harvey.'

'But it sounds like a party.'

'It is a party, Harvey. For Dave Cartwright – you remember? You gave your blessing to it.'

'But what I had in mind was some quiet and reverent affair. A cup of tea – a slice of cake – something like that. This sounds like a Bacchanalian orgy. Come along, Jane. We must put a stop to it.'

Laying down his ballpoint, Harvey rose and stalked purposefully out of his office while Jane scuttled dutifully along behind him. Down the corridor they went and then descended a short flight of stairs and so along another corridor until they reached the dining room. Its door was closed and the din, while loud, was as nothing to the blast of sound that struck them the moment Harvey threw it open. Then the two new arrivals were virtually overwhelmed by cheerful uproar.

Standing like Nemesis in the doorway, Harvey, with Jane cowering beside him, surveyed the depraved scene sternly. A geriatric pianist was pounding the piano. Geriatric dancers were, with astonishing vigour considering their years, moving about the floor in time to the music. And everywhere were little knots of wrinklies gulping whisky and champagne and roaring with laughter. Clearly audible above the rest of the din came the voice of Basil, the Bayview Stallion, addressing a gang of his disciples.

'You may laugh. You may jeer,' he challenged them, 'but it is nonetheless true. The prostate operation works wonders for one's sex life at our age. Just you ask Dave Cartwright about it. After his prostate operation he thought every day was Christmas. Yes, you ask old Dave about it.'

Jane shuddered fastidiously and remarked: 'So tasteless —'

Tom, who was in the circle around Basil, pointed out, 'Basil, we can't ask Dave Cartwright about it. This is his wake, remember?'

Basil smote his brow and conceded the point.

'Oh, so it is. Poor old Dave. Still, I bet they had a job getting the lid down on him.'

And he chortled with glee at his own lewd jest.

Diana called impatiently, 'Tom, will you please get on with it?'

'Oh right,' said Tom.

He picked up two glasses and tinkled them together for silence. Then he boomed, 'Ladies and gentlemen – er, and Diana.'

Diana made a rude sound. Tom continued.

'Let us all raise our glasses in memory of Dave Cartwright who was not only a splendid fellow but also left us two hundred pounds so that we could all get – and I quote from his will – "completely legless in memory of me". Well now, we don't want to let him down, do we? So – charge your glasses for a toast!'

There was a roar of applause and a good deal of laughter and filling up of glasses. The pianist struck up 'For He's a Jolly Good Fellow' and soon the whole company was roaring out the song and gulping their drinks.

It was at this point that Harvey chose to intervene.

'Excuse me,' he called out, but ineffectually in that uproar. 'Could I have a spot of hush, please? I say. Could I have your attention, please – oh hell. Jane?'

Seeing Harvey snubbed was more than Jane could bear. She cupped her hands around her mouth and, at a volume surprising for one of her sex and build, bawled: 'QUIET!'

There was an immediate hush and Harvey said:

'Thank you. Now then —'

But before he could get to the point of his intervention, Tom looked round, saw him and called: 'Oh hello, Harvey. Have you come for a drink to celebrate Cartwright's last stand?'

There was a burst of loud laughter. When it had subsided Harvey said primly:

'As it happens I do not drink at this time of day.'

'Well, that's understandable,' commented Basil. 'He doesn't normally emerge from his coffin until sunset.'

'All right, all right,' said Harvey with a tight smile. 'But may I remind you that you are senior citizens and not a lawless rabble? Is this appropriate behaviour? And not only here and now but at nights too? Oh, I know what goes on. I hear the Zimmer frames clinking along the corridors in the dead of night. But thus far I have done nothing about it. Why? Because I'm a nice guy, that's why.'

'Oh no you're not,' carolled the company ritually.

'Oh yes, I —' began Harvey but then realized it would serve

no useful purpose for him to get involved in a nursery slanging match. 'The point I wish to make is that Bayview has always been, and so long as I'm in charge will always remain, a haven of gentility. There is no place here for drunken carousing. So I would just like to request that you all – aaargh!'

The strangled exclamation had been wrung from Harvey by the curved handle of a walking stick that shot out and caught him round the neck. At the other end of the stick was Diana who now pulled hard, causing Harvey to fall sideways onto a chair with his hands at his throat trying desperately to dislodge the stick.

'Now listen here, you pustule,' began Diana genially, 'how many times does it have to be dinned into the lump of soggy blancmange you use for a brain that we are the paying customers? You are not the overseer of a cotton plantation but a member of the staff of a residential establishment. Your sole purpose in life is to look after our needs and wellbeing. And if we wish to enjoy ourselves, so long as we remain within the law of the land, we are free to do so in any way we choose – with tearful memories, drunken revelry or bedtime frolics. Is that clear, Harvey?'

In reply, Harvey made noises suggestive of a cat choking on a fishbone and Diana eased up on the stick slightly.

'Harvey? Have you taken my point?'

'Yes, Diana,' gasped Harvey gratefully. 'Certainly, Diana. Of course, Diana.'

'Very well then, stay and join the conga line that was about to begin before your uninvited intrusion or slink off to your puritanical bed. But do not attempt any further interference with our legitimate recreational activities. Got it?'

And Diana with a neat flick of the wrist, released Harvey from his uncomfortable plight. Once free, he stood up, rubbing his neck and smiling ruefully.

'All right then,' he said in a surprisingly resigned voice. 'Have a good night everyone. Come along, Jane.'

'So tasteless,' muttered Jane, shaking her head in bottomless disgust.

'Yes, well you heard what Diana said,' observed Harvey humbly. 'If they wish to frolic all night it's their decision. You and I, Jane, are just here to do the donkey work.' At this point,

Harvey paused and smiled in a gentle and compassionate way upon the company. Then he continued, 'And, of course, Jane, someone has to stay sober in order to 'phone for the ambulances when the revellers start to collapse from strokes and heart attacks. As, of course, good old Dave Cartwright did so very recently.'

And he and Jane departed leaving a momentary chill behind them. This, however, was soon broken by Basil calling, 'Come on, Arthur, tickle the ivories. Let's get the conga line going.'

And within a minute or two, a long line of vigorously kicking wrinklies was circling the room and then snaking out through the building and into the grounds. As he passed through the door to the dining room, Tom detached himself from the line and joined a figure who was standing in the corridor watching.

'Come on, Diana,' he urged, 'it's for you too.'

'True, but only as a spectator. I have an idea that if I kicked up my leg it might fly off. And then what would I use for kicking the idiot Bains with? Still, this is certainly a wonderful sight to behold.'

'It is indeed,' agreed Tom, as the stamping and shouting old folk went frolicking past. 'We've never had this kind of fun and games at Bayview before.'

'It's the dawn of revolution in England,' said Diana firmly. 'As the population gets older the GLF will become the dominant power in the land.'

'What's the GLF?'

'The Geriatric Liberation Front. Just think of it, Tom – grey-haired terrorists forcing people to play bridge at gunpoint.'

Tom was quick to pick up the idea and limp with it.

'Jumbo jets hijacked to Torquay. Riots on bowling greens as dry sherry louts stage pitch invasions.'

'Zimmer-frame thefts by tea-crazed joy-hobblers,' contributed Diana. 'Rap-happy grannies hurling orthopaedic corsets at superannuated male strippers.'

'God, how tame our little conga line seems compared to the glorious future that beckons, comrade,' said Tom with a sigh. 'Still, I think I'll get back into it.'

'And I think I'll split to the pad and grab a little shuteye ready for more fast-lane action tomorrow.'

And with a quick spit on their palms and a hand-slap the two went their separate ways.

The fun and frolics went on long into the night. But finally the last fun-satiated reveller collapsed into his or her bed and, not long after that, the clock struck ten. Bayview slept.

At about nine the following morning, Jane bustled cheerfully into Diana's bedroom, prattling as she did so, 'Morning, Diana. Well, I'm glad it's a new day. Harvey was right, of course. The excitement was altogether too much for a lot of people. The doctor is seeing Clifford Lutton at this very moment. He's suffering from acute wine retention. Bill Cox caught a chill sleeping in a tree wearing a baby doll nightie. No one knows where he got it from. Vi Phillips is looking – oh!'

The exclamation of surprise had been caused by the fact that, having drawn the curtains and straightened out one or two pieces of furniture, Jane had glanced towards the bed and found, to her surprise, that there was no one in it. Since it was still fully made, it was obvious that not only was it empty now but that no one had slept in it that night. Where then was Diana?

Jane frowned uneasily. In spite of the hard time the older woman often gave her, Jane liked and respected Diana. Could something really serious have happened to her in the aftermath of last night's dreadful party? Jane turned with the intention of hurrying to the office in order to notify Harvey of the situation. But then she paused. Tom Ballard often knew about Diana's movements and his flat was a lot closer than the office. Jane decided that she would just call in at Tom's place and make inquiries before notifying Harvey.

Jane thereupon hurried into Diana's conservatory and then through it into Tom's conservatory and on until she reached Tom's living room. And there, in the middle of the room, clad in a smart red-felt dressing gown over striped pyjamas and sipping a cup of tea, stood Tom himself.

'Hello, Jane,' he said warmly, beaming at his uninvited guest. 'Do come in. Would you like a cup of tea?'

'No thanks, Tom,' said Jane hurriedly. 'I can't stop. Amongst other things I have to go down to the laundrette and rescue Horace Wilmott. He spent the night in a tumble drier. But what's worrying me is – I can't find Diana. She's not in her room and her bed hasn't been slept in. Do you happen to know where she is?'

'Yes, I do,' said Tom. And, like a stage magician, he took a dramatic step to one side and made a theatrical gesture towards his bedroom. *'Voilà!'*

Jane gazed and saw that the door to Tom's bedroom was open, revealing Tom's bed. The bed was a bit ruffled as one might have expected since Tom had clearly only recently risen from it. But what on earth was Tom insinuating with his smug smile and —

'Oh, my goodness!' exclaimed Jane. 'Oh dear. Oh no. Oh what will Harvey say? Oh, how tasteless!'

For the covers had heaved slightly and Jane had seen a figure in the bed under the sheets and blankets. And even while she was watching, the figure had rolled over and revealed, as the face became visible, that it was none other than Diana Trent. Worse, in the brief moment permitted to her for observation, Jane had received the distinct impression that Diana was as naked as Eve in Eden.

'I would never ever have thought this possible, Tom,' stammered Jane. 'I just don't know what to say. I don't know what Harvey will say. I don't know what anyone will say. The truth is I'm quite – quite – quite – speechless.'

And Jane span round and hurried away. Tom watched her go with a broad grin on his face. Then he turned and went into his bedroom. He approached the bed and looked down complacently at the still-sleeping figure. Then he bent over and gently shook Diana's shoulder.

'A cup of tea, old thing?' he asked pleasantly. 'It might help to clear the cobwebs?'

'Hmm?' asked Diana, opening her eyes and blinking. 'Could you possibly switch off that searchlight?'

'There isn't any searchlight on. In fact, it's really quite dark in here.'

'Is it? And I suppose there isn't any brass band playing either? I was dreaming that I was in Wembley Stadium and a military tattoo was taking place.' But then suddenly Diana's eyes opened wide and she stared at Tom in dismay. 'Yes, but what the hell are you doing in my bedroom, Tom?' she asked angrily.

'This isn't your bedroom, Diana,' Tom explained pleasantly. 'It's mine.'

'Yours? Are you sure? But then how did your bedroom get into my flat?'

'No, no, let's try and get the measure of this thing, shall we? This is not your flat, Diana. It is my flat and my bedroom and my bed.'

A look of grim reproach formed on Diana's face and she said bitterly.

'So that's it, is it? You beast! What did you do? Drug me and drag me in here?'

'Oh, don't be silly, Diana. No drugging and dragging were called for. When I got back from the party I found you tucked up in my little beddy-bye, sleeping your tiny head off.'

'What? But that's completely impos —' But then Diana, essentially a fair-minded person, broke off, thinking hard.

'No, it's not, is it? Oh my God, yes, it's coming back to me now. I undressed in my bedroom and then I found my bedside book was missing. I always read for at least ten minutes before going to sleep. Then I remembered bringing the book in here the day before to read you a passage from it – and so naturally I came in here to find it.'

'Oh, that's a bit of a letdown,' said Tom ruefully. 'I assumed when I got home that you'd simply been overcome with an irresistible desire for my embraces.'

'Silence, you cad. To continue, I found the book and then – oh dear. Yes, I forgot I was in your flat and not mine. After all, I'd drunk enough wine to float Harvey Bains. So I just climbed into your bed by mistake.'

'Oh well,' said Tom. 'All roads lead to – er – Rome. There is just one thing that puzzles me. Don't you usually wear a nightie?'

'Of course I do,' said Diana firmly. But then an uneasy look came into her eyes. 'Why do you ask?'

'Because, you weren't wearing one when I got home.'

'Utter rubbish!' There was a pause while Diana, as could be discerned from delicate movements under the covers, explored the situation. Then she asked in a small voice, 'Tom, did you remove my nightie?'

'Certainly not.'

'Then how —' but then again a look of understanding appeared on Diana's face. She turned slightly and looked up towards a corner of the room and then she gave a little scream.

'What's the matter?' asked Tom.

'I've remembered. I was so hot in the night that I took it off and flung it away from me – and look, that's where it ended up.'

Diana pointed. Tom looked in the direction in which she was pointing and sure enough there was Diana's nightie on top of his wardrobe with a section of it dangling down.

'Of course,' nodded Tom. 'At night you keep your bedroom at what is virtually an arctic temperature. No wonder my bedroom seemed very warm to you. And all that explains why I assumed – well —'

'Yes?' asked Diana with grim urgency. 'Don't stop. You assumed what exactly?'

'Well, what most gentlemen would assume if they found a naked lady in their bed.'

Diana swallowed and then said very carefully, 'Tom, whatever the curious circumstances that brought me here – we didn't actually make love did we?'

'Well, of course we did,' affirmed Tom positively.

'Oh my God!' exclaimed Diana tragically.

Tom frowned.

'Is there some kind of problem?'

'Well, what do you think? There's you. And there's me. And then there's sex,' and her expression hardened once more. 'My God, you swine, you took advantage of me.'

'Hardly.'

'Yes, you did. You're simply a heartless beast, Tom. A woman who has perhaps taken a little more wine than she is accustomed to accidentally takes a short nap in your bed and you come thundering in and practically rape her. You should be in jail.'

'No, I shouldn't. If anyone should be in jail it's you. You made the running.'

'What's that supposed to mean?'

'Well, as I've already explained, I came home and found you asleep in my bed naked. So I chuckled at the thought of what an impetuous little thing you can be when your desires are roused, but naturally I was far too much of a gentleman to take advantage of the situation. So I went to sleep in the armchair. A little later I was awakened by your groping me.

And while you were happily occupied in this way you regaled me with a long and persuasive lecture along the lines of, "There are only a few happy times possible in any of our lives and so we must grab them with both hands," which, in fact, was what you were doing. Finally, you almost dragged me to the bed and pulled off my clothes. If anyone was ravished last night, Diana —'

Tom broke off meaningfully. But no further protestations of innocence were required from him. Diana had remembered all.

'You're right,' she exclaimed. 'That's how it happened. It's all come back to me now. And what I said – I recognize that too. It was my early feminist speech. Every time I fancied a chap and there wasn't time for the usual fiddle faddle, I'd tell them we had to grab happiness with both hands and that women had just as much right as men to initiate sex and – so on. Oh Tom, can you ever forgive me?'

'Eh?' asked Tom, looking a trifle perplexed.

'Well – your wife – Maggie. You've always been so faithful to her memory. I hope I haven't made you sully it.'

'Oh, not at all,' Tom generously assured her. 'After all, it's been seventeen years. And Maggie always enjoyed a good laugh.'

'That's not very —'

'No, I meant at both of us. At our tumultuous embraces, as someone said of Dr Johnson and his wife.'

'Very nice embraces I seem to recall.'

'Oh, they were. They were indeed.'

'But for all that,' said Diana, trying to sound sensible, 'we must keep this thing in proportion.'

'Absolutely. Very much in proportion.'

'Tom, can I borrow your dressing gown?'

'Of course. Naturally.' Tom removed the garment and placed it on the bed. Then, feeling a little foolish after the night they had spent, he turned in a gentlemanly way and went into his living room. A moment or two later, Diana, quite fetchingly immersed like a waif in what for her was his huge dressing gown, joined him.

'Very becoming,' Tom said with a tender smile. 'Diana —'

'Yes?'

'About what you said – keeping it in proportion. I'm all for that, of course.'

'Good.'

'But I do hope we can do it again.'

'Oh, don't be absurd. It was an accident.'

'Next time it won't be. Think about it. It was jolly good fun. A lot better than upsetting the mobile library lady.'

'Now look Tom —'

'Or baiting Harvey Bains.'

'Tom —'

'Of course, it would be a lot more convenient for doing it if you and I were shacked up together.'

'Well, there is absolutely no chance of that,' asserted Diana vehemently. 'I will never relinquish my freedom of action and thought.'

'Well, you wouldn't have to,' Tom assured her. 'It's your body I'm interested in.'

Diana smiled.

'Forget it, Tom, and make me another cup of tea. I forgot to drink the last one.'

Tom said willingly, 'Certainly, but before I do, just reassure me, Diana: we will be able to do it again some time, won't we?'

Diana sighed and said thoughtfully, 'We'll just have to see, won't we?'

At about half past two that afternoon, Tom, with a warm, reminiscent light in his eyes, was seated, enjoying the sunshine, on one of the many attractive benches scattered throughout the grounds of Bayview. He did not see Basil approaching and was not aware of the Bayview Stallion's proximity before the other man spoke.

'Tom, I want a word,' said Basil, somewhat peremptorily.

'Hm?' Tom looked down from the branches he had been contemplating and saw who had addressed him. 'Oh, it's you, Basil. Yes, of course. Why don't you join me and tell me how I can be of service?'

'Right.'

Basil seated himself next to Tom on the bench, cleared his throat and said firmly, 'I think you are aware, Tom, that when it comes to anything connected with sex I am top dude around here.'

'Good heavens, yes, Basil,' Tom assured him earnestly. 'Why, your achievements are legendary. I still tremble with admiration whenever I recall the time you had intimate relations in turn with every single one of the Dagenham Girl Pipers in their dressing room during a Burns Night banquet, between the piping in of the haggis and the arrival of the ambulance to take you to hospital suffering from acute exhaustion syndrome. I am also proud to be the friend of a man whom Errol Flynn, amongst many other celebrated studs, used to write to for advice in amatory matters. And I am also well aware that since you've been here at Bayview no woman has felt dismally safe – except possibly Diana because of her celebrated left hook.'

'As it happens, Tom,' said Basil, still sounding rather severe despite Tom's outrageous flattery, 'it's Diana that I wish to talk to you about.'

'Really? Fire away then.'

'It's just that I won't have you or anyone else muscling in on my turf.'

'God forbid.'

'And Diana is part of my turf. So you would greatly oblige me, Tom, if you stopped trying to emulate my achievements and slung your hook.'

Tom gazed at him in amazement and said feebly, 'I can't imagine what you can be talking about, Basil.'

'Balls!' said Basil crudely. 'Your balls, as it happens. I am sick to death of hearing references to their activities. All day long it's been Tom Ballard this and Tom Ballard that from all the hot chicks about here. Anyone would think you invented copulation.'

Tom shook his head in disbelief.

'Basil, you're not suggesting that people know? About me and Diana?'

'Oh yes, I am. It's the lead item in the local news roundup. Jane's rushing around blabbing to everyone.'

'Oh God, that's awful!' said Tom feelingly.

'It certainly is!' Basil echoed him indignantly. 'I haven't scored all day. And I've got five dozen condoms with a use-by date of next Wednesday. I really don't want to have to chuck half of them away.'

'But this is incredible, Basil. I mean everyone knows that you've always been the greatest – the Muhammed Ali, the Edmund Hillary, even the Fanny Craddock of the sexual revolution. So it hardly seems possible that the time might finally have come —' Tom broke off, with wrinkled brow, apparently thinking deeply.

'The time might finally have come for what?' asked Basil suspiciously.

'No, it's not possible, is it?' murmured Tom almost to himself.

'What's not possible?' demanded Basil, looking slightly alarmed.

'That the hour could really have struck for you, Basil? The hour for yielding your crown graciously to a younger man?'

'What younger man?' asked Basil, now sounding distinctly panicky.

Tom grinned broadly.

'Why me, of course, Basil. Yes, me – Tom Ballard, superstud extraordinary.'

And as Basil watched angrily, Tom got to his feet and shook his clasped hands in the air like a boxer that has just knocked out the champion.

Some two hours after this encounter, Diana, with a faint reminiscent smile playing about her lips, sat painting in her conservatory. Before long Jane issued from Tom's flat and began clearing his conservatory table.

'Afternoon, Jane,' Diana greeted the new arrival civilly.

But Jane failed to acknowledge the greeting with word or look. Diana smiled knowingly.

'Jane?' she said.

At this Jane heaved a sigh and, still without looking in Diana's direction, said, 'I'm sorry but I just don't feel I can talk to you today, Diana.'

Diana shook her head wearily and laid down her brush.

'Jane,' she ordered, 'come here and sit down.'

'I'd rather not, thank you.'

'Jane,' said Diana sweetly, 'sit down or I will chop off your legs and nail the stumps to the chair.'

With a martyred look, Jane did as she had been ordered.

'Now then —' said Diana. 'What exactly is the matter?'

'I suspect you know that only too well, Diana.'

'Jane, how do you see me?' asked Diana in quite a kindly voice.

And at this Jane finally did raise her eyes and look at the older woman.

'Oh, I've always seen you as a pillar of strength, Diana,' she confessed. 'I know we have our differences and that you're often terribly cruel to Harvey, but you're the senior statesman of Bayview. That's why it's so tragic that you've gone and besmirched your reputation and —'

'Jane, Jane,' cried Diana maternally. 'Why are you such a dismal twisted dimwit? Have you been so completely brainwashed by the constant drip of kiddy TV that you think sex only ever takes place between beautiful young people?'

Jane sighed deeply and said, rather grandly, 'But you – you're an icon, Diana.'

'Bollocks,' returned Diana, rather less grandly. 'I'm a woman. Until quite recently I had resigned myself to being just an old person. But now thanks to some cheap plonk and a fully functioning Tom Ballard, I am rediscovering the fact that I am still firing on all cylinders. And if I can still feel that then why can't all the other zombies around here who have prematurely copped out of life feel it too? Perhaps from now on instead of bridge nights we should have orgy nights. Just because we sag and bag a bit and no longer fancy doing it in the back of a mini with one foot out of the window does not mean that we shouldn't enjoy a sex life in the privacy of our own homes, does it?'

'The thing is, Diana —' Jane attempted to reply but the other rather unfairly held up a stern hand and continued.

'Now, I didn't ask you to barge in this morning – or indeed any morning – Jane. But since you have done, what have you seen that is so terrible? If Tom and I had been roasting a schoolboy on a spit you might have had some justification for your revulsion – although most of the schoolboys I know would greatly benefit from the treatment. But my main point is this: do you really consider simple lovemaking to be such an unforgivable activity, Jane, that you are prepared to stop speaking to me just because I very occasionally indulge in it?'

For a long moment, Jane continued to look doubtful and unhappy, but finally a tremulous smile of complicity flickered across her features.

'Oh, all right, Diana,' she began, and then surprised the other by continuing rather coarsely. 'Just so long as you don't do it in the grounds and frighten the gardener. And incidentally, I don't know if it's of any interest to you, but Tom Ballard is at this very moment being given tea by the whole of the ladies' bowling team.'

'What? Those trollops? It most decidedly is of interest to me. Where is this outrageous event taking place, Jane? Lead me to it at once.'

And so Jane led Diana to the Bowls Club where Tom Ballard had been installed in the sunshine in a comfortable deckchair surrounded by an adoring circle of athletic women, some of whom were very attractive. The ladies were engaged in listening to Tom's tall tales while drinking tea and eating gooey cakes.

'It was at about this time,' Tom was saying majestically, 'that MGM signed me up to play Tarzan. Actually in those days my name was Weissmuller, but I changed it to Ballard in 1939 since Weissmuller was not then considered quite the most suitable name for a fighter pilot in the RAF. I now began to acquire my international reputation as a sexual athlete and all through the Blitz, when not zapping Jerry from the skies, I was breaking bedroom records throughout the length and breadth of England.'

'Tom,' said Diana sweetly, and yet somehow ominously, as she hove into sight on the fringes of the ring of adoring bowlers.

Tom started and then, seeing who it was that had arrived, stammered, 'Oh dear, I think it's Bette Davis. The trouble is she's never forgiven me for having had an affair with Gina Lollobrigida and —'

'Tom, what the hell are you doing?' asked Diana pointedly.

'Well – er – just telling these ladies the history of my life as one of the century's leading sex symbols.'

'Rubbish!' said Diana crisply. She looked around at the circle of women, who were now tut-tutting at the interruption, and began. 'Now, listen you lot, it just so happens that by some fluke of genetic justice we women tend to live longer than the men creatures. And as a result the men are outnumbered by the women. This means that a good man is bloody hard to find. I would therefore like all you harpies to take notice that I have found me a good man and if any one of you so much as glances in his direction you will end up being cut into small pieces and sent home in a matchbox. Is that clearly understood?'

And Diana glared round at them so fiercely that several of the doughty bowlers drew back in alarm. Diana held out her hand to her new mate and said quietly, 'Come along, Tom.'

Tom grinned sheepishly at the bowlers as he rose obediently.

'As you see,' he admitted, 'it's not always all that wonderful being wonderful. Goodbye, ladies.'

Whereupon Tom and Diana departed and then walked slowly through the grounds of Bayview towards their adjoining homes. After a while, Diana said, 'Aren't you showing a slight tendency to trespass on Basil's territory, Tom?'

'Oh, he's yesterday's stud,' said Tom confidently. 'I'm the new cock of the walk around here.'

'Good, good,' said Diana gently. 'But I hope you don't mind if I point out that we're not talking about inventing the wheel here?'

'How do you mean?'

'I mean that you might perhaps cool it a bit. You're going round like a young teenager grinning from ear to ear because he has just joined the oldest club in the world. Making love is no very big deal, Tom.'

'Well, I'm not too sure about that, Diana,' said Tom, a shade sullenly. 'It's quite a big deal for me.'

'Really?' asked Diana. 'Why?'

'Well, it provides a spot of additional proof that I might really be alive and not just a figment of your imagination.'

They walked on in silence. The sun was warm. A gentle

breeze stirred in the topmost branches. The hum of bees filled the air.

'What about your heart?' asked Diana, referring candidly to the slight medical problems Tom occasionally had with that organ.

'Oh, who cares about a spot of angina?' asked Tom rhetorically. 'Suggest a better way to go and I'll show you a liar.'

'Yes, well there's another consideration too. I have always liked to be known as a person in my own right. But I gather from Jane that Basil is buzzing about the place referring to me as "Tom Ballard's bit of crumpet".'

'Don't you worry about Basil, little lady,' said Tom in the tones of a Hollywood gunslinger. 'I can take him out any time I choose.'

'I'd prefer it if you would just keep your trap shut about us. Our business should remain ours and nobody else's.'

'All right,' agreed Tom with a sigh. 'I'll keep mum from now on. But – er – Diana, you never did give me a proper answer – what about us?'

'I don't know,' said Diana shortly. 'What about us?'

'Well, I mean – do we have a future? In bed?'

'I doubt it.'

'You don't mean that.'

'Yes, I do,' said Diana calmly.

The humming of the bees became fainter. The sun, too, became a few degrees cooler as the two senior citizens drew near to the home that they partly shared.

'But I was hoping – I mean – I was thinking – I mean – it's such a lovely day —' said Tom.

'And you had designs on me again, is that it?' asked Diana scathingly.

'Well, I wouldn't have put it like that, but —'

'Forget it Ballard. I may not be in the first flush of youth but the heart of a maiden still beats beneath these veteran ribs. I will not be taken advantage of by you or anyone else.'

'Oh dear,' said Tom glumly. 'I never thought of it as taking advantage but rather as joyously sharing.'

But Diana did not comment. They again walked in silence for some time. And then Diana said quite softly, 'No, I will not be taken advantage of ever again – except perhaps on very rare occasions such as saints' days and other religious holidays.'

'Do you mean it?' asked Tom, brightening. 'Do you really mean that, Diana?' But then he shook his head and pointed out sadly, 'Yes, but there probably won't be one of those for ages.'

They had reached their flats. Tom turned the key in his lock and pushed open his front door.

'Oh, I don't know,' said Diana, 'just remind me: what's the date today, Tom?'

'Today? Erm – oh yes, it's the seventeenth.'

'Exactly,' said Diana, advancing confidently through Tom's open door and continuing on into his living room, 'and the seventeenth happens to be the Feast of St Kermit of All the Frogs, doesn't it ?'

'What on earth,' asked Tom, with a puzzled look, 'is the Feast of – oh.' His puzzled expression gave way to a delighted smile. 'But of course. Of course it is,' he exclaimed. 'And – by heaven – tomorrow is the Feast of St Donald of All the Ducks.'

'Exactly,' agreed Diana. 'It's astonishing how many of these saints' days you can find if you really pore over the calendar.'

Chuckling happily, Tom followed Diana as she walked purposefully into his bedroom.

'Praise be to St Kermit,' Tom murmured reverently as he closed the bedroom door behind them, 'and to St Donald as well.'

EIGHT

Autumn had come to Bayview and, beneath the oak trees, acorns lay thickly on the ground. Tom was gathering some of these up while Diana tested the elastic of a stout catapult that she was holding.

'What are you doing?' she asked.

Tom snapped to attention and saluted.

'Getting the ammunition, sah,' he replied.

'Acorns? Don't be such a wimp. I want pebbles or, ideally, glass marbles.'

Tom shook his head sadly as he reverted from being a daring captain of commandos to plain Tom Ballard once more.

'Don't be silly. That's a powerful catapult. You could put his eye out with a pebble.'

'Precisely.'

'Good heavens, Diana, he's only doing his job.'

'He's an insolent puppy. He called me a sweet old thing.'

'Which, I have to concede, is not only patronizing but quite astonishingly inaccurate. But if you put his eye out you'll only have to buy him a new one.'

Diana sighed unhappily.

'I suppose you're right. Pity, because I utterly loathe and despise postmen. They never bring you anything but bad news.'

'That's not their fault.'

'Well, it's not mine. All right, give me your wimpish acorns and get back to your observation post. At least let's try to raise a decent sized lump on his fat head.'

Tom obediently handed Diana his acorn harvest and then moved to a place behind an oak where he could not be seen from the approach road. Diana stationed herself behind another oak.

They had only a few minutes to wait before Tom raised an arm – the pre-arranged signal – to indicate that the postman was puffing up the hill on his bike. Diana promptly inserted the hardest and most gnarled acorn in her collection into the leather pouch of the catapult and drew the pouch back a little to get it tensioned properly.

She waited a few seconds more and then peeped round the tree. The postman was now virtually within range. She drew the acorn back to its fullest extent but just as she was going to release it the postman stopped his bike, reached into his big canvas bag and withdrew a crash helmet. He placed this on his head and then set off on his bike again. As he pedalled past the tree behind which Tom was hiding, he raised two fingers in a derisive salute. Diana dispiritedly let fly her acorn but it only pinged harmlessly off the postman's helmet. He turned and gave Diana too a mocking salute. He then continued on up towards the main building of Bayview.

'He knew. He'd been tipped off,' Diana exclaimed disconsolately. 'We must have been penetrated. The question is: who is the mole?'

'It must be you,' said Tom firmly.

'How do you work that one out?'

'Well, there are only two of us in the organization. And since I know that I'm not the mole it can't be anyone but you.'

'I suppose that figures,' admitted Diana glumly. 'Yes, but hang on, since I also know that I'm not the mole then, by the same reasoning, it has to be you.'

'Perhaps we're both moles,' suggested Tom, 'which is all right by me. I like moles. Although it might be more sensible, with all these acorns around, if we were both squirrels.'

'What we squirrels really need is a flame-thrower to take out that bloody postman,' said Diana firmly. 'See to it, would you, number two?'

'All right, number one. But it'll take a couple of days to get a flame-thrower out here from Blighty. Parachute drop, I'd suggest. Jerry has got the straits covered with his gigantic naval guns. Incidentally, shouldn't we blow those up before we bring in the flame-throwers?'

'One thing at a time,' urged Diana excitedly. 'Listen, he's got to come back down the drive, hasn't he?'

'Unless he's picked up by a night-flying Auster —'

'No, no, stop the game for a moment! I'm being serious. What we need is a rope and then we'll have him.'

'You mean we lassoo him as he goes past?'

'Nothing of the sort,' exclaimed Diana impatiently. 'We'll stretch the rope low down across the drive. He'll hit it when he comes zooming down the hill and he'll go flying over the handlebars. With any luck he'll land on his head.'

'But he could be badly hurt.'

'Serve him right for all the rotten letters he delivers.'

'Yes, but —'

'In Antonio's hut over there – bound to be a rope. Fetch it, number two —'

'But I still think —'

'Insubordination? That, number two, is a court martial offence.'

'Oh, all right. But I really do think we'll have to review our war aims as regards postmen.'

While this minor skirmish in the long-standing struggle between Diana Trent and the postman was going on, Harvey Bains was distressing Jane by his strenuous activity.

'Is this wise, Harvey?' Jane asked anxiously.

'Is what – wise – Jane?' Harvey gasped between strokes.

'All this exercise? Your lips are turning blue and your eyes are popping out.'

'Oh my God – really?' exclaimed Bains.

He pushed away the oars and jumped up. A fierce pain shot up his arms causing him to cry out in anguish. Then his arms went numb. Harvey had just rowed the simulated distance from Putney Bridge to the Tower of London and, what's more, against a simulated incoming tide.

'Great heavens!' Harvey cried. 'I think you're right! I've overdone it. Search around for my arms, would you, Jane? And when you've found them 'phone the hospital and tell them to prepare an operating theatre where they can be sewn back on.'

'Your arms are still attached to you, Harvey,' Jane reassured him.

'Are they?' asked Harvey. He glanced down. 'So they are.

Amazing. I can't feel them any more. But what about my face? Oh! You're right, Jane. My lips are blue and my eyes are popping out. God, I look ghastly!'

'No, no, Harvey, that's not a mirror. That's a framed picture of Bob Hoskins in my favourite film, *Who Killed Roger Rabbit?*. The mirror is next to it.'

Harvey located the mirror and gazed critically at his reflection.

'Well – my lips aren't really all that blue, Jane, and my eyes are hardly popping out at all. Aren't we being a tiny bit alarmist here?'

'It's just that I do worry about you, Harvey. All this jogging and rowing and weightlifting – why? What's it all for? What's come over you?'

Harvey seated himself in his executive swivel chair and wiped the sweat from his face with a paper tissue.

'Would you really like to know, Jane?'

'Yes, I would, Harvey.'

'The fact is that I'm trying to make myself worthy of someone, Jane. It's someone who is very dear to me.'

'Oh?' asked Jane, conscious of a tremor of excitement which experience should have taught her to mistrust. 'And who would that be, Harvey? I suppose it's some – some relative, is it? Your mother perhaps?'

'No, Jane, it's not a relative. It is a young woman. A young woman I have known for a long time but whose many fine qualities I have to my shame only recently come to appreciate.'

Jane was conscious of a pulse of sheer delight but strove to suppress it.

'Really, Harvey?' she asked. 'And would I be right in thinking that you see this – this young woman a good deal?'

'Almost every day, Jane. But our relationship has thus far been almost purely professional and thus impersonal. It was only about a fortnight ago that, suddenly and unexpectedly, I realized what a very wonderful person she really is.'

'Oh, Harvey, I – oh, I don't know what to say.'

'Then, don't say anything, Jane. Just listen. It pains me to admit it but I have often treated this young woman in a very casual way. I have even sometimes been rude and peremptory towards her. I am now, of course, deeply ashamed of my former unkind behaviour.'

Jane gulped and asked, 'But there is still one thing I don't quite understand, Harvey, what has all the heavy exercise got to do with this young woman?'

'It is simply that she is a superbly healthy and physically desirable person, Jane, and so I too want to glow with rude health – so that I can be worthy of her, you see, Jane?'

'But, Harvey, quite honestly – I'm sure this – this hypothetical young woman would like you just as much if you didn't do quite so much rowing and jogging and all that.'

'Really, Jane? Naturally, I value your opinion in this matter. But I can't help wondering if you'd feel the same if you knew who it is that I'm talking about.'

'Oh, I – I'm sure I would feel the same, Harvey. And actually I feel pretty confident that I can guess who it really is. So you needn't hesitate to tell me her name, Harvey.'

'All right then, Jane. It's Helga.'

Jane stared blankly at Harvey for a moment.

'I'm sorry, Harvey,' she stammered finally. 'I don't think I can have heard you right. I thought you said Helga. But my name isn't Helga, Harvey – it's Jane.'

'Well, my goodness I know what *your* name is, don't I, Jane? But what on earth has that got to do with it? I mean, you could hardly have imagined that I was talking about you, could you?' Harvey laughed merrily for a moment at the mere idea.

Jane looked crestfallen. Harvey continued, 'I'm talking about Helga Wildfrau, the receptionist at Stubbins Bakery where I purchase all our bread and other bakery products because they're the only bakery around here to give us a realistic discount. Now until recently, Jane, I thought of Helga as being just another dumb Kraut with corn-yellow hair. But then about a month ago I bumped into her by chance when we were both out jogging and it was a revelation. In shorts and T-shirt she reveals a superb figure with two of the very finest – er – ornaments that I have ever seen in my life. And that is why I bought this splendid rowing machine. Helga is clearly a seriously athletic type and so I – Jane? Are you all right, Jane? What is it, Jane? Is something wrong, Jane? Good heavens, whatever has come over you?'

But Jane was no longer present. With her hands over her streaming eyes she had rushed headlong from the office. For a moment Harvey gazed after her, shaking his head at this baffling behaviour and sighing. Then, aware of a faint rising effluvium, he frowned, raised both his arms in turn and sniffed delicately at each of his armpits. It would never do if all this rowing were to give him BO.

'Well?' asked Tom impatiently.

Diana was perched on a chair, peering out of a small, high window that was in a corner of Tom's living room. It was the only window that clearly surveyed the approach road where they had stretched the rope. She was waiting for the postman to pedal past so that she would be able to see him fly off his bike and land with a crunch on the tarmac.

'Nothing,' said Diana gloomily. 'I suppose Jenny's given him a cup of tea. That girl is far too kind-heart — Hang on, here he comes. Quick Tom, or you'll miss the fun. He's going like the clappers. He's getting near the rope. He – oh no!'

'What?' asked Tom, who was attempting to see what was going on through a lower window but finding that too many shrubs were in the way.

'What a sell!' exclaimed Diana in disgust. 'There is definitely a traitor in our ranks, comrade. The bourgeois swine has stopped his bike and removed the rope. He could never have seen it at the speed he was going. So he must have been tipped off.'

'Jenny probably spotted us setting the trap,' suggested Tom.

'Possibly,' said Diana doubtfully, looking down at Tom with thoughtful eyes, 'but I wouldn't put it past you to have forewarned Jenny. You have never had a true stomach for revolutionary violence, comrade. All right, help me down.'

Tom went to the chair on which Diana was standing and held up his hand. Diana took it and began to descend but something went wrong with the operation. She slipped slightly and the unexpected increase in weight caused Tom to stumble backwards with her in his arms. Then, precariously carrying Diana, Tom managed to lurch a few feet across the room before dumping her unceremoniously into an armchair.

'Ow! You great oaf!' cried Diana. 'What the hell do you think you're doing?'

'Now, there's gratitude,' commented Tom ruefully. 'I could have dropped you but instead, by summoning up the strength and determination of my old friend and colleague, Superman, I managed to make it to the chair.'

'I think you've broken my back,' groaned Diana. 'I landed on something hard. What the hell is on this chair anyway?'

With some difficulty she reached round behind her and tugged out a strange contraption. It was a plastic box that had a window in it which showed a calibrated dial and needle. The box was also equipped with a short length of plastic tube ending in a nozzle.

'Good God,' exclaimed Diana, contemplating it. 'It's a DIY enema, isn't it?'

'No, it is not,' urged Tom with some asperity. 'And I hope you haven't broken it. It cost a pretty penny. It's my new damp meter.'

'I see,' said Diana grimly. 'You want to establish just how wet you really are, is that it?'

'I want to find out where it's damp.'

'Well, you great steaming twit, I can tell you exactly where it's damp. It's damp in the sea. It's damp in the rain and it's damp in the bloody bath.'

Tom grinned, went over to her and took the meter from her hand. He then applied the nozzle to her knee and watched as the needle in the window began to waver a little.

'There you are – it's registering,' he said triumphantly. 'You must have water on the knee.'

'Oh, bollocks,' exclaimed Diana ungraciously.

'There's only one cure for water on the knee,' persisted Tom. 'Drainpipe trousers.'

He chortled at this feeble joke while Diana glared at him. Then he put the nozzle to Diana's head and exclaimed, 'Good heavens, it's registering again. It seems you have water on the brain too. You know what the cure for that is, don't you? A tap on the head. Get it? A tap on the head.' And he burbled loudly with childish amusement. 'I got those jokes from the *Beano*,' he explained.

'Well, you should return them,' said Diana coldly. 'Some five-year-old is probably missing them horribly. Tom, have you taken leave of your senses? Why are you shelling out good whisky money for idiotic gadgets?'

'It's damp in here,' explained Tom. 'It gets into my bones. So I sent away for this so that I can prove that it's damp and compel Harvey to give me another flat.'

'Fat chance,' said Diana. 'And that reminds me. I had a letter too. It'll be bad news, of course, but I suppose I'd better peruse it.'

'I'm going to check the bedroom,' proclaimed Tom. 'That's where the damp is worst.'

He stumped off with the damp meter into his bedroom. Diana opened her bag and took out a white envelope with her name and address typed on it and with the sender's address printed along the top. She examined it for a moment.

'It's from the bloody investment people,' she murmured contemptuously. 'What do they want?'

She tore open the envelope, withdrew the letter and read it. Now Diana Trent, as the reader will by now be abundantly aware, was someone who greeted the minor hazards and pitfalls of life with loud and prolonged moans and complaints. However, on those rare occasions when something truly disastrous cropped up, it was her perverse habit to react by becoming steely and silent. She was therefore sitting, steely and silent, with the letter in her hand when, a few minutes later, Tom came back from his bedroom still holding his meter.

'You won't believe this,' he proclaimed bitterly, 'but it's seven point three in there.'

There was no answer and Tom said reproachfully, 'Diana? Did you hear what I said?'

Diana shook her head, but did not speak or move.

'I said it's damp enough in my bedroom to start a salmon farm. And that means it's unlikely to be as dry as a bone in your bedroom. Let's check it with my meter, shall we?'

'Yes, all right,' Diana murmured mechanically.

'Well, no time like the present,' proclaimed Tom. 'Let's go.'

'Hmm?' asked Diana, glancing round at him. 'Go where?'

'To check your room and then give Harvey hell about the damp.'

'Oh – it'll have to wait, I'm afraid,' said Diana briskly. 'The thing is, I have to go up to town.'

'Really? Up to what town?'

'London, of course.'

'London? But you haven't said anything about going up to London today?'

'No, I – I forgot. Anyway, I shouldn't be away more than a few hours. With any luck. So I'll see you at dinner if not before.'

And Diana rose and went out through Tom's conservatory towards her own quarters.

Tom stared after her with a puzzled expression for a moment. Then he noticed an envelope on the arm of the chair in which Diana had been sitting. He went and picked it up and realized that it must have contained the letter that Diana had received. He read the name of the sender and frowned slightly. Then he put the envelope on his mantlepiece, took up his damp meter again and went off to test his kitchen for damp.

'Harvey,' said Jane.

'Yes, Jane?' replied Harvey absently.

'Look what I've found,' urged Jane.

Harvey looked up from a sheet of paper on which he was making notes and saw that Jane was waving some kind of document towards him.

'What's that, Jane?' he asked, without much interest.

'It's a receipt, Harvey,' said Jane meaningfully.

'Really? Well, it'll keep, won't it? I'm trying to finalize my speech for the annual dinner of the Young Yuppies of Bournemouth Professional and Social Society which takes place next week.'

'Oh yes, it'll keep, Harvey,' said Jane. 'I was just surprised to find it in your room.'

This announcement caused Harvey to look up again with a slight frown.

'Find what in my room? What are you talking about, Jane?'

'Well, you see, I've just been giving your room a bit of a clean, Harvey, and I found this receipt while I was doing so.'

Harvey cocked his head slightly and asked:

'And what receipt would that be exactly, Jane?'

'It's the receipt for your rowing machine, Harvey. Gosh, it did cost an awful lot of money didn't it?'

'That's right, Jane. State-of-the-art products usually do.'

'But what I don't understand Harvey is why this receipt was in your room? Bayview receipts are normally filed here in the office, aren't they?'

'Indeed they are, Jane,' said Harvey with a reassuring smile, although a wrinkle or two on his brow suggested that he might not really be feeling quite so nonchalant as he was striving to seem, 'but this is my machine, not Bayview's.'

'That's just why it's so strange, Harvey. You see the receipt states: "One rowing machine for Bayview Gym". We don't have a gym, Harvey.'

'Just a form of words, Jane.'

'But the receipt is made out to the Bayview Number Two account, Harvey. That means you didn't pay for the machine at all. It came out of Bayview funds.'

'Oh, for goodness' sake, Jane,' exclaimed Harvey, shaking his head in exasperation. 'You don't understand the first thing about accounting. It's often desirable, for tax reasons and so forth, to process debts through a number of different accounts. It's a pure formality.'

'Oh, that is a relief, Harvey,' said Jane, exhaling deeply, 'because I would hate to think that you might get into trouble for misappropriating funds or anything like that.'

'Well, you can put your mind at rest, Jane. Everything is completely above board.'

'Oh, I'm so glad,' said Jane. 'Then if the committee should ever question me about this purchase, as they have done once or twice about others, it will be all right if I tell them that – just for tax reasons – you bought yourself that machine with Bayview funds?'

Harvey started slightly and said quickly, 'Ah – well now, what would be the point of doing that, Jane? It would just create complications – involve a great deal of tedious explanation and so on. No, it would be much simpler if you just forgot you'd ever seen this receipt. I may say that the rowing machine really is intended for the residents and once I've – well – completed my preliminary trials of it, then it will be moved down to the gym.'

'There isn't a gym, Harvey,' murmured Jane.

'That's exactly my point, Jane,' protested Harvey excitedly.

'I intend to start one. Wrinklies need sport and exercise just like real people do. It might even help them to stay alive longer and that wouldn't upset the committee, would it? Where did you find that receipt anyway, Jane? I suppose I just carelessly left it lying about, did I?'

'No, you didn't, Harvey. But when I was dusting your mantlepiece I knocked over that little jar decorated with robins and out tumbled several receipts like this one. But, of course, now I understand that all the purchases were for the residents. That is right, isn't it, Harvey?'

'Absolutely, Jane.'

'There was one receipt for Janet Reger underwear. Which resident wears Janet Reger underwear, Harvey?'

'Ah, well —' said Harvey, gulping slightly, 'that must have got in there by mistake. It was a purchase I made for – for a friend – and he – well, he paid me for those stunning knickers in cash and so everything – well – worked out in the end, do you see?'

'Of course I do, Harvey,' Jane reassured him. She then produced another receipt from the pocket of her cleaning smock and held it up. 'And what about this one, Harvey?' she asked. 'It's for a weekend break at the "Fast Fun and Frolic Honeymoon Hotel" in Torquay. It was also paid for on a Bayview account. Which resident did you take there for —' and Jane read from the receipt, '"three wild days and nights of ultra-sensual luxury"?'

Harvey sighed deeply. There was a brief silence and then he asked simply, 'All right, Jane, how much do you want to seal your lips?'

Jane shook her head in apparent horror at this query.

'Harvey!' she exclaimed. 'What can you mean? You seem to be suggesting that I'm trying to – and I can hardly bring myself even to use the word – to blackmail you! Oh, Harvey! What a dreadful idea. As you should know, your best interests are my only concern.'

'Really?' asked Harvey doubtfully. He gazed hard at Jane. And at that moment the door to his office flew open and Tom Ballard lunged into the room. He looked red and cross and he was holding up a curious piece of apparatus that looked rather like a DIY enema kit.

'It's a disgrace!' he thundered. 'An absolute disgrace. And I demand that something be done about it.'

Jane and Harvey blinked at the new arrival for a moment. Then Harvey frowned slightly and asked, 'Is something the matter, Tom?'

'Yes, something is the matter,' returned Tom fervently. 'My flat is wetter than the English Channel, that's what's the matter. I want another and drier flat.'

'What are you talking about, Tom?' asked Harvey with a faint sigh of impatience.

'Do you see this piece of equipment?' asked Tom, holding up his little damp meter. 'It cost me a pretty penny but it was worth it. It proves what I have been maintaining for some time now, which is that my flat is more suitable for whales and haddocks than for people. I want to be moved, Harvey.'

'I'm afraid that's impossible, Tom.'

'My residency contract states that if there are structural problems in the premises the management must provide me with another place.'

'It will soon be spring, Tom,' said Harvey soothingly, 'and no doubt your place will dry out then. And now if there's nothing more—'

'But there is: I insist on being moved.'

'The trouble is, Tom, that there isn't another single apartment available.'

'Well, it doesn't have to be a single,' exclaimed Tom firmly. 'I'm quite prepared to take a double.'

'None of those either, Tom,' said Harvey, shaking his head positively.

But oddly enough, considering how reticent she normally was, at this point Jane intervened, saying, 'Harvey, I think perhaps you're forgetting. The Baileys' apartment became vacant yesterday. You remember, they've gone back to Carlisle?'

'Leave this to me, Jane,' said Harvey peremptorily. He turned to Tom again. 'That particular apartment is already taken, Tom. But I'll put you down on the waiting list for the next one that becomes free.'

'Well, I don't know,' said Tom pathetically. 'I mean, you should hear me cough at nights. I'll be lucky to survive the winter at this rate.'

'You look fit enough to me,' observed Harvey briskly as Tom moved disconsolately towards the door. 'But don't hesitate to let me know whenever you have some little problem, Tom. After all, that's what we're here for.'

Tom opened the office door preparatory to departing. Jane said, 'Hang on a minute, Tom. I think perhaps we can find some solution to your problem.'

'Jane!' said Harvey severely, and gave her a heavy frown.

'But no one has actually moved into the Baileys' apartment yet, Harvey,' said Jane pointedly. 'So it would be possible for Tom to occupy it.'

'Jane —' began Harvey, and his frown had now become a scowl.

'After all,' added Jane brightly, 'we don't want Tom having to row about his flat, do we?'

'Now look here, Jane – what?'

'I said "row", Harvey.' said Jane sweetly but pointedly. 'It's what you do with a boat or with that rowing machine over there.' And she pointed to Harvey's state-of-the-art purchase.

For a moment Jane's and Harvey's eyes were locked. Then a small, weary smile appeared on Harvey's face. He gave a faint, resigned shrug.

'All right,' he said. 'Yes, very neat. It seems you win this one, Jane. Come back in and sit down, Tom,' he urged the older man. 'And we'll see if we can't come up with something helpful for you.'

A quarter of an hour later, Tom hurried through his conservatory and burst into Diana's living room.

'I say, old thing,' he began excitedly, 'you'll never guess what's happened? Bains has agreed —'

Then he paused in astonishment as he realized what was going on. Diana was packing. Three cardboard boxes were on the living-room table and Diana was wrapping small vases and other breakable items in newspaper and placing them in the boxes.

'What on earth are you doing?' asked Tom in a mixture of dismay and astonishment.

'Well,' began Diana, glancing round, 'I should have thought it was obvious. I'm packing.'

'Yes, but I mean – why?' asked Tom, shaking his head in bewilderment.

'Why do people pack?' asked Diana tartly. 'The answer is, of course, because they are moving.'

'But you're not moving, are you? I say, is it the damp? Has Harvey agreed to give you another flat too?'

'No, it is not the damp. I – I've taken a decision, that's all.'

'Decision? What decision?' probed Tom, feeling a cloud of dismay starting to form along the horizons of his mind.

'A decision to get the hell out of this graveyard while I can still walk and talk.'

'But why have you never said anything about it? I didn't know you were feeling like that.'

'Well, perhaps you should have known,' exclaimed Diana irritably. 'Perhaps your insensitivity is part of the problem.'

'My insensitivity?' asked Tom, baffled and hurt. 'What on earth do you mean?'

'Think about it, Tom. What happened just now? You charged into my flat as if it was a public place. You simply wouldn't do that if we were neighbours in London. You would respect my privacy which is what normal people do. But it's impossible to be a normal person in Bayview. You lose all sense of civilized living. Well, I'm getting back to the big city where I belong – where ordinary human values still prevail and where one can still be part of the living world.'

Tom nodded slowly. He was smiling but it was a strained, almost an agonized, smile.

'I see. And I suppose if I hadn't come back when I did, you'd have just slipped away – without even saying goodbye?'

'Well, why on earth not?'

But Diana saw the way Tom looked. She went over to him and took his big hands in her smaller ones.

'Oh no, of course I wouldn't. I'd have stayed to say goodbye. Look, this is no big deal, Tom. We'll still be friends. We'll be able to see each other whenever we want. And we'll have fun weekends in London with you as my guest.'

'Yes, that does sound jolly,' said Tom, not very heartily.

'Anyway,' said Diana, 'it's the best I can offer. Take it or leave it.'

'Then I suppose I'll have to take it.'

'Exactly. Oh, for God's sake don't look so pathetic. Please, Tom, don't make this any harder for me than it need be.'

'Is it hard?'

'Yes, yes of course it is. If you must know, it's one of the hardest things I've ever done in my life.'

'Then why on earth – good Lord, I'd forgotten. Of course – that's it, isn't it?'

'What are you talking about?' asked Diana irritably.

'Wait here,' said Tom. He hurried off through Diana's conservatory and on into his own flat.

He was only gone a couple of minutes while Diana, instead of resuming her packing, awaited his return with a thoughtful expression.

'This is it, isn't it?' asked Tom urgently, charging back into Diana's living room waving the envelope he had found that morning. 'You left it in my flat. It's got the address of some finance house on it. That's where you've been today, isn't it? To see these people in the City? And that's why you're talking of leaving?'

'All right,' said Diana, smiling a trifle deliberately. 'It's true. I've had a spot of luck. Some of my shares have shot up in value and I now have enough money to buy a small house in a good part of London and —'

'Diana,' said Tom gently, 'cut the crap.'

There was a long pause and then Diana sighed deeply and murmured.

'I'm broke.'

'Go on.'

'They've gone bust – the finance house – into receivership. If I'm lucky I'll get ten pence or so to the pound but even that will take years. As of today I'm a pauper.'

Tom nodded and smiled.

'So that's all it is?' he said, sounding deeply relieved.

'All?' asked Diana fiercely. 'What the hell is that supposed to mean? After a lifetime of work, of independence, of settling my own debts, I'm reduced to abject poverty. And you say, "that's all"!'

'No, I apologize. It's terrible for you, Diana. But it's not actually disastrous because, you see, I've got quite enough money for both of us.'

'You're an old crackpot, that's what you are,' urged Diana crossly.

'It is the most amazing coincidence,' said Tom in a wondering kind of voice. 'You see, I have just come back from seeing Bains and he has reluctantly agreed, because of the risk of drowning in my present flat, to give me another one. There are no singles available and so he has been obliged, much against his greedy impulses, to give me a double. Don't you see what that means? We can share it.'

Diana snorted and said fiercely, 'Don't be ridiculous!'

'Oh you mustn't think,' Tom reassured her quickly, 'that I'm suggesting true cohabitation. There are two bedrooms.'

'You don't understand, do you, Ballard? The fact is that I don't want to share a flat with you. I may not be able to afford a house but I intend to get a nice little room somewhere in London.'

'Rooms cost money, Diana —'

'I have my old age pension.'

'People who only have old age pensions live in cold hovels and regard baked beans as a luxury. You simply don't know anything about poverty.'

'Well then, I'll go and live with Sarah. I had lunch with her today after I'd seen the financial demons and she begged me to move in. I can't imagine anything nicer – being with Diana the Second all day.'

'Oh, Diana, can't you see – it's destiny? You and I were bound to live together sooner or later.'

'I will not accept charity.'

'And I would not dream of offering it. I will keep accounts. And when that new edition of your war photos comes out next year or the year after – and you're richer than Polly Peck whoever she may be – you can pay me back every penny. Meanwhile, you will accept not my charity but my hospitality.'

'Tom, I can't. I just – can't —'

'Give it a try,' urged Tom tenderly. 'That's all I ask. Try it for a month and if you're not completely satisfied you can have your money back – no, I mean you can well – make alternative arrangements.'

Diana sighed deeply. She walked towards the window and

looked out onto the green and not all that unattractive grounds of Bayview.

'Oh God,' she asked rhetorically, 'has it come to this? After all these years of barnstorming about the world? Of being feted, wounded, sleeping with seventeen world leaders? All the campaigns, the battles, the gins and tonics. After being the leading photo-journalist of 1973, am I to end my days shacked up with a dog-eared old golf bag?'

'Woof, woof,' said Tom, easing up beside her.

Absent-mindedly, she reached up and scratched him behind the ear.

Two days later, Harvey was just passing Grantchester as he skulled expertly up the Cam. While rowing he glanced from side to side at the fascinating river-bank life he was passing. On his left were two pretty undergraduates on bicycles showing a good deal of leg and on his right a young fogey of a don was arranging his first TV appearance on a hand-held telephone as he jogged past wearing King's College jockey shorts. After a brief glance at the don, Harvey returned his attention to the cyclists. He was nodding appreciatively as he pulled rhythmically on the oars when his side screens suddenly went blank. Jane had entered his office and switched off his hi-tech, virtual-reality rowing machine.

'Oh Harvey, it's so touching,' she purred. 'Tom and Diana are bidding farewell to their old quarters before moving into their new ones.'

'Really, Jane?' asked Harvey, rising from his sliding seat in the simulator. 'But may I say that I can't help wishing you would let me know when you're about to pull the plug on my rowing. I mean, I concede that you hold the whip hand now and I must cringe before you but —'

'Oh, Harvey!' exclaimed Jane, looking distressed and shocked. 'That's not true. Why you're still my prince and my hero. I wouldn't do anything to cause you a single moment of unhappiness and you should know that.'

'Really?' asked Harvey, brightening somewhat.

'Of course, Harvey. I've always had your best interests at heart.'

'In that case, why don't you just give me back those – those slightly indiscreet receipts you rather naughtily took from my room and then our relationship can get back to normal?'

'Oh, I'd just love to, Harvey, but you see —'

'Yes, Jane?'

'Well, it's just that I sometimes wonder if you really know exactly what your best interests are.'

'Oh, I think I do.'

'I'm not so sure, Harvey. I mean, take this business of Tom and Diana. You didn't want to give Tom the double flat and then you didn't want to let Diana move in with him. Isn't that true?'

'Perfectly true, Jane.'

'And so if I hadn't – well, used my poor influence over you to help you to change your mind, you would have been overwhelmed by guilt at a later date.'

'No, I wouldn't.'

'Yes, you would, Harvey.'

'No, I wouldn't. I have never felt a moment's guilt in my entire life.'

'That's just the problem, Harvey. It's all building up. One day you'll probably suddenly collapse under an intolerable load of guilt. Then you'll decide that you must retire into a monastery or something in order to expiate your sins. And I'll never see you again.'

Harvey sighed and said wearily, 'Jane, can I tell you something?'

'Of course you can.'

'It's something that all blackmailers should learn. But you're new to the game and possibly haven't grasped it yet. You can push the thing too far.'

'How do you mean, Harvey?'

'If you try to squeeze too much out of your victim then ultimately he will turn on you whatever the consequences. Now you've done pretty well so far. I've given Tom and Diana one of the best double flats in Bayview at what almost amounts to a peppercorn rent. If I were you, Jane, I wouldn't push my luck. I'd call it a day and give me the receipts back.'

Jane nodded soberly and said, 'You may be right, Harvey. But there is just one slight problem —'

'What would that be?'

'Well, correct me if I'm wrong, Harvey, and I admit that you know far more about these criminal matters than I do – but aren't blackmailers supposed to get something for themselves as a result of their heinous activities?'

Harvey shrugged and shook his head faintly.

'Well – not always. Not if they're philanthropists like you.'

'But I'm not just a philanthropist. There really are a few things that I'd appreciate having for myself and – well, if you could perhaps see your way to granting me just one of them, Harvey, then I could give you back the receipts with a good heart.'

'What is it that you want, Jane?' asked Harvey.

'Send back the rowing machine.'

Harvey gave a little sigh of relief and said lightly, 'Consider it done, Jane.'

'And promise me you'll never see Helga again.'

'Now, just hang on a minute,' said Harvey indignantly. 'To begin with, that's two things.'

'Really, Harvey? Mathematics was never my strong point. Oh yes, and there's just one more: I'd like you to take me for a weekend to Torquay.'

Harvey gazed at her in wide-eyed horror.

'You don't mean – no it's too hideous to contemplate – not the "Fast Fun Hotel"?'

'No, of course not, Harvey,' protested Jane primly. 'So tasteless. I mean, to some respectable but luxurious hotel on the seafront where we can have separate rooms – although they could perhaps be adjoining ones – and we would just walk along the promenade in the sunshine breathing in the sea air and dine together and – well, that's about all really.'

'But, Jane, you must appreciate —'

'All right, if you won't grant me the least little —'

'Done,' said Harvey quickly.

Jane beamed at him.

'And as soon as we return from Torquay, I'll give you back those silly receipts. And I'm sure you'll be much more careful in future about your financial arrangements.'

Harvey managed to muster a weak smile as he nodded agreement.

Tom and Diana stood in front of a low building in the grounds of Bayview. It was divided into several flats and was not, in fact, very different from the structure they had just vacated.

'This is it,' said Tom proudly. 'What do you think?'

'I think it is a classic example of the Bayview Catastrophic School of Architecture,' affirmed Diana. 'Pallid, lifeless, fifties modernism. What do *you* think?'

'I think,' said Tom, dampened by her response but not over-whelmed by it, 'I think – that it could turn out to be a little corner of heaven.'

'Oh, how wonderful!' lisped Diana, clasping her hands in front of her like Shirley Temple. 'And wouldn't you also say, Unca Tom, that every time it rains it rains pennies from heaven? Just so we old paupers can hobble out joyously and gather up the pennies so that we can pour them into the pockets of greedy swine like Harvey Bains and —'

'Diana!'

'Yes, Tom?'

'Wrong note!'

'Really? Well, you can't seriously be expecting moist-eyed gratitude from a sick old turkey like me, can you?'

'It's our new home, Diana.'

'Your new home, Tom. I'm just the skivvy. And I only hope and pray that maister will be satisfied with my humble services.'

'Oh dear —'

'Come on, let's totter in and inspect the fridge or something.'

'It's full of champagne and smoked salmon,' announced Tom.

'Is it now? Has Harvey been renting it out as a cold store to some local deli or what?'

'I put the goodies there, Diana, to celebrate our first night in our new quarters. There's also a duck roasting in the oven.'

'Oh my God!' exclaimed Diana in apparent dismay, 'of all sentimentalists a senile one is the worst.'

'And we're going to have a wonderful evening whether you like it or not,' concluded Tom complacently.

Diana said glumly, 'I'd like it if we could have a simple sand-wich and a cup of coffee and watch something halfway decent on the box. Of course there won't be anything halfway decent on the box. There never is. But still.'

'We are going to feast and drink,' maintained Tom. 'But before that I am going to carry you across the threshold.'

And Tom reached down to pick up Diana.

However, she successfully beat him off, crying, 'Stop it! Stop it you old fool. You'll make me drop it and it could easily break!'

'What could easily break?' asked Tom, puzzled.

Diana was carrying a plastic shopping bag which Tom had assumed contained a few personal effects from the old flat.

'Nothing,' said Diana cagily. 'Nothing important.'

'Let's see,' said Tom and made a snatch at the bag. Diana pulled it back out of his reach. A short tussle ensued but in the end Tom obtained possession of the bag. Diana watched sullenly as he reached into it and withdrew a bottle of six-year-old first-growth claret from a famous château.

'I see,' he said. 'I suppose this was for the cat?'

'I do hope that's a feeble joke,' said Diana testily, 'because there is no way I am going to live in the same flat as a flaming cat.'

'There is no cat,' said Tom. 'And if there were one I wouldn't even give it a single glass of this stuff. Because Pomerol of this calibre is quite definitely my favourite claret – as I think you knew.'

'I'm not sure,' murmured Diana distantly. 'Possibly you may have mentioned it. Do you suppose it will go all right with the duck?'

'It will go magnificently with the duck,' said Tom. He thereupon carefully replaced the bottle in the bag and put the bag down beside the door to the new flat. He then unlocked the door and pushed it open to reveal quite a spacious entrance hall leading into an attractive living room. He said, 'I am now either going to carry you across the threshold or we're not going in at all. You choose.'

'Oh well, it's your heart on the line,' said Diana ungraciously. 'And I have no objection to the ride.'

Tom bent down and picked Diana up quite easily. He was a burly man and Diana was slight. He moved forwards into the hall and then on into the living room – which was where disaster struck. Tom stepped on something which he had failed to spot and which crunched ominously beneath his foot. He stumbled and nearly fell, succeeded in partly recovering his balance and then staggered on for three or four more steps. At that point, he collapsed finally onto the sofa with Diana beneath him. She immediately beat him lustily on the back.

'Gerroff,' she growled. 'I thought you agreed. No funny business.'

'For God's sake, I stumbled,' said Tom. 'That was not a seduction ploy.'

He stood upright.

'But what on earth did I stumble over?' he asked crossly.

He went back across the room and soon found the object. He bent down and picked it up. He contemplated it wryly. Yes, now he remembered. Earlier in the day it had suddenly occurred to him that the new flat might suffer from the same serious fault as the old one.

'Well, what is it?' called Diana, who had been trying to settle herself in a more dignified position on the sofa.

Tom turned and held it up for her to see.

'Oh my God!' she exclaimed. 'Are we going to have to live with that horror? On the whole I'd prefer a cat.'

'Don't worry,' said Tom. 'I've wrecked the poor thing. But you must admit that it's been an important influence in our lives.'

He then walked over to the neat, new wastepaper basket and dropped into it the ruins of the damp meter.

NINE

Tom was watering the plants in the living room. Diana was seated in one of the armchairs reading *The Times*.

'I hate funerals!' said Diana in reply to a suggestion that Tom had just made.

'Yes, well, on the whole I agree with you,' said Tom diplomatically. 'But I want you to meet someone – someone who will be there.'

'Really? Who?'

'Well, he will be the centre of attention.'

'Oh, the corpse?'

'No, of course not,' protested Tom. 'I mean the vicar, Dennis Sparrow.'

'On the whole I think I'd prefer to meet the corpse,' said Diana crisply. 'Vicars are usually even duller.'

'Ah but not Dennis. He's witty and charming and deeply understanding.'

Tom poked his finger into the soil of a *ficus* and shook his head. He then watered the parched plant liberally.

'Well,' said Diana, 'in the unlikely event of that being true, why don't we just have him to tea?'

'Perhaps we will later. But I thought it might be a good idea if you saw him doing his stuff first.'

Diana shook her head and asked, 'Why, for heaven's sake?'

'Well, just to see if you think he might be able to – oh, to cheer us up a bit,' replied Tom uncertainly.

'Will he try to cheer the corpse up a bit? Who is the corpse, anyway?'

Tom looked surprised and asked: 'Oh, don't you know? It's Jimmy Addison. You remember Jimmy, surely?'

Diana nodded and said, 'Yes, although I hardly exchanged a

word with him.' Then she laid down her paper, gazed hard at Tom and said challengingly, 'You're up to something, aren't you?'

'Not at all,' protested Tom. 'It's just that I respect and admire Dennis Sparrow.'

'And there's nothing more to it than that?'

'No, not really,' insisted Tom. 'Oh, except possibly – well people do speak highly of Dennis's – well, of his counselling ability.'

'His what?' asked Diana incredulously.

'It's just that – well – he sometimes counsels couples whose relationship is – well – getting a bit rocky.'

Diana said fiercely, 'I just don't believe this. You're scheming to have us treated by a marriage guidance counsellor, aren't you?'

Tom looked uncomfortable as he maintained, 'No, of course not. Dennis isn't a real marriage guidance counsellor. He's just a part-time and voluntary one. He does it out of a sense of – well, Christian duty.'

'I see. Well, if he ever crosses my threshold with counselling in his heart I might just feel compelled, out of a sense of Christian duty, to smother him with his own chasuble. Have you gone mad?'

Tom sighed and went on watering a yucca although he had already almost drowned it.

'I think we've both gone a bit mad, Diana. We do nothing but quarrel.'

'That's because you're so bloody difficult to live with.'

'No, I'm not,' protested Tom.

'You vacuum three times a day. It drives me crazy.'

'I like a neat house.'

'I like a messy one.'

'Exactly,' said Tom, as if Diana had made his point for him. 'Whatever I want or suggest you demand the opposite.'

'Well, if that's what you really think, why are we living under the same roof?'

'Because you haven't got any other,' said Tom candidly, and immediately regretted it.

'Damn your arrogance!' said Diana savagely. 'I only moved in here because you begged me to. I could have been very comfortable in London.'

'No you couldn't —'

'Really? Well, just watch my smoke.'

And she rose and stumped off towards her bedroom.

'Where are you going?'

'To pack.'

'Oh, not again. Diana you march off and pack about three times a week. We can't go on like this.'

'I agree.'

'Well then, sit down again. At least let's talk it over.'

After a long moment of hesitation and of head-shaking to indicate that she felt it was a mistake, Diana resumed her seat.

'We're always talking it over,' she said wearily, 'and it never does a blind bit of good. Frankly, Tom, I think we should admit that this experiment in communal living has been a failure. We've had six weeks of pure hell. Hadn't we better call it a day?'

Tom sighed deeply and said, 'Come to the funeral tomorrow. See what you make of Dennis.'

'I will not be counselled,' insisted Diana. 'I would not subject myself to such a humiliation even if the prospective counsellor were Sigmund Freud himself.'

'Understood,' said Tom, 'but just come along and meet Dennis. I'm sure you'll find him sympathetic.'

There was a long silence. Diana started reading *The Times* again.

'Well?' asked Tom.

'Good heavens,' exclaimed Diana. 'I see that Duncan Corcoran, who worked under me on the old *News Chronicle*, has been knighted. I taught that half-wit everything he ever knew about photography. So would some ingenious male chauvinist please explain to me why I am invariably ignored by the monarch when she doles out the honours?'

'Diana, will you come to the funeral?' asked Tom desperately.

'Oh all right. But if anyone, vicars included, tries to counsel me I shall quite certainly biff them.'

At half-past eleven the following morning, in a light drizzle, Tom and Diana strolled slowly through the churchyard of St Botolph's Church in the suburbs of Bournemouth. Along with a handful of other guests, mainly residents of Bayview, they were there for the interment of James Addison who had lived at the retirement home for just three days before the Grim Reaper had paid an unexpected visit and gathered him in.

'Poor old Jim seems to have been one of Harvey Bains' smarter moves,' commented Diana. 'As soon as Harvey cashed the deposit the poor old sod snuffed it.'

'A little reverence, please,' said Tom.

Diana turned on him crossly and urged, 'For God's sake, Tom, we don't have to feel reverence for fellow passengers on the sinking ship! I mean, what the hell are we all doing at Bayview if not waiting to die?'

'I wouldn't put it like that,' Tom protested mildly.

'Oh really? Well are you under the impression that we're on a youth-training scheme? Tom, Bayview is the hard shoulder of life and we're just waiting for the bloody tow-truck to drag us off to the dump. It so happens that, because of the peculiarities of the route, poor mutton-headed old Jimmy Addison was carted away first.'

'Diana, *de mortuis nil nisi bonum*. Which, should your Latin be a little rusty, translates as: speak nothing of the dead unless it be complimentary.'

'That's a trifle odd coming from you,' said Diana with a snort. 'After all, when Jimmy first came amongst us, I seem to recall you remarking, almost in disbelief, that he struck you as being even more boring than Geoffrey.'

Tom smiled uneasily and protested, 'Oh, I hardly think —'

'Oh, but you did,' insisted Diana. 'And you went on to say that Jimmy was a man who had lived for nearly ninety years but had done nothing of any significance throughout that entire span. You said you were damned if you could work out his place in the great scheme of things and you concluded by stating that you had known more interesting artichokes.'

Tom coughed with faint embarrassment and said hopefully, 'Ah, but that was on his first night at Bayview. I thought then that he was going to be with us for years.'

'And now that he's dead, he's become Noel Coward, has he?'

Tom sighed.

'No, but he deserves the benefit of a reasonable place in the collective memory of mankind.'

'You mean, we should lie about him?'

'Yes,' pleaded Tom desperately. 'That's the way it is, Diana. And since you seem in the mood for metaphors, kind words are the cushion that protects our earthly bottoms from the stone bench of reality.'

'Get knotted. I mean just look at these —' Diana waved about at the ancient gravestones that surrounded them. 'You can't even make out the names on half of them. Their only reason for existing was to pass on the genetic baton.'

'Well, I'm quite sure of one thing, Diana. When you hear Dennis memorializing Jimmy in terms that are both understanding and compassionate, you'll perceive that there is a core of nobility in every one of us.'

But it didn't turn out quite like that.

The Reverend Sparrow, Diana discovered twenty minutes or so later, was a man in early middle age, quite tall, reasonably attractive and possessed of a pleasant voice. However, the use to which he was putting his pleasant voice in church that morning was extraordinary.

After climbing to his lofty pulpit the Reverend Sparrow began resonantly, 'James Addison, or Jimmy as he was known to his multitude of friends, travelled the globe in his dual role of surfing champion and record producer. I am sure there must be many here in the congregation today who will have vivid memories of his wild parties and his even wilder women. Old Jimmy wasn't known as Screeching Jim Addison for nothing.'

'Who on earth is he talking about?' whispered Diana from the corner of her mouth, as gasps of amazement rose from the pews.

'God knows,' Tom whispered back, 'or then again perhaps He doesn't. I wonder if Dennis could have flipped his lid?'

Diana chuckled faintly and returned: 'I'm beginning to enjoy this.'

'But the good Lord,' the reverend continued, 'giveth and the good Lord taketh away although I personally have never understood why he bothers to do either. Anyway, just as Screeching Jim's career was really getting into orbit the good Lord decided that it was time for him to cash in his chips and our hero, who was hang-gliding in the Alps at the time, plummeted to earth from ten thousand feet and gave up the ghost.'

More gasps and a faint undertone of protest began to sound throughout the congregation. Jane, from a front-row pew, called out, nervously but urgently, 'Excuse me, Reverend Sparrow, but Jimmy was eighty-eight and he was in insurance.'

'Rubbish!' pronounced the reverend loudly. 'I've heard that slanderous tale put about before. It clearly represents an attempt by Jim's many talentless rivals to discredit him. The fact is that Screeching Jim was a real rooting, tooting raver and no bones about it. And while we're on the subject of bones, why don't we get Jim's underground as quickly as we can manage so that we can all plod down to the White Hart and get outside a few much-needed pints of real, or even unreal, ale?'

With which the Reverend Dennis Sparrow, blowing kisses at the congregation, descended from his pulpit, performed a dainty little pirouette, bowed and then headed for the disrobing room.

'Bravo!' called Diana rising to her feet in unfeigned admiration. She raised both her hands, clearly intending to applaud, but Tom seized one of them and hung onto it grimly.

'Why on earth did you stop me?' asked Diana a few hours later when she and Tom were back in their flat discussing the morning's remarkable events. 'He deserved a round of applause. He gave what was undoubtedly the most gripping pulpit performance I've ever been privileged to hear. Oh, you were absolutely right, Tom.'

'What about?'

'About how wonderful Dennis is.'

'Yes, but I meant the old Dennis before he went round the twist. It turns out he shouldn't have been in the pulpit at all. He's been sacked.'

'What? How do you know?'

'Harvey told me in the bus on the way home. Well, not sacked exactly but instructed to take a rest from his parochial duties.'

'But how can the bishop have been so quick off the mark? Dennis only cracked up this morning.'

'No, he's apparently been behaving – well – eccentrically for some weeks. Only a couple of days ago, he christened a child: "Ugly Little Bastard Jones".'

'Golly,' exclaimed Diana. 'Although you must admit it has a certain Cromwellian ring to it. But why was Dennis allowed to put on that splendid show today if he's been dropping his marbles right and left?'

'That's just it. He wasn't supposed to officiate at all. But the substitute vicar's car broke down on the motorway and Dennis sneaked into church before anyone could stop him. Anyway, I'm glad you took to him because he may be coming to tea the day after tomorrow?'

Diana frowned.

'Oh? Why should he be coming to tea?' she asked suspiciously.

Tom looked sheepish as he explained, 'Well, I invited him last week – before he went bonkers of course.'

'And for what purpose did you invite him, Tom?'

Tom looked embarrassed.

'Well – we don't have all that many guests, do we? And I just thought —'

'I can guess what you just thought. You just thought it might give him a chance to do a spot of counselling, didn't you?'

'Good heavens, no,' said Tom positively. 'My motives were purely social.'

'Anyway, it doesn't matter too much now, does it?' said Diana tolerantly. 'Dennis isn't going to be in counselling fettle for some little time, is he?'

'It doesn't seem very likely,' agreed Tom. 'And I don't suppose he'll be in any condition to come to tea either.'

'Oh, don't say that,' protested Diana, 'Dennis is the best thing to happen around here for years. He's a one-man ecclesiastical black comedy.'

'Diana, that's very cruel.'

'Not at all. I just meant —'

But at this point, there came an interruption. A voice, apparently stemming from the letter box in the front door, called, 'Hello? Anyone in?'

'My God!' hissed Tom. 'It's Geoffrey.'

In unison Tom and Diana replied loudly, 'No, we're both out.'

But the tactic failed. The door, as was common in the relatively safe grounds of Bayview, had been left unlocked. It now opened and in walked Tom's son looking like a gigantic pigeon wearing a blue, chalk-striped suit.

'Hello, Dad. Hello, Diana,' said Geoffrey glumly.

'Hello, Geoffrey,' exclaimed Tom as buoyantly as he could manage. 'What a pleasant surprise. Isn't it, Diana?'

'Ecstatic. And now I think it's time for my aerobics class —'

'That's not for another hour,' said Tom firmly. 'Sit down.'

Sighing, Diana did as instructed. Geoffrey simply stood sunk in thought.

'Is anything wrong, Geoffrey?' asked Tom uneasily.

'Hm?' asked Geoffrey, stirring slightly. 'Oh yes, there is something wrong, Dad. It's Marion. She's having some kind of crisis. She just stands in a corner for hours, gazing blankly at nothing.'

'Well, you're an accomplished handyman, Geoffrey,' said Diana helpfully. 'So why don't you just wall her in and —'

'Be quiet, Diana,' ordered Tom. 'Now sit down, Geoffrey, and tell us all about it.'

Geoffrey glanced around, saw several chairs but for some reason rejected them in favour of a small occasional table upon which, despite its creaks of protest, he deposited his substantial form. He shook his head in a puzzled kind of way and said: 'The funny thing is that I told Marion that I'd stick by her whatever problems she had, but it didn't seem to help.'

Tom nodded understandingly. 'You mean,' he queried, 'that you assured her that you'd always be there for her and it seemed to make her even more depressed?'

Geoffrey looked at his father with respect.

'That's exactly right, Dad. How do you explain it?'

'Perhaps,' began Diana, 'it's because you are such a crashing —'

'I'll handle this, Diana,' said Tom quickly. And then to his son, 'Geoffrey, I thought Marion was seeing a psychiatrist?'

'Well,' said Geoffrey, 'she did see a psychiatrist but only once.'

'Oh, why is that?'

'He refused to see her again. He said that she was the most unpleasant person that had ever walked into his consulting room.'

'That doesn't sound like a very professional attitude,' pointed out Tom.

'I know,' agreed Geoffrey. 'I think it may have had something to do with the fact that Marion ran over his cat when she was parking the car.'

'Yes, that could easily have affected his attitude towards her,' conceded Tom. 'Still, the sad truth, as I have always frankly admitted to you, Geoffrey, is that I have not always seen eye to eye with Marion myself.'

'No one else has either, Dad, so that needn't bother you.'

'Well, actually it doesn't bother me all that much. But to develop the theme, I have sometimes caught myself thinking that mankind need hardly have bothered to drag itself out of the primordial soup if the best it could then come up with was Marion.'

'Quite a reasonable point, Dad,' agreed Geoffrey, nodding thoughtfully. 'But the fact is that she is still my wife and I love her.'

'Are you quite sure about that, Geoffrey?'

'Oh, absolutely, Dad.'

Tom contemplated his son with something approaching awe and said, 'You certainly have some – well, remarkable qualities, Geoffrey.'

'Thank you, Dad. The point is, can you help me?'

'It's a big challenge, son. But I will try.'

'You're a brick, Dad,' said Geoffrey warmly. 'And you too, Diana. You're another brick.'

'And talking of bricks,' said Diana with sudden inspiration, 'has it occurred to you two that the simplest thing might be for us to get hold of some and just heave them at Ma —'

'Diana,' Tom rebuked her once more, 'it behoves us to be compassionate to our afflicted brothers and sisters.'

'You're right, of course,' agreed Diana surprisingly. 'Well now, can I make you a cup of tea, Geoffrey?' she asked hospitably.

'Yes, thank you, Diana,' said Geoffrey. 'And I would just like to compliment you on the new shelving above the sofa. It's very handsome and beautifully mounted.'

Tom and Diana exchanged a glance.

Two days later, at twenty-five minutes to five in the afternoon, Diana looked at her watch and said sadly, 'He's five minutes late.'

'Well, of course, he may not come at all. He might even be in a – well, in a rest-home by now.'

'A loony bin, you mean?' said Diana with a sigh. 'What a waste. Three quarters of the most entertaining people in the world are incarcerated in bins. They should be out and about spreading hilarity and illumination but instead we lock them away where they can't be of any use to the rest of us.'

'Talking of doing good —' began Tom, with a slight cough of embarrassment.

Diana picked up his tone immediately and, smiling a shade grimly, asked, 'Yes?'

'Well, since Dennis has gone loopy and probably won't turn up in any case, I feel that I should confess something.'

'Oh, don't bother,' said Diana lightly.

'I think I felt that when you got to know him you'd agree that Dennis just might have been able to help us.'

'Tom, when will you learn that I am essentially a reticent and even a shrinking kind of person? I would no more allow my intimate relationships to be picked over by an outsider than I would my underwear. Still, I'm sure you meant well.'

'Well, I'm glad you think that. Because if Dennis should still turn up —'

At this point the doorbell rang.

'And here he is,' Tom exclaimed, sounding surprised.

'All right then,' said Diana somewhat tensely, 'this puts a different complexion on things. Before we let him in you'd better just finish what you were about to say.'

'Well, it's merely that – well, I suppose that I did mention to Dennis when inviting him here that you and I were going through – oh – rather a tricky patch in our relationship. Mind you, I can't actually recall having said anything about counselling.'

The doorbell rang again.

'That doesn't actually sound too bad,' said Diana as she headed for the front door, 'and anyway he probably won't remember. In his present state he'll be more likely to announce that he's Anna Pavlova and offer to dance *Swan Lake* for us.'

She thereupon opened the door to reveal the Reverend Sparrow, wearing ordinary clothes but with his necktie awry and a slightly deranged smile on his face.

'Hello?' he said. 'Were you expecting me to tea?'

'We were indeed,' said Diana warmly. 'Come in, Reverend, and give us the benefit of your immense wisdom and experience.'

'I'll try but it might be a bit difficult,' said Dennis crisply. 'You see, I've lost my faith.'

'Have you really?' asked Diana, evincing great interest. 'How fascinating. Now you two boys chat between yourselves for a few minutes while I make the tea and then, Dennis, you must tell us all about your loss.'

'All right,' said Dennis.

'Come and sit down, Dennis,' said Tom hospitably.

'Thank you, Tom,' returned Dennis, taking a seat on the sofa. 'How are you?'

'Rather fatigued, as a matter of fact,' explained Tom. 'From tunnelling, you know. I was on late shift in Colditz this morning and —'

'Tom!' called Diana warningly from the open plan kitchen. 'Dennis is the top fruitcake around here just at present. So stay off his turf. Talk about cricket or something like that.'

'Oh, righto,' said Tom. 'Do you like cricket, Dennis?'

'No, but I like cricket bats. They're perfect for smashing glass.'

'Yes, they would be, wouldn't they?' said Tom interestedly. 'Do you know that never occurred to me before? Do you smash a lot of glass then, Dennis?'

'No, not much,' admitted Dennis confusingly.

And after this exchange, conversation flagged a bit until Diana turned up with the tea tray.

As she poured, she asked civilly, 'So what is it like, Dennis, losing your faith?'

'It's absolutely dreadful,' proclaimed Dennis with a shudder. 'I look up, like St Paul, but instead of seeing the blinding light of faith I see the outer darkness, the empty chasms of the soul, the snakes writhing in the bowels of hell.'

'No, that doesn't sound too jolly,' conceded Diana. 'Try one of those little butterfly cakes, Dennis. They're home-made and quite delicious.'

'Thank you,' said Dennis, taking one.

Tom now asked earnestly, 'When exactly did you lose your faith, Dennis? It seemed to be in place last month when you broke your finger and I drove you on your rounds.'

Dennis sighed deeply and said, 'You know, I sometimes wonder if I ever really had true faith. Oh, I do my best. I perform all the ceremonies. I scuttle around the parish picking up the bits missed out by the welfare state. But deep down I know it means nothing. Were you aware that more people go to the pub quiz night than to church?'

'That might be because the questions are easier to answer,' pointed out Diana. 'More tea, Dennis?'

'Yes, thank you,' said Dennis, holding out his cup. 'And you're right about the butterfly cakes – they are delicious. No, the fact of the matter is that I'm just not what I set out to be. I'm not a vital, central part of the community. In the last resort I'm simply an untrained social worker trying to prop up yesterday's ideologies. I feel like a character in an Ealing comedy half the time and it makes me behave oddly.'

'Yes, we've noticed,' said Diana. 'Although I must say that I think "Ugly Little Bastard Jones" beats anything in an Ealing comedy.'

'Nice of you to say so,' said Dennis, sounding gratified. 'Another thing I find hard to bear is that Americans sometimes take photographs of me with their aunts or their hideous children. So what does that make me? A kind of tourist attraction? A flesh and blood Windsor Castle?'

'Well, make sure you don't burn down,' urged Tom, sounding concerned. 'Always carry a full quota of fire extinguishers on your person, Dennis.'

'Tom!' said Diana warningly. Then to Dennis, 'If it's any comfort to you, Dennis, I can assure you that it's perfectly possible to get by without faith. I do it.'

'Really?' asked Dennis in mild awe. 'But don't you find your life to be an empty void – a kind of non-statement?'

'Yes, I do,' said Diana. 'But it doesn't bother me specially. Oh dear, I'm afraid there are no more cakes, Dennis, but I could always make you some buttered toast?'

'No, it would be sheer greed,' protested Dennis, 'and anyway, I don't need buttered toast. I need a cause.'

'A what?' asked Diana nervously, dropping her teaspoon into her saucer with a loud clink.

'Work. Christian work to do. That's what my whole being craves. A soul to save. A heart to heal. Tom – Diana, you've no idea how much your anguish calls out to me. Counselling you two could actually be my salvation.'

'Yes, but half a mo,' said Diana desperately. 'Tom, what is this? I thought you said —'

'Yes, yes,' stammered Tom desperately, 'don't worry. I can straighten it out. Dennis, you haven't got things quite right.'

'Oh? Why not?' asked Dennis, frowning in a reproachful sort of way.

'Well, you see,' continued Tom a shade desperately, 'it's not actually me and Diana that require counselling. I mean we're just having a few trivial disagreements – nothing unusual about that. Par for the course. No, the actual heart that is in need, the desperate soul, the one crying out for succour and who could perhaps help you to find your own way back onto the path of faith once more is – well is —'

'Yes?' asked Dennis eagerly. 'Is who? Don't keep me in suspense, Tom. This could be one of the key moments of my life.'

'Is my daughter-in-law Marion,' said Tom in a rush.

'Masterly,' murmured Diana under her breath.

'Your daughter-in-law?' repeated Dennis, looking tense and excited. 'Good heavens, I would never have guessed. She's the nymphomaniac, isn't she?'

'That's right,' said Tom.

'And she has problems, does she? What kind?'

'Just about every kind. She's a drunk and a pill addict. She's a frightful wife and mother. She has no inner life. She lacks self-knowledge, understanding and culture. In fact, I would say, Dennis, that in Marion you may easily have found your Everest —'

'Tom!' said Diana warningly.

'Your supreme challenge then,' amended Tom.

'I can't wait to get started,' said Dennis looking wrapt and primed for action. 'Take me to her, would you?'

'Of course we will, Dennis,' said Diana soothingly. 'Just as soon as we've finished our tea. I'll put the kettle on now for seconds and – I've just remembered – we've got some scones.'

Two days later, about mid-afternoon, Tom strode buoyantly into the flat and called: 'Diana, where are you?'

'In here,' called Diana from the conservatory.

Tom strode through the living room into the conservatory and found Diana painting. The half-finished canvas on the easel in front of her showed a centaur cantering across a plain with a classical city in the background. It struck Tom as a competent and even evocative painting. But what he found surprising was that Diana would look frowning out through the glass walls of the conservatory as if fixing a scene in her mind but then what she actually placed upon the canvas was a purely imaginary landscape.

'What do you look at when you gaze out like that?' he asked curiously.

'Hm?' asked Diana, applying a dash or two of white to the centaur's mane. 'Whatever's out there, of course.'

'Yes, but then you paint something quite different.'

'Well, of course I do. I'm not a crass realist.'

'No, but – oh, never mind.'

'How's Dennis?'

'Wonderful. The doctors say he can leave hospital tomorrow. It was only a mild concussion after all – not a fracture.'

Diana stopped painting and gazed at Tom in astonishment.

'Really? He must have a skull like a bull's. Marion brought that vodka bottle down on his head with all her force.'

'I know. And he'll have to keep his head bandaged for a week or two. But the big news about Dennis is: he's recovered his faith.'

'What?' asked Diana in astonishment. 'You mean, because Marion beaned him with a bottle when he offered to counsel her?'

'No, because she has now shown true repentance. And it actually happened while I was there in the ward. I've never seen true repentance before. It was rather impressive.'

'Tell me exactly what happened?' ordered Diana, clearly keenly interested in this new and improbable development.

'Well, one minute Dennis was muttering darkly to me about the pitfalls of this world and the next moment Marion suddenly appeared. She rushed down the ward to his bed, fell on her knees beside him and said: "Father, forgive me. I am only a poor sinner."'

'Marion said that?' exclaimed Diana astounded.

'She did. But that was only the start. She then clasped Dennis's feet and kissed them and then began working her way up his body kissing all the time and pleading for forgiveness. After a while Dennis suggested that I should pull the curtains round the bed to give them a spot of privacy for their devotions. I did so and departed.'

'Hm,' said Diana. 'Devotions, you say?'

'Oh, it was clear that Marion was in a spiritually exalted state. You realize this could be the salvation of both her and Dennis? Geoffrey will be overjoyed when he learns about it.'

'Possibly,' said Diana. 'Anyway, did you remember my crisps and peanuts?'

'Yes,' Tom glanced at his watch. 'Ah, I see that my programme starts in ten minutes. I've just time to make myself a cup of tea before then. Would you like one?'

'No thanks,' said Diana. 'Just leave the crisps and the peanuts on the kitchen table, would you, Tom?'

Ten minutes later Tom settled down happily in front of his television set to watch a documentary about the search for the abominable snowman. He had been looking forward to the programme ever since he had seen it announced in the Sunday paper. He had himself several times encountered strange footprints on the upper slopes of the Himalayas and he was eager to discover the latest scientific evidence concerning the so-called Yeti.

The programme had just begun and the commentator was saying: 'We must go back to the fifties for the first indication of the existence of a mysterious lifeform high above the snow line in the Himalayas. This was when an Italian expedition saw and photographed this line of footsteps in the snow.'

There was a pause in the commentary while the camera tracked along what looked like a line of small pits on a mountainside. And just at this point – causing Tom to start violently in alarm – a jazz band started playing very loudly.

'What on earth —' he exclaimed. He then glanced about and found that Diana had seated herself in her own armchair which was immediately next to his. She had switched on her

own television set and it was this which was emitting the rau-
cous music.

'You're not going to play that while I'm watching my documentary, are you?' asked Tom beseechingly.

'Well, of course I am,' said Diana indignantly. 'It's a programme about Spike "Fatboy" Philips, the New Orleans trumpeter who is very possibly my favourite musician in the world.
And I wish you'd turn down your silly documentary so I can
hear the music properly.'

'But Diana,' pleaded Tom, 'I told you days ago about this
programme on the Yeti and how much I wanted to see it.'

'And I told you weeks ago about my concert and how much
I wanted to hear it.'

'Oh, this is ridiculous,' said Tom, sighing unhappily.

He rose, went to his set and turned up the volume. For a
while he managed to hear the commentary about the Yeti
above the sound of the jazz band, but then Diana also got up
and turned the sound up on her television set.

Tom bore the mixed din for some time, then he became
aware of yet another disagreeable sound. It was a munching,
crunching kind of sound and when he glanced at the chair
beside him, he saw that Diana was now noisily eating potato
crisps. He got up, went to the two television sets and turned
them both off.

'What are you doing?' exclaimed Diana.

'This is impossible,' said Tom.

'Well then, why don't you take your set into your bedroom
as I suggested weeks ago and that way we will both be able to
watch what we want?'

'I'm damned if I will,' protested Tom. 'This is my flat and I
think, as I said when you first moved in, that you should take
your set into your room. It's absurd having two televisions in a
living room.'

'I'm not taking orders from you,' said Diana. She thereupon
ate the last potato crisp in the plastic bag, screwed up the bag
and threw it onto the floor. Tom stiffened.

'Pick that up!' he ordered.

'Get stuffed,' said Diana.

'Diana, I —' Tom began furiously but he restrained himself
and, with an effort of will, bent down and picked up the

crumpled bit of plastic. He carried it through into the kitchen and put it into the rubbish bin there.

'Damn your neurotic tidiness!' said Diana. She got up, hurried into the kitchen and returned a moment later carrying the rubbish bin itself. With a grim smile, she then ostentatiously emptied the bin's contents onto the carpet in front of Tom.

Tom contemplated the mess and shook his head sadly.

'It's no good, is it?' he asked rhetorically.

'That's what I've been saying for weeks,' said Diana.

'Do you know the truth?' asked Tom sombrely.

'A fair amount of it,' said Diana. 'Which bit did you have in mind?'

'The bit which states that you and I could be very happy together in this flat but for one thing.'

'And what would that one thing be?'

'Your stupid pride.'

'I don't understand what you mean by that,' declared Diana firmly, 'and I suspect that if I did I wouldn't accept it.'

'Diana, just think for a moment – why do you suppose that you have this compulsion to upset me all the time?'

'I have no such compulsion. The discord between us arises solely from the fact that you are impossible to live with.'

Tom shook his head sombrely. 'No,' he said sadly. 'It's because you can't come to terms with the fact that you're living in my flat. You have a psychological need to keep demonstrating that you're completely independent. But, of course, you're not – any more than I am. We share this space and that means we should both show ordinary human courtesy and consideration towards each other.'

'I agree about the courtesy and consideration,' said Diana, quite cheerfully, 'but it seems to me that our values are simply so utterly different that there's no hope of our ever being able to live harmoniously together. Anyway, in the last resort it doesn't really matter which one of us is right or wrong because there's clearly only one solution to the problem.'

'And what would that be?' asked Tom, not sounding very hopeful.

'For me to move out,' said Diana simply. 'Actually, I should never have moved in in the first place.'

'Oh for goodness' sake, Diana, can't you see that —'

But Tom's protest was almost immediately drowned out by renewed din from Diana's television set. She had switched it on again and turned the sound up to full volume. The resulting uproar from "Fatboy's" trumpet was so fierce that a squirrel which had been scampering about in a tree just beyond the open window froze in sheer terror.

At about mid-morning on the next day a large and comfortable saloon car stood waiting on the drive outside Tom's flat. It belonged to Diana's niece, Sarah, who had come to collect Diana, and was the replacement for the red Porsche in which Tom and Diana had once had a memorable, high-speed outing to Brighton. Feeling that maternity required something a little less meteoric than the Porsche, Sarah had changed her car soon after the birth of Diana the Second.

Tom, Sarah and Diana were standing beside the car saying awkward farewells. Antonio, the gardener, was lugging a number of large suitcases out of the flat and placing them in the car's boot. Having completed this task he turned with a scowl to depart.

'Antonio,' called Diana.

The gardener swung round and glared at his old antagonist.

'I have something for you,' said Diana graciously. 'Hold out your hands.'

Antonio frowned in a mixture of challenge and incomprehension.

'Oh, do wake up you tiresome grape-treader,' urged Diana. *'Mettez vos mains* out in front of you. *Voyez* – like this.'

And, as a demonstration, Diana held out her own cupped hands.

Looking deeply suspicious Antonio tentatively did the same.

'Now then,' said Diana, 'what you are about to receive is a collection derived from a professional lifetime of globe-trotting. There is money here – *argent, vous comprenez?* – from thirty or forty different countries. You'll probably be able to sell it to a museum and retire on the proceeds.'

Diana thereupon bent down and picked up a small and quite heavy canvas bag that she had a moment before placed on the ground. Then, in a clinking cascade, she poured a stream of coins into Antonio's cupped hands. It seemed unlikely to Tom that the whole collection of what were clearly very low-denomination coins would equal the value of a bottle of wine but Antonio's eyes widened in wonder and gratitude.

'There,' said Diana graciously and then quoted some mangled Kipling at Antonio. '"Though I've belted you and flayed you by the living God that made you you're a better Portuguese gardener than I am, Antonio."'

'Thang oo, thang oo!' stammered Antonio.

'Now scamper off and get your new found wealth securely stashed in a bank vault,' urged Diana genially. She then turned to Tom. 'Goodbye Tom,' she said with a wry smile. 'You'll be able to watch any programme you like from now on.'

'But, Diana, that is not what I meant. It does not have to end like this.'

'Oh, I fear it does,' said Diana. 'Sarah would kill me if it turned out that I'd dragged her all the way out here for nothing.'

'No, I wouldn't, Diana,' protested Sarah.

'Oh, don't you start,' urged Diana wearily, 'or I may decide just to walk to London and doss down amongst the vagrants.'

Sarah shook her head and made a wry face at Tom.

'Sorry, Tom,' she said.

Diana thereupon got into the front of the luxury German car and Sarah slipped in behind the wheel. A moment later the big machine came to life and, almost immediately afterwards, began to roll smoothly off down the drive and away from Bayview. Tom watched, waving feebly, until it was out of sight and then, shaking his head sadly, went back into his flat.

That night, Tom sat eating a modest dinner of sandwiches and a glass of wine and watching television. One of his favourite programmes was on. It was a soap opera about the intertwined lives of a number of families who lived on the same street in Sydney, Australia. Tom normally found it hilarious. This was perhaps a little odd since the serial was considered to be searing human drama by most of the millions addicted to it. Perhaps only Tom habitually viewed it as a mixture of slapstick comedy and witty satire. On this particular night, however,

Tom was finding that the programme seemed to have lost its humorous appeal for him. Even when kindly old grandfather O'Halloran, suffering from the first twinges of as yet undiagnosed Parkinson's disease, stumbled through a second floor window and crashed to the ground, fracturing his tibia, Tom could hardly dredge up a chuckle.

As he put aside his half-eaten sandwich and began mechanically to peel the silver foil from the top of a raspberry yoghurt, a sepulchral voice said: 'Hello, Dad.'

'Geoffrey,' gasped Tom, looking up from the screen. 'What on earth are you doing here?'

'I've come to try and ease the loneliness, Dad,' explained Geoffrey, shutting the front door behind him and advancing towards the armchair where Tom was sitting.

Tom, whose spirits had sunk a degree or two further when he had first recognized Geoffrey's voice, was nevertheless touched by his son's concern.

'Well, that's jolly kind of you, Geoffrey,' he said gratefully. 'But it's not really necessary. Diana's only been gone a few hours and I seem to be coping —'

'No, it's not your loneliness I mean, Dad. It's mine,' said Geoffrey, sighing heavily. 'May I sit?'

And without waiting for an answer, Geoffrey plonked himself down into the other armchair, the one Diana normally used.

'Yes, but hang on,' said Tom, aiming his remote control at the set and obliterating the Australians. 'What exactly are you talking about, Geoffrey?' he asked. 'Why should you be lonely?'

'Because Marion's gone off on a spiritual retreat,' droned Geoffrey.

'Really?' asked Tom. 'Well, she'll doubtless return a better and wiser person.'

'I'm not so sure about that, Dad,' said Geoffrey. 'Dennis Sparrow is with her. They're in Wales.'

'I see,' said Tom thoughtfully. 'Some church establishment, is it? A quiet institution devoted to prayer and meditation?'

'That wasn't the impression I got when I spoke to Marion on the 'phone about an hour ago, Dad.'

'Oh? What impression did you get, Geoffrey?'

171

'Well – something like a Roman orgy would about cover it. I could hear laughing and screaming in the background and Dennis singing rude hymns. There was also the clink of glasses, the squeals of girls and a combo playing hot music.'

'One of these modern charismatic places, I suppose?' urged Tom desperately.

'Marion gave me the name for forwarding letters —' said Geoffrey. He thereupon took out his wallet and foraged in it for a slip of paper. He then read from the slip, 'It's called "The Ravers' Retreat".'

'Oh? Well – after all, what's in a name?' asked Tom, as buoyantly as he could manage. 'Still, I don't quite see why Marion should need her letters forwarding.'

'Because she's left me, Dad. She says Dennis is the man she's been waiting for all her life. She proposes to become a woman priest so that she and Dennis can do a double act. She claims that between them they'll be able to save loads of sinners and that it won't matter in the least if they fail because they'll have such wonderful fun trying. I have to say it, Dad: this is all your fault.'

'I consider that most unfair, Geoffrey,' protested Tom warmly. 'I was only trying to help.'

'All right, I accept that you meant well, Dad. But I simply can't stay in that house alone. I seem to hear Marion everywhere – the gulping sound she makes drinking vodka and those screeches of anger I know so well. No, it's simply more than I can bear. Harvey told me that you're alone again too now, Dad. So I'm going to move in with you until either Marion comes to her senses or I decide to commit suicide.'

'Now, hang on, Geoffrey,' urged Tom in acute alarm. 'This is no time for snap decisions. I mean surely we should talk it over carefully. It's a very delicate situation. I mean we're both chaps who have been abandoned and – well, we could get on each other's nerves and make matters worse.'

'That's true, Dad,' agreed Geoffrey, 'but on the other hand we're father and son and we should try to support each other in our time of need. Anyway, I vote we try it. I've got my necessaries in the car. I'll just pop out and get them.'

Geoffrey got to his feet and smiled tremulously at Tom. It made him look, Tom noted, rather like a pigeon striving to be brave. Tom struggled desperately to think of some new argument for preventing Geoffrey from carrying out his threat. But nothing came to him. Finally he called out in sheer desperation: 'Geoffrey, Geoffrey, have you considered —'

But the words died on his lips. It was too late. Geoffrey had left the flat. And a minute or two later, with the full horror of the situation now finally apparent to him, Tom watched Geoffrey plod stolidly back in through the front door carrying two huge suitcases.

TEN

Diana the First sat rocking Diana the Second on her lap. As she rocked, she sang: '"Rock a bye, baby, on the tree top. When the wind blows the cradle will rock."'

She stopped singing and frowned.

'Now what was that silly baby doing on a tree top, eh, my little Di Di Diddle Dumpkins? Can you tell me that?'

The plump one-year-old in her arms gurgled happily in reply and casually hit Diana on the nose with her rattle.

'Ouch,' said Diana as her eyes began to water. 'Oh, golly, I hope your mummy's not going to wallop me like that when she gets home and finds out what I've done. Now, listen, Di Di Diddle Dumpkins – and, by the way, would you mind if I simply called you Dumpy for short? No, I didn't think you would. And as for that silly baby on the tree top, we don't give a toss about her, do we? No, of course we don't. What we want from Aunty Di Di Diddle – let's say Aunty Dumpy – is surely a really good song, like this one by Spike "Fatboy" Philips, the New Orleans wizard of the trumpet. It goes like this: "Oh, you ain't nothin' but an ole' houn' dawg, No, you ain't nothin' but an ole' houn' dawg. If you was somethin' different from an ole' houn' dawg, Why then perhaps I wouldn't love you quite so much —" Now why does that song always remind me of Tom?'

The baby suddenly let out a piercing yell.

'Good Lord, my voice can't be that bad,' protested Diana. 'Or is it possible that you're hungry again already? What time is it? My God, yes, it's feeding time once more. You don't need a nanny, you need a conveyor belt —'

At that moment, there was the sound of a key in the front door and then of the door opening and shutting. A moment later the living-room door also opened and into the room tottered Diana's attractive niece Sarah, laden with parcels.

'Golly, what have you got there?' asked Diana, surprised.

'Oh, Christmas presents mostly,' said Sarah, dumping her armful of packages onto the dainty, embroidered sofa.

'Christmas presents?' exclaimed Diana. 'But it's only mid-November?'

'Yes, but time always goes so quickly at this season. And I always have so many presents to buy – customers and staff and so on.' At this point Sarah plucked Dumpy from Diana's arms, hugged her fiercely and smothered her face in kisses, making appropriately ecstatic maternal exclamations as she did so. She then returned the baby to Diana and collapsed exhausted into an armchair. She asked, 'Where's Mary? Perhaps she could make me a cup of tea. I'm completely knackered.'

'Tea?' asked Diana. And at that moment, Diana the Second, who had stopped crying while being petted by her mummy, once more set up a hullaballoo. 'Well, I could make it for you myself. But you'd have to feed Dumpy here. Her bottle's in the —'

'Oh, Diana, honestly. Deeply as I yearn to be a proper mum, I'm absolutely knocked out. Perhaps you could feed her and Mary could make the tea?' Sarah assumed the nanny was doing something upstairs and called loudly, 'Mary? Any chance of a cup of tea?'

'I don't think she'll be able to hear you,' said Diana thoughtfully, as she placed the teat of a feeding bottle into Dumpy's mouth and thus silenced the baby.

'Really? Why not?'

'Well, I estimate that she's probably about halfway to Halifax by now.'

'She's what?' asked Sarah in astonishment.

'On her way home. She comes from Halifax, you know.'

'I don't think I did know,' said Sarah, bewildered. 'But why's she going home? Some emergency in her family?'

'No,' said Diana judiciously. 'The emergency actually happened right here in this room.'

'In this room?' repeated Sarah, astonished. 'But what kind of emergency?'

'Well, the fact is,' said Diana, rather deliberately, 'that Mary suddenly found herself in danger of being beaten black and blue with a walking stick.'

'Good God – whose walking stick?'

'Mine actually,' admitted Diana. 'I didn't think there was any point in messing about with tact or diplomacy. I always feel that it's so much better in these situations to go straight to the nub of the matter. So I told Mary that this doll's house just wasn't big enough for the two of us, that I was Dumpy's new official nanny and that if she wasn't out of the front door within an hour I would be compelled to punish her severely with my trusty cane.'

Sarah gazed at her aunt in appalled amazement.

'I simply don't believe this!' she exclaimed. 'Did you know that Mary was a Swiss-trained nanny and that they're harder to get hold of than top executives? They get paid a merchant banker's wages too.'

'Well, there you are then,' said Diana complacently. 'You're quids in. You won't have to pay me a cent and you'll get a better service.'

'You can't get a better service than that provided by a Mutterkraft nanny. They're the tops.'

Diana sighed deeply.

'Sarah,' she pointed out, 'I'm family.'

'Yes, but you're —' began Sarah but then broke off just in time.

'You were going to say?' asked Diana frostily and then, when Sarah remained silent, went on. 'Could it have been that in your opinion I am past my sell-by date, over the top, superannuated, too antique for the job?'

'No, no, Aunty, nothing like that,' protested Sarah. 'It's just that – well, I lead a very stressful life and I – I really need to feel absolutely confident that little Diana is getting – well the very best care going. I'll just have to try and persuade Mary to come back. And that will probably mean upping her already astronomical wages but still —'

'No, you can't do that, my dear,' said Diana with quiet authority.

'But, it won't affect your status, Diana,' insisted Sarah. 'As you said, you're family. You can do as much as you like for little Diana but I really do want Mary to be here too.'

'I'm afraid I did mean what I said to her,' said Diana firmly, 'about there not being room in this place for both of us. If she comes back, then I go.'

'But why?'

'Because I am not a charity case – not while I have the use of my limbs anyway. I will gladly live here with you if I can pull my weight but not otherwise. And the only way that I can see of pulling my weight is by taking over as Dumpy's nanny. Still, if my services aren't good enough for you, then go ahead and 'phone —'

'Oh, Diana, why are you so infernally proud?' grumbled Sarah. 'Well all right, we'll give it a try but you must be responsible about it. If it proves too much for you, you must be prepared to tell me.'

'Of course I will. I wouldn't let Dumpy get second-class treatment, even if it was my own. So if it really should turn out that I can't handle the job then you're at liberty to bring in another Swiss wonder.'

Sarah nodded and said grimly, 'Assuming another one has come onto the market by then. Mutterkraft nannies are rarer than pink diamonds.' Then she heaved herself to her feet with a sigh and said ruefully to the baby, 'Well then, little Di, in the circumstances, it looks like Mummy will have to make tea for nanny rather than the other way round, doesn't it?'

And she limped away to the little kitchen.

Tom was watching an episode of his favourite Australian soap. The television set was now in his room. Geoffrey's presence in the flat had succeeded in doing what Diana's nagging had failed to do. It had induced Tom to retreat deeper into his own space.

The episode of *Kangaroo Street* that Tom was viewing was a particularly hilarious one. Young Nell Folderoo had discovered that she was pregnant by Bucko McFizz who had just proposed to lissom Doll Dinkum, the neighbourhood tart. But Doll, after falling secretly in love with Father Koala, the outback flying priest, had been overdosing on religion and had applied for admission to a very strict convent. Meanwhile Tiger Kelly, the speedway king, had broken both his legs and his callous wife, Sharleen, had run off with 'Diamond Jim'

Billabong, the cricket umpire. All of these characters were distraught and several of them were suicidal. Almost limitless hilarity should thus have been guaranteed. But although Tom smiled appreciatively now and then, he realized that these days he was somehow failing to enjoy all that the programme had to offer.

'Dad,' said Geoffrey, quietly entering the bedroom without knocking.

'Ah, Geoffrey,' replied Tom, trying to suppress a faint shudder. 'I thought we'd agreed that you'd knock before coming in?'

'Normally, I would have done, Dad. But I think you're forgetting that I told you a little while ago that I'd pop in when I'd finished. Well, I'm finished now and so you can inspect what I've done.'

'Oh good,' said Tom, trying to sound enthusiastic. 'Yes, it's true, I had forgotten you were nearing the completion of your mammoth undertaking.'

Tom thereupon aimed his death ray at the screen and, pressing the appropriate button, wiped out the lovelorn Australians. He then turned and gaped for a moment at the spectacle of Geoffrey wearing a white workman's coat and carrying a saw and a spirit level. His son looked rather like a pigeon that had just graduated from an alternative employment training scheme.

'Come along then, Dad,' said Geoffrey calmly. 'I've just put up the last one.'

Tom rose obediently and followed Geoffrey into the communal living room. He had, however, only taken a few steps into the room when he felt a kind of giddiness and raising his hand to his head swayed slightly. A moment later he shook his head to clear it, but when he looked again there they all still were. Shelves! Good Lord, the spectacle was almost surreal. Shelves climbed the walls, roamed over the fireplace, swirled in complicated patterns round fixtures and fittings.

'All grade-one, knot-free pine, Dad,' said Geoffrey with quiet pride. 'And I suspect you're still below your optimum capacity. If you were prepared to invest in a wheeled library-style ladder, I could get another two, and possibly even three, tiers of shelves —'

'No,' gasped Tom. 'I think not, Geoffrey. There's already far more shelving in here than I can possibly use.'

'What about the hall, Dad?' asked Geoffrey, sounding wistful.

'No, I prefer the hall to be passable —'

'Then the bathroom, Dad? You can never have too many shelves in bathrooms.'

'Yes, you can, Geoffrey. Look here, there's already far more shelving in the flat than I will ever need and so —'

'But, Dad,' pointed out Geoffrey, 'you can always store extra shelves on the existing shelves and that way when you require new shelves —'

'Enough!' cried Tom sternly.

Geoffrey sighed and a rueful smile appeared on his face.

'You're right, Dad,' he acknowledged. 'The truth is that up to this point I've always been a proponent of the moderation theory of shelving. I've even written an article on it for a DIY magazine. I know really that I'm just using shelving as a substitute for Marion. And there's no real comparison. After all shelves don't run off with other men. They don't get drunk. They don't make your life a hell. And yet, for all that, I somehow feel closer to her when I'm putting up shelves.'

Tom looked at his son with a flicker of sympathy.

'Oh, all right then, Geoffrey,' he said. 'Put up some more shelves in the bathroom if it will help.'

Geoffrey shook his head sadly.

'No, Dad, you're right. It only postpones the decisions I will sooner or later have to make. I think I'll go for a little walk and try to make some of them today.'

'You do that, Geoffrey,' said Tom. 'And I'll make a 'phone call.'

Diana stood in the middle of the tiny living room of Sarah's mews cottage surrounded by the baby things that covered the floor. They had been consigned to the floor because there were, frustratingly and exhaustingly, practically no surfaces in the room. Diana would, in fact, have been grateful for as many of Geoffrey's shelves as she could get.

She was occupied in sorting the garments into two piles: one of clean and one of dirty clothes. Somehow in the few days since nanny Mary had fled back to Halifax all of Dumpy's clothing had got dreadfully mixed up.

Diana picked up a small woollen garment, lifted it to her nose, sniffed it and then, making a face expressive of distaste, put it on the pile of dirty things.

Sarah came into the room and gazed about.

'I say, you are in a state,' she said. 'Can I give you a hand?'

'No, no, all under control,' Diana assured her. 'Dumpy is my department. You just go off and run your brothel.'

'Actually it's a model agency, Diana,' said Sarah just a shade reproachfully.

'Same thing,' said Diana, kicking some tiny vests into a heap. 'A whorehouse of the mind.'

'Not quite my image of it,' said Sarah with slightly forced amiability as she put on her outdoor coat. 'You wouldn't be getting just a tiny bit fed up with nannying would you, Diana?'

'Good Lord, no,' protested Diana. 'I love it. Who wouldn't? Getting up in the middle of the night, being peed on and bitten, spending half one's time up to the elbows in poo. Oh, it's the good life all right.' She looked around with a slight frown. 'The only slight problem is that there's never anywhere to put things in this impractical Wendy house.'

'Well, stay with it,' urged Sarah, heading for the door. 'But don't forget, if you should decide to settle for a life of ease and relaxation, I can always phone Mary —'

'In a pig's ear,' said Diana indignantly. 'Just run along and marshall your tarts.'

Sarah smiled a shade tightly and departed. Diana resumed sorting Dumpy's things. The 'phone rang.

Diana picked up the handset and said wearily: 'Hello? Lady Muck's residence. Nanny Diana speaking.'

A familiar voice said, 'Diana?'

There was a second's pause and then Diana, in a carefully casual voice, said, 'Oh, hello, Tom.'

'So – how are you, old thing?' asked Tom, also sounding easy and natural.

'Oh fine – fine,' Diana assured him. 'Yes, everything is fine here —'

'So – it's fine, is it?' asked Tom, a shade unnecessarily.

'Yes, it quite definitely is. Very fine indeed.'

'Good, good,' commented Tom. 'And how are things here?'

'Oh they're – I'm sorry?' asked Diana.

'I said, how are things – oh no, I'm here, aren't I? So I know, don't I?'

'Well, yes – at least – you should do. Don't you?'

'Yes, naturally. I know exactly how things are here. And I'm thus in a position to assure you that things here are every bit as fine as they are there. Perhaps ever finer.'

'Well, that's fine then, isn't it?' summed up Diana. 'For both of us?'

'Definitely,' confirmed Tom. 'And since everything is so fine for both of us it means that we can't be missing each other very much. And that's a big relief, isn't it?'

'An incredible relief,' agreed Diana. 'But the thing that I like best about it is that it proves we made the right decision.'

'Yes, that's always a splendid thing to have proved. I would really hate to feel that you were missing me even to the smallest extent.'

'Which makes it a delight for me to be able to assure you that I'm not. Indeed, I can go so far as to insist with complete candour that you hardly ever cross my mind.'

'Well,' that's marvellous,' exclaimed Tom with a sigh of relief. 'And I am able to set your mind at rest too. Almost the last thing I ever think about is you.'

'Then we're both in clover, aren't we?' said Diana happily.

'We are indeed. Well then – I mean – have you been doing anything exciting?'

'Oh, oodles of things,' maintained Diana rapturously. 'Going to shows, to dinners, on outings with old friends – best of all, playing with my lovely little Dumpy.'

'Really? And just which Dumpty would that be,' asked Tom with keen interest. 'Would it be a relative of Humpty Dumpty's?'

'No, it's Dumpy, not Dumpty. And anyway Humpty Dumpty was a fictional character. Dumpy is my new pet name for Diana the Second. Oh, we have simply tons of fun together and I'm now her official nanny.'

'Well, that is simply splendid,' Tom said gladly. 'But you will make sure she doesn't sit on any walls, won't you? We wouldn't want any tragic breakages. You'll be glad to know that I'm really enjoying myself too. Geoffrey's come to stay for a while and he's – well, he's transforming the flat.'

'But why is he staying with you?' asked Diana, sounding puzzled. 'Doesn't Marion object?'

'Oh, didn't you know?' asked Tom, sounding surprised. 'Marion's run off with Dennis, the rogue vicar, and they're living it up all over Wales.'

'Really? And you're actually saying —' asked Diana trying not to sound too incredulous, 'that you're enjoying living with Geoffrey?'

'Oh splendid stuff,' affirmed Tom, determined to sound convincing. 'You know, father and son together, jolly shared meals, lots of shelves. Yes, it's a wonderful world all right.'

'Well we both really seem to have fallen on our feet, Tom,' declared Diana positively. 'And because of that there's no urgency about it but still – I mean perhaps next spring or autumn, or some time like that we might – well – just have a drink together to – well to —'

'Yes, perhaps we should,' said Tom helpfully, 'that is if we both happen to have a free evening at the same time. Yes, actually, it might really be quite pleasant.'

'Good, that's settled then. And now – oh dear, there's Dumpy crying. She can be a real little dictator – in the sweetest way of course. When she wants a drink she really lets you know – a bit like Marion. 'Phone again, any time, Tom.'

'I will, Diana. And feel free to 'phone me too, if you feel the impulse.'

'Will do – bye.'

'Bye.'

And they both hung up. But then, oddly enough, they both sat without moving for several minutes. This was most remarkable in the case of Diana because Dumpy was screaming like ten car alarms for a feed.

'Aren't you going to move, Dad?' asked Geoffrey a few days later.

They were playing Scrabble.

'Mm? How do you mean, Geoffrey?' asked Tom, looking up with a frown.

'You've been gazing at your pieces for a quarter of an hour or so. Can't you make a word?'

'Certainly,' said Tom with dignity.

Tom almost always won at Scrabble, a game which the two of them had been playing quite a lot recently. He now removed five tiles from a little holder on the table in front of him and laid them out on the board. He began to count the score which this move gave him but Geoffrey protested:

'That's not allowed, Dad.'

'What isn't?' asked Tom irritably.

'That word. It's a proper name. Proper names aren't allowed.'

'But this isn't —' Tom began but then he saw what he'd put down and exclaimed, 'Good heavens!'

The five letters he had placed on the board spelled out the name: DIANA.

But I'll tell you what, Dad,' urged Geoffrey, 'with those letters you could make AND or DIN or —'

'Thank you very much, Geoffrey,' said Tom stiffly, 'but when I require your help, I'll request it.' He took up the tiles again. 'That was just an oversight. What I meant to put down was – ah – yes, here we are – using the E that's already there – DRAINAGE. See? And I've used all my letters too, which gives me a tremendous premium and just about wraps this game up.'

Geoffrey sighed and admitted, 'You're just too good for me, Dad. Still, that was funny, wasn't it?'

'What was?'

'Well, putting down a proper name like that. And you being such an experienced Scrabble player.' He frowned thoughtfully. 'I say, I wonder if it's significant that the proper name you put down was Diana?'

'No, no,' said Tom dismissively. 'No significance whatsoever. It was pure coincidence.'

'I wouldn't be too sure, Dad. The mind plays funny tricks sometimes. When I made out a shopping list yesterday I found later that I'd written: "a half pound of minced Marion". Possibly you're still missing Diana more than you realize.'

'Not at all. Why I never even think about her. I'm much happier without having her bossing me about.'

'If you say so, Dad. But I certainly still miss Marion. All the time. There's hardly an hour goes by when I don't imagine I hear some noise of the kind she used to make. You know, a cork popping out of a bottle or the clatter of her falling downstairs drunk. But to go back to Diana, did I tell you that I bumped into Sister Sheila and she asked after her?'

'You bumped into who?' asked Tom, mystified by the name.

'Sister Sheila, the nun that puts on the Christmas entertainments for the pensioners. She asked me if I would ask Diana if she would direct another pantomime this year like she did last year. But I told her Diana had gone back to London. Sister Sheila seemed quite disappointed.'

Tom grew rather excited.

'But why didn't you mention this to me, Geoffrey? When did it happen?'

'Oh, yesterday or the day before. Time means very little to me these days.'

'Really? And just where did you bump into Sister Sheila?'

'I was passing St Anthony's and Sister Sheila was just going in. She's in charge of the novices there, I believe.'

'Is she, indeed? Well – thanks for the stimulating Scrabble game, Geoffrey. And now I think I'll take a little stroll. It's a glorious afternoon.'

'I'll come with you, Dad,' said Geoffrey obligingly.

'No, no, it's not necessary,' exclaimed Tom quickly. 'It looks like rain or possibly hail. And anyway, Geoffrey, weren't you going to start – er – redecorating something? The kitchen, possibly?'

'Oh, there's no rush —'

'No rush?' echoed Tom reproachfully. 'Good heavens, Geoffrey, I don't think you realize how much it matters to me! You've got me all worked up with your – well, your visionary ideas for the work surfaces. I simply can't wait to see the finished result.'

'Really, Dad?' asked Geoffrey, looking distinctly cheered. 'I always thought you didn't really give a damn about my DIY stuff. But if you're that keen, I'll make a start immediately —'

'Good – good. And when I get back from my little stroll I'll come straight into the kitchen to inspect progress. See you soon, Geoffrey.'

About half an hour later, Tom was conferring with Sister Sheila, a diminutive but forceful Irish nun, in the grounds of St Anthony's which was a large church with an associated convent. Their feet rustled over the carpet of fallen leaves which thickly covered the lawn on which they were walking.

'I quite understand, Sister,' Tom was saying. 'As an old folk myself I can't tell you how much I depend on a Christmas pantomime to keep me content and chuckling until well into the New Year. Last year, indeed, the benign effect lasted until it was almost summer and was probably the main influence in keeping me from despair throughout the entire year.'

'That's very gratifying, Mr Ballard,' said Sister Sheila, sounding a little surprised by the intensity of the commendation. 'I only hope this year's pantomime will be just as effective.'

'But unhappily, it can't be, can it? Not without Diana Trent to direct it?'

'Oh, I'm not too sure, Mr Ballard. You see, we've found another lady who will almost certainly be just as good. She might even be better since she was in show business herself – a stage manager, I think, in the West End of London.'

Tom shook his head doubtfully.

'Yes, but surely the truth must be that however talented this new person is she just won't be Diana Trent, will she?'

'That would seem to be self-evident, Mr Ballard.'

'And it was, in fact, Diana Trent that put on last year's superb pantomime?'

'Well —'

'So for the purposes of mounting a pantomime of the same quality as Diana did last year it would be accurate to say that Diana is irreplaceable, wouldn't it?'

'Well, I'm not quite sure if I would —'

Tom smiled gently and explained, 'I only ask, Sister, because I happen to be going up to London tomorrow morning and I could easily call in and tell Miss Trent that you consider her services indispensable for providing a Christmas pantomime this year.'

'Yes, but that would not be quite —'

'Don't worry, Sister,' purred Tom. 'I can be very persuasive when I try. And moreover I happen to know that Diana Trent has a very tender heart and when she hears of the dismay and sorrow caused in the parish by the news that she is not going to direct this year's Christmas pantomime —'

'But hang on, Mr Ballard,' protested Sister Sheila. 'There has been no dismay and sorrow in the parish.'

'Oh, but there has, Sister Sheila. I myself feel enormous dismay and sorrow. And when Diana realizes how everyone is depending on her then I feel quite sure that she will relent and return to us in order to direct the pantomime.'

Sister Sheila shook her head uncertainly. She felt that she was being outmanoeuvred in some way but wasn't quite sure how it was being done. She sighed and conceded, 'Yes, well, I'm sure that Miss Trent has a good Christian heart in her —'

'Oh she has. And a good Christian liver and pancreas too. Do you know she spends much of her time trying to dream up ways of improving the lot of widows and orphans? And when I tell her that you're distraught by her decision my guess is that she'll change her mind.'

'Yes, but I'm not exactly distraught, Mr Ballard. Besides, there's Miss Tomkins to consider.'

'Who?'

'The lady who has now agreed to direct the show.'

'Don't worry about Miss Tomkins, Sister Sheila. I'm sure that once she's been reinstated, Miss Trent will be able to deal with Miss Tomkins.'

'You mean,' asked Sister Sheila, recalling some of the stormier passages during last year's pantomime rehearsals, 'that she'll put out a contract on her?'

'She will reason with her and if reason fails she will discourage her by other firm but humane methods. And now I must dash Sister Sheila. But be of good cheer. I feel confident that tomorrow I will bring you tidings of great joy.'

'Yes, but hang on, Mr Ballard. Mr Ballard, please come back. Mr Ballard —'

But Tom was already loping swiftly away towards the gate.

'Surprise, surprise!' announced Tom with his biggest, juiciest grin when, after he had knocked several times, Diana finally opened the front door of Sarah's mews cottage the next day.

Glazed with exhaustion, having only managed to secure three hours' sleep the night before, Diana blinked at him.

'Who the hell are you?' she asked blearily.

'Oh come now – you can't have forgotten me already,' protested Tom, his grin evaporating.

'Tom Ballard!' exclaimed Diana reproachfully. 'How dare you come here unexpectedly when I'm looking as if I've just been fed through a threshing machine.'

'You look all right,' Tom assured her. 'In fact, you look wonderful.'

'Liar!' exclaimed Diana. 'I'm pale and drawn and my hair is floating about like cobwebs in a haunted castle. My dress is covered with assorted human secretions and I'm on the point of collapse.'

'Good heavens, why?' asked Tom.

'Because I've been up all night with Dumpy. She gets through more milk between dusk and dawn than an ice-cream factory. And when she's not guzzling she's screaming with wind pains.'

'Well, be of good cheer – relief is here,' said Tom, breaking into merry doggerel. 'May I come in?'

'Certainly not. The living room is knee deep in soiled nappies and—'

'Oh come on, we can't talk on the doorstep.'

Diana sighed deeply, stepped back and pulled open the door. Tom entered. The living room was indeed somewhat untidy but nothing like as disorderly as Diana had suggested. It only required brushing a few lightly stained garments from its seat for Tom to be able to sink into an armchair. Diana followed him into the living room and, without bothering to brush away the garments, sank down into the other armchair.

'What do you want?' she asked unceremoniously.

'Well, I haven't had breakfast yet,' began Tom a trifle archly, 'and so perhaps some bacon and eggs with a few grilled tomatoes – only joking, only joking,' he concluded hastily, noticing a homicidal light beginning to shine in Diana's eyes. 'No, the truth is I've come to take you home.'

'Home? What do you mean – home? This is home.'

'No, it's not. Bayview is your home and you're needed there.'

Diana contemplated him icily for a moment but then surprisingly asked quite mildly, 'And just why am I needed there?'

'Because you are unique. And because you can do what no one else can do.'

Diana's eyes took on a rather distant look as she asked, 'And what would that be exactly?'

'Put on the Christmas pantomime,' said Tom triumphantly. 'Your *Puss-in-Boots* last year was a triumph beyond anything Andrew Lloyd Webber has ever dreamed of. But your many fans are convinced that your *Dick Whittington* this year will be an even more memorable theatrical occasion.'

'What the hell are you talking about?' asked Diana.

'We want you to come back to Bayview and direct the Christmas pantomime.'

Diana nodded. 'I see,' she said. 'And who exactly is "we"?'

'Why everyone, Diana. Sister Sheila for a start. And then Harvey and Jane and Basil and – oh, everyone.'

'You included?'

'Absolutely.'

'But not you in particular?'

'Oh good heavens, no,' Tom hastened to reassure her. 'This was definitely not my idea. I'm just conveying to you the overwhelming will of the people.'

'I see,' said Diana, although looking, Tom felt, a trifle grim. 'Well then, the least I can do is acknowledge this popular demand and ask you to take back my reply.'

'Which is?' asked Tom complacently.

'You can tell everyone to get stuffed. I have, as I thought you were aware, Tom, cast the dust of Bayview from my feet forever and I hope from now on you will always remember that.'

'Yes, but,' stammered Tom, crestfallen, 'surely the pantomime —'

'Bugger the pantomime,' roared Diana. 'Tell them to have a barn dance instead. My place is here with Dumpy and now, I don't wish to be rude, but as you can see every square inch of this hutch is rather mysteriously required for looking after one small baby and so would you kindly remove yourself from the premises?'

'But – is that your last word?'

'First, last and forever. Goodbye, Tom, and if I don't see you before, have a very merry Christmas.'

With which, Diana rose, went to the door, opened it and held it open. Tom, now a mere shadow of the ebullient self that had arrived, tugged himself wearily to his feet and, shaking his head with a rueful and puzzled smile, departed.

It turned out to be a day for puzzles. When he got home he found a puzzling note that had been left for him on the living-room table. It read,

Dad
You will recall that I told you some time ago that, in my present marital difficulties, I had two alternatives: 1) to wait until Marion came to her senses and 2) to commit suicide. While I was working on the new work surface for the kitchen sideboard (and please do not disturb the underlay of special latex waterproofing I have applied), I suddenly realized that there is in fact a third alternative. I have therefore gone off to implement it. It may take a few days. So do not worry about my absence (and under no circumstances tamper with the latex underlay in the kitchen). I will visit you as soon as I return, to report on the success or failure of my mission.
Devotedly,
Geoffrey

What on earth could it mean? Oh well, Tom assured himself, there was clearly nothing to worry about. If Geoffrey had been contemplating anything desperate he would hardly have been so concerned about his latex underlay. At this point, Tom wandered curiously into the kitchen and glumly inspected a kind of dull glaze on the sideboard. He then probed it with an experimental finger and was appalled to find a moment later that a thin film of rubbery material had become attached to his finger and peeled completely off the surface to which it had been applied when he moved away. After a frantic few minutes of attempting, with increasingly messy and frustrating results, to replace the film, Tom abandoned the effort. Geoffrey would, of course, be furious when he returned and found his handiwork ruined. Or would he? Tom thought about it for a moment. No, it was virtually impossible to imagine Geoffrey furious – who has ever seen a pigeon in a rage?

Anyway, notwithstanding this DIY catastrophe, what Tom essentially felt was a great sense of relief. Tom had been finding that sharing a roof with his son was quite a strain. There was something about Geoffrey – calm and industrious though he was – that jangled Tom's nerves like an out-of-tune xylophone. With Geoffrey gone, Tom would at long last be able to rediscover what living alone was really like.

It was, he decided after two days, pretty bloody. True, he could watch what he wanted on television, vacuum as often as he thought necessary, cook and eat the food he liked best, but somehow nothing that he did or ate or watched had any savour any more. Without someone – even an old curmudgeon (could a person, he wondered briefly, be a young curmudgeon?) like Diana – to share things with, they all seemed flavourless. This discovery set Tom to wondering why Diana had given him such short shrift when he had visited her about the pantomime. He had been sure that vanity, if nothing else, would have induced her to return. But it hadn't. Well then, perhaps the problem was to be found with the messenger rather than the message. Perhaps if Sister Sheila herself were to ask Diana to come back the good nun might get long shrift and —

It was while Tom was turning over in his mind the possibility of getting Sister Sheila to 'phone Diana with a renewed appeal for help that Geoffrey returned. Tom heard his Volvo pull up outside and a moment later, looking like a pigeon that's won the pools, Geoffrey walked in.

'Hello, Dad,' he said. 'I have some bad news for you.'

'Really?' asked Tom, frowning slightly. 'What is it?'

'I won't be able to finish the work surfaces in the kitchen. But I can tell you how to do them yourself. It's not really all that difficult if you strictly observe the drying times of the various special emulsions which you'll need.'

'Geoffrey, where have you been?' asked Tom impatiently.

'Well, as I said in my note, I realized that there was a third alternative open to me.'

'And what was that?' Tom wanted to know.

'To go and bring Marion back myself,' explained Geoffrey. 'I can't imagine why it took me so long to think of it. Pretty obvious really.'

Tom gazed at him in unfeigned astonishment.

'And that's where you've been? To Wales?'

'Exactly. None too soon either. That was a terrible place they were living in —'

'In what way?'

'It was full of strange people called hippies who were supposed to have died out in the sixties.'

'I see. And what did you do, Geoffrey?'

'Well, it was about ten o'clock at night when I got there and Dennis and Marion were carrying on with these hippies in the main lounge of the hotel. Everyone was either drinking or smoking something with a funny smell which I assume must have been marijuana. Marion was sitting on Dennis's lap. I went up to her and told her that I'd come to take her home. She laughed in a funny way. I grabbed her hand and pulled her to her feet. She shouted at me to stop. Dennis got to his feet but I punched him on the jaw and knocked him out. I then pulled Marion behind me to the car, threw her into the front passenger seat and drove her back here.'

Tom gazed at his son in mixed awe and amazement.

'You just – went in – and plucked her out of that wild mob?'

'That's right, Dad. It wasn't really very difficult.'

'It beats anything I've ever done in my fantasies, Geoffrey,' said Tom respectfully. 'You know there's a side to you I've never really appreciated.'

'There is to most people, Dad. Anyway, Marion and I are going home now —'

'Marion?' asked Tom in disbelief. 'Do you mean that she's here? With you?'

'Oh yes, Dad, she's in the car.'

'But why can't I hear any screams of rage? Isn't she howling like a wolf and clawing like a tiger?'

'No, not really, Dad. Come and see,' invited Geoffrey.

He turned and went back out the way he had come in. Tom followed him. As they approached the Volvo a female figure jumped out of the passenger seat, went round the car and opened the driver's door. It was Marion and she was watching

Geoffrey approach with something quite like worship in her eyes.

'Oh, I am glad you're back, Geoffrey,' she sighed. 'I missed you.'

Geoffrey consulted his watch.

'I've only been gone seven and a half minutes,' he said.

'I know but every minute seems an hour.' She glanced at Tom with a faint smile. 'Hello, Tom,' she greeted him. 'Have you heard about the magnificent exploits of your marvellous son?'

'Well – yes – I have,' stammered Tom. 'I never realized he had it in him.'

'Geoffrey is a sleeping lion,' said Marion softly. 'And when he wakes fully the world will tremble.'

'I'd be quite satisfied,' said Geoffrey firmly, 'to be made area manager of the dairy.'

'And so you will be, dear,' Marion assured him. 'If that's what you want. Now climb into the car and we'll go home where I'll make you a lovely supper and put a hot water bottle in your bed. Bye, Tom – see you around —' concluded Marion with something like her old breeziness.

Tom smiled and nodded.

'Goodbye, Marion,' he said.

'Bye, Dad,' said Geoffrey, 'and I'll 'phone you about those work surfaces tomorrow.'

'Thank you, Geoffrey,' said Tom humbly.

Whereupon the Volvo started and eased away down the drive. Tom gazed after it shaking his head in wonder.

That night Tom jumped off Mount Everest. A little while before, he had reached the summit on stilts, the first time it had ever been done. He was being congratulated by a reception committee headed by the Prime Minister when it suddenly occurred to him that anything that Geoffrey could do he should be able to do at least as well. If Geoffrey could come over all masterful with Marion and bend her to his will, why couldn't he do the same with Diana?

'We are awarding you this special medal,' said the Prime Minister, holding out a solid gold disc about the size of a beach umbrella, 'in recognition of your superb achievement —'

At which point Tom interrupted with a wild cry of, 'Sorry, got to go. Must bring Diana back. But thanks in any case.'

And before the wondering eyes of the assembled dignitaries, he crouched down and then, with one mighty spring, leapt off the summit of Mount Everest and landed in his bed at Bayview. There he woke up, noted that it was pitch dark in the room, switched on the light and discovered that it was just 3.15am. For the rest of the night, he tried to sleep but without much success. It would, he realized, prejudice his chances of success with Diana, no matter how masterful he was, if he arrived at the mews house in the middle of the night.

At about 11.30 the next morning, as Tom's train from Bournemouth drew in at Victoria, Diana was wheeling Dumpy through Hyde Park. It was a sparkling winter day and surprisingly warm in the bright sunshine. After a while, Diana said to the little girl in the pram, 'How about a nice rest, Dumpy, on this bench? As usual I only managed to get about thirty seconds' sleep last night and so I'm utterly knackered.'

Diana sat down on the bench and pulled a rug warmly over the girl baby who was smiling seraphically at nothing. While doing this, Diana became aware that another nanny with a pram had arrived at the bench and had also seated herself. When she had finished her task, Diana glanced round and smiled in a neighbourly way at the new arrival, remarking civilly, 'Hello, nanny. Lovely morning.'

She was surprised, however, when the other nanny totally ignored her and instead addressed Dumpy.

'And who is your mummy?' she asked the baby.

Diana frowned slightly and then, in a falsetto lisp, said, 'Oh my mummy is Sarah Parry.'

The other nanny, who was resplendent in a very posh, starched uniform, still did not look at Diana but again spoke to the baby, 'Oh yes,' she said positively, 'I know Mrs Parry. And I knew her former nanny too. She would have known better than to sit on this particular bench.'

Diana frowned at this remark and, again speaking like an infant, asked: 'Why would other nanny not sit on this nice comfortable bench?'

'Because,' explained the grand nanny, 'this bench is reserved for the nannies of titled mummies. And Mrs Parry is only a commoner, isn't she?'

Diana stopped talking in falsetto but still pretended to be Dumpy.

'Oh no, my mummy isn't a commoner at all,' she proclaimed very firmly. 'She is, on the contrary, a very uncommon lady who has made a success of herself purely by her own efforts and not just by marrying a titled imbecile. And if this incredible fossil of a snobbish nanny persists in her idiotic remarks, new nanny is quite likely to flatten her with a straight right to the jaw.'

The smart nanny rose with commendable speed and wheeled her charge away, calling back, 'Mrs Parry will hear about this.'

Diana sighed and said despondently, 'I don't think I'm really cut out for this nannying lark, Dumpy. I can just about handle the nappies and the nonstop feeding but my sister nannies must be the dimmest, snobbiest bunch of females that exist anywhere in the known universe.'

She rose and, turning the pram about, set off back to the mews house. When she got there, she was surprised to find Tom sitting on the doorstep.

'What the hell are you doing here?' she asked.

'I've come to take you home, Diana,' said Tom masterfully.

'That's what you said last time,' said Diana, as she lifted Dumpy out of the pram. 'Bring that pram in for me, would you?'

'Yes but – oh, all right,' said Tom.

They entered the house together and Diana took Dumpy upstairs and deposited her in her cot. Then she went back downstairs and confronted Tom.

'I told you when you were last here,' Diana said wearily, 'this is my home now.'

'Oh no, it's not,' said Tom. 'You belong at Bayview and you're coming with me.'

He reached forwards and grabbed Diana's hand. He gave it a tug. Diana stumbled, recovered her balance and immediately hit Tom in the eye with her balled fist. He gave a shout of pain.

'Are you crazy?' asked Diana calmly.

'Probably,' said Tom, with his hand over his punished eye. 'But how on earth did Geoffrey pull it off?'

'What did Geoffrey – hang on, let's have a look at that eye.'

Tom uncovered his damaged eye and Diana inspected it closely.

'Yes, well you might end up with a shiner,' she said thoughtfully. 'But I don't think it's very likely. I just haven't got the clout I once had. Sit down and I'll get you an ice bag and then you can tell me why you're acting so weirdly.'

'All right,' said Tom, his aspirations towards being masterful having totally evaporated. A little later, with a cup of tea beside him and an ice bag pressed to his eye, he sat opposite Diana who asked: 'So what did you mean about Geoffrey?'

Tom thereupon told Diana how Geoffrey had journeyed to Wales where he had penetrated the castle of the Wild Hippies, vanquished the dragon, Dennis, and returned in triumph with the captive princess, Marion.

'Who would have believed it?' asked Diana in wonder.

'I know,' said Tom. He removed the ice bag, blinked and then replaced it, remarking, 'My eye feels a bit better. But what I simply can't understand is why Geoffrey's technique didn't work with you.'

'Because,' said Diana with a sigh of wonder at his lack of understanding, 'I am not a glop-headed goop like Marion who would be utterly bowled over by B-picture heroics. And I would have thought you might have realized that after knowing me as long as you have done. Tom, why are you so anxious to get me back to Bayview anyway?'

'Well because – because —'

'You can get someone else to direct the pantomime. It's not as if it was a try out for the West End.'

'No but —' Tom removed the ice bag from his eye, sighed and said glumly, 'Oh, it's nothing to do with the pantomime really.'

'Then what is it?'

'I miss you. That's what it is.'

'Oh you do, do you?'

'Yes, I do. I miss you in the day and I miss you in the night. I'd got used to having you there.'

'Just like an old dog?'

'Yes – no. Just like a friend and companion if you really want to know. Just like the person I want to hold in my arms. Just like, in the last resort, the woman I love.'

Diana blinked and shook her head slightly.

'I – er – I don't think I can have heard you correctly. It seemed to me just then that you stated softly but distinctly that I am the woman you love.'

'Well, so I did. Oh, not the very first woman that I've ever loved, I have to admit. The first love of my life was, as you know, Maggie and I shall always love her with that part of me which lived with her. But, with the part of me that now goes on living, I love you, Diana.'

'Then may I ask why you've never, when trying to coax me back to Bayview, mentioned this, at the very least, pertinent fact before?'

'Yes, it's quite simply that I wasn't actually aware of it before. In fact, I didn't really know it until a minute ago when I spoke it out loud. Oh, I knew well enough that I wanted you back and I thought of all kinds of crazy schemes to get you back. But it had simply never occurred to me that the real reason I wanted you back was because I loved you.'

'I see,' Diana nodded thoughtfully and continued, 'well, it certainly puts a different complexion on things.'

'I don't suppose,' said Tom wistfully. 'I don't suppose there's the remotest chance that you might – well – might reciprocate a little?'

'Yes, I think there is,' said Diana. 'Quite a good chance in fact – just so long as you don't object to being loved like an ole houn' dawg?'

'A what?'

'Oh God, this is ridiculous. One had hoped that of all the indignities that this world heaps on us wrinklies romantic love was something one might have grown out of. What are we supposed to do now? Hold hands in the cinema? Gaze soulfully into each other's eyes? And when the end approaches, whisper endearments as we clank towards eternity on our Zimmer frames?'

'Well, why not?' exclaimed Tom heartily. 'And also feed each other titbits with our forks. And kiss and cuddle like kids. And have eyes for no one else at dinner parties if only we could get someone to invite us to some dinner parties and —'

'Yes, all right,' said Diana. 'And don't forget holding out the puking bowl when the sentimentality levels get too high – as they're threatening to do right now. Anyway, what does it mean in practice? That I come back and live in your flat in Bayview?'

'Exactly. But this time we'll have just a few ground rules —'

'You were right,' said Diana firmly, 'when you said in effect that I was just an ungrateful brat who couldn't bear to be in your debt. I knew it at the time but I still couldn't seem to help myself. You may be surprised to learn that I don't actually enjoy living knee-deep in rubbish. So perhaps it will be different this time round.'

'What about Dumpy?' asked Tom, a shade anxiously.

'Oh, she'll be no problem. I've blotted my copybook with the nannies' union in any case. And Sarah can afford the finest Swiss-trained nanny in Europe to replace me. Of course, I'll have to hang on until one arrives.'

'All right,' said Tom. 'Then I'll get back to Bayview and get the work surface ready for use.'

'Are you being obscene?'

'Eh?' asked Tom in surprise. 'Oh no, it's just the kitchen. Geoffrey made a start on it but I'll have to finish it. How long do you think it will be before you can join me?'

'A week, perhaps less,' said Diana thoughtfully. Then something occurred to her. 'And, Tom, when you get home, why don't you check on whether Sister Sheila has signed that other female for the pantomime yet? If she hasn't, I might still take on the job myself. I quite like keeping a toehold in showbiz.'

The pantomime, which Diana did indeed direct, was a great success. It was held in the dining room at Bayview and the audience of old folks applauded so long and loudly that several had to be treated by the St John's Ambulance men who were standing by. After the final curtain had descended – or rather been pulled across the stage since it consisted of blankets on a pulley arrangement – there was a party at Tom and Diana's place for the entire cast. Since the performers all came in their costumes, the occasion had the air of a fancy dress ball.

Tom was dressed as Dick Whittington and Basil as his lascivious cat. Harvey Bains was the demon king. Jane was a Babe in Bayview. Marion was the principal boy. Geoffrey was Old Mother Hubbard, although Diana admitted that strictly speaking Old Mother Hubbard had no business in the pantomime at all. And there was a wonderful chorus of Zimmer-frame geriatrics in sequin-glittering short skirts and tiaras. Basil had a very rewarding time crawling about on all fours and rubbing himself against them.

Vast amounts of champagne were drunk and delicious titbits were consumed. The disco music pounded out but promptly at midnight it was turned off and everyone fell silent as the recorded strains of 'Adeste Fidelis' sung by the choir of King's College Chapel swelled through the flat. Christmas Day had arrived.

When the carol had ended, the guests began to drift, or perhaps hobble, away. When they were finally alone together again, Tom filled Diana's glass and also his own. He held his up: 'You did real good,' he said proudly in a comic American accent.

'Yeah?' asked Diana with a wry smile.

'The best pantomime I've ever been in.'

'And how many have you been in?'

'Just this one. But it was a big success. You could tell by the audience reaction.'

'Seven collapses and three fatalities,' said Diana grimly.

Tom looked shocked.

'I had no idea!' he exclaimed.

'Only joking,' said Diana quickly. 'Although one or two of the octogenarians did laugh so heartily they had to be medically straightened out. Yes, if I do say so myself, it wasn't a bad show.'

'Jane was amazing, didn't you think?' chuckled Tom reminiscently.

'Rather wooden, I thought.'

'No, I meant the neat way she kept managing to get close to Bains. At one point, Harvey bent to kiss that Helga woman from the bakery who was playing the Wicked Stepmother and Jane managed to intercept the kiss.'

Diana laughed and said, 'I missed that. However, I did see Marion pinching Roger the stagehand's bum. Has the effect of Geoffrey's masterly rescue worn off then?'

'Good Lord, no,' maintained Tom. 'But Marion was so nervous about playing her part well that she popped a handful of pills for the first time in weeks. It may have produced a temporary relapse.'

'You were excellent as Dick Whittington,' Diana said affectionately.

'Oh, really? I wondered how I'd struck you.'

'Ambitious and noble at the same time,' asserted Diana. 'Every inch a fifteenth-century yuppy. A pity about the cartwheel.'

'Yes, it was a little overambitious perhaps,' said Tom, rubbing his leg. 'But I thought it would dramatize my delight at being made Mayor of London. And I don't think I hurt any of those in the front row that I fell on, did I?'

'No, it wasn't them,' Diana reassured him. 'It was you I was worried about. Didn't you damage yourself at all?'

'Only a bruise on my right thigh. Would you care to see it?'

'No way.'

'I see,' said Tom. There was a thoughtful pause. 'Don't you ever want to see it again?'

'See what exactly?'

'Well – my right thigh. Or my left, come to that. I know they're not in the same class as Cary Grant's in his prime but we used to go to bed together – before you ran off to London.'

'And we will again,' said Diana accommodatingly. 'Just – give me a bit more time.'

'It's been more than a month since you came back here,' Tom pointed out. 'And, of course, time is the one thing we haven't got unlimited supplies of. What's up, Diana?'

'Nothing's up.'

'Which is just what I'm complain – no, joking apart, aren't we going to resume our sex life?'

'Of course we are,' insisted Diana. 'And now, hadn't we better tidy up before we go to bed?'

'I don't believe this.'

'Believe what?'

Tom shook his head and explained, 'I know that you are the

new, fully reformed, all purpose, infinitely helpful Diana Trent but I never thought I'd hear you actually suggest tidying up at two in the morning after a party. Or could there be an ulterior motive?'

'Such as?'

'Oh, what we were talking about – bed. Bed together. A way of postponing it again. If there is some problem we really should talk about it, you know.'

Diana poured herself some more champagne.

'All right,' she said. 'I admit it. I'm afraid.'

'Of me? But we've done it before – quite a lot.'

'No, of me. Of completely losing my independence. Of – of loving you too much.'

'No one has ever loved anyone too much, Diana.'

'True, true —' agreed Diana but with a hint of desperation in her voice. 'But still – give me a little more time, Tom.'

'No problem. All right then, let's tidy up a bit. Shall I put on another record?'

'Yes. Something really hot. How about "Fatboy"?'

Tom said indulgently, 'I don't actually share your rapturous appreciation of that New Orleans trumpeter but all right.'

Tom put the record on. Diana started tidying up and in a moment the music started. It was at once clear that Tom, possibly because he was just a shade drunk, had made a mistake. He had not put on 'Fatboy' Philips singing 'I ain't nothin' but a no-good hawg'. He had put on 'Heilige Nacht' sung by the choir of King's College Chapel.

'Oh, I'm sorry —' Tom said, realizing his error. 'I'll change it.'

'No, leave it,' said Diana.

So they listened to the limpid carol for a while, sipping their champagne. It was the hackneyed, overfamiliar, almost vulgar anthem of Christmas in a mercantile culture but it was also a wondrous progression of swelling cadences.

After a while Diana said softly: 'Well, I suppose we did have an agreement.'

'Oh? What agreement?' asked Tom.

'Don't you remember? We made it months ago. An agreement to get together on high days and holy days. Well, if challenged, I would have to concede that they don't really come much higher or holier than this.'

Tom stared at her. Then, as he slowly realized what she was implying, he began to smile. Soon he rose to his feet and held out his hand. Diana took it. He helped her to her feet. And then the two old people went off hand in hand together into the bedroom to sleep and quite possibly to make love.